FREYJA'S DAUGHTER

P

CITY OWL
PRESS

FREYJA'S DAUGHTER
Wild Women, Book 1

CITY OWL PRESS
www.cityowlpress.com

Cover Design by Mibl Art and Tina Moss. All stock photos licensed appropriately.

Edited by Heather McCorkle.

Map by Dani Woodruff.

For information on subsidiary rights, please contact the publisher at info@cityowlpress.com.

Print Edition ISBN: 978-1-944728-68-7

Digital Edition ISBN: 978-1-944728-67-0

Printed in the United States of America

To my sisters.

"Freyja's Daughter is a fast-paced, thrilling tale of women reclaiming their power in a folkloric battle of the sexes. I can't wait to spend more time in Pudelek's exciting and enchanting world."
– *Cass Morris, Authof of From Unseen Fire.*

Huldra—Forest women, able to cover their skin in bark and grow branches from their hands and feet, created by the goddess Freyja.

Washington Coterie

- Faline

- Shawna

- Olivia

- Celeste

- Patricia

- Renee

- Abigale

- Naomi (missing)

Succubi—Empathic women, able to manipulate and absorb energy, created by the goddess Lilith.

Oregon Galere

- Marie

- Heather (missing)

Mermaids—Aquatic women, able to shift their legs to a tail and cover their skin with scales, created by the goddess Atargatis.

California Shoal

- Gabrielle

- Azul

- Elaine

- Sarah

Harpies—Women able to sprout bird-like wings, feathers, and talons, created by the goddess Inanna.

Rusalki—Women tied to nature, able to read minds, practice divination and cut lives short, created by the goddess Mokosh.

PREFACE

Many years ago, the Wild Women—huldra, succubi, harpies, mermaids, and others—warred to near extinction before the Hunters rescued them from their own demise. These men, born into a lineage of strength and bravery, separated the Wild Women, placed them into territories to protect them, tame them, and train them.

This is my history, according to the Hunters.
My mother's whispers told a different tale.

ONE

MY PREY, a five-foot-ten Caucasian male, ordered a double shot mocha as he tapped his pointer finger on the counter. I eyed him from a little round table near the door. His faint scent of nervous sweat called to me.

I preferred the scent of fear wafting from my prey, but nervousness would have to do. Fear would soon join the mix. It was only a matter of time.

"Do you go to school near here?" he asked the barista. She looked to be in high school, more than twenty years younger than the man I followed.

The barista nodded. "I graduate in June." On a paper cup, she wrote the fake name he'd given and shifted her attention to the next customer in line.

He failed to notice the hint.

"You like your teachers? I bet you like teachers." He shook his pointer finger at her.

I choked on my coffee.

This bail-jumper hadn't risked capture to satiate his caffeine fix. No, the fix he was jonesing for was a female of the unwilling sort.

A male barista brought the man's drink to the counter and stood protectively beside the girl. The object of my current hunt, Samuel Woodry, picked up the cup with the fake name on it and struck out. He left the coffee shop, careful not to make eye contact with anyone. As he walked past, I stared at that pointer finger he'd been tapping on the counter and decided to break that one first...on accident.

As a bounty hunter, I still had rules to uphold, proper conduct when bringing in a perp. Though, if he fought me—and he would, since I only selected bail-runners who got off on victimizing others— then a tussle resulting in a broken bone would be perfectly understandable.

According to his file, Samuel Woodry had never learned that it's not polite to point. His victim, a college student who'd escaped from his capture, will forever remember his scarred finger. The way he shook it in her face when she begged to go home. How he pretended to be a teacher in his sick idea of role playing.

My heart beat a little faster as I downed the rest of my drink and exited the coffee shop. Samuel's black hoody—so different from the blazer and khakis his most recent victim had met him in—didn't exactly stand out in the misty Seattle rain. Between his outfit and the swarm of downtown pedestrians, I had to follow closer than I would have liked. At least the crowd served to protect me from his gaze the few times he glanced over his shoulder.

As I followed him into Pike Place Market, the salty scent of Puget Sound thickened the air. Everything from fresh flowers to figurines created from Mt. St. Helen ash were sealed into containers. The semi-outdoor shops were shutting down for the night.

Unlike the open-air market upstairs, the lower level shops had already closed for the day. With shop doors locked and lights off, fewer people mingled. As we left the crowd, Samuel Woodry slowed his pace and whistled a tune. A bittersweet scent wafted from his skin. Excitement. He had noticed me, a lone woman, and he was pleased.

He couldn't wait to point that finger in my face. And I couldn't wait for him to try.

I was a female, yes. But not like any woman he'd ever met. Let's just say, out of the two of us in the now-empty hall of closed-up shops, I was the more deadly monster. Not that he knew he was salivating over a huldra. If I even so much as tree-jumped in front of a human the Hunters would peel the bark from my back...or worse.

Samuel Woodry stopped short and spun, ready to rush me.

Oh, I hoped he would.

The leather from my black steel-toed boots reached up to my knees, pressing a dagger into each calf. A maroon leather bomber jacket hid my gun, holstered at my ribs over a black tank top. But tonight, my weapon of choice was my hands. I figured since he liked using his on others so much, maybe I'd give it a go.

"Like what you see?" Samuel crooned. "I should teach you the dangers of following strange men into strange places." He smiled widely and his eyes darkened.

This is the fun part. The part where my prey thinks he's the predator. Where he relishes the few moments of absolute bliss before reality—also known as the steel toe of my right boot—slams into him.

"I thought you'd never offer," I said under my breath.

"I brought you someplace special." He stepped toward me.

So, he thought he had been luring me. Nice. Twisted, yes, but nice.

I cowered to draw him in. I couldn't help myself. He got off on victimizing others just like I got off on bringing people like him to justice.

The scent of arousal filled the air between us. Sick bastard.

Any normal human with half a brain would question why I followed him, ask who I was, question if I was a cop with backup just around the poorly lit corner. But Mr. Samuel Woodry wasn't a normal human. He was arrested years ago in connection to missing women, but let off due to insufficient evidence. This time one of his victims got away, which I assumed had a lot to do with why he skipped bail—her testimony held enough proof to put him in jail for a very long time. Still, all his poorly wired brain wanted was to find his next victim. And seeing as his seduce-the-underage-barista plan hadn't worked, I would have to do.

My inner huldra begged to come out and play.

He rushed forward, grabbed my shoulders, and slammed my back into the front of a darkened used book store. I let my body respond like a rag doll. It led him to believe he had the upper hand, and I wanted to play that card a little longer.

The thrum of my heart beat wildly in my ears.

Samuel drew his tongue from the side of my lower neck to right below my ear. I hid a smile. I'd get to show him his mistake in three...two...

"I'm gonna teach you your first lesson," he promised. "Class is in session." He pulled his face away from mine to waggle his pointer finger toward my nose.

One!

I removed my right hand from his grasp and caught hold of his finger. While still holding onto him, my boot—Reality—kicked him in the gut. Samuel screamed out. Steel toes were hell on the innards. I grinned.

He staggered back, cupping his finger and cursing me.

Was that the faint trace of fear I smelled? I lingered as the scent of musty iron filled my nostrils; I allowed it to fuel me, allowed it to tease my inner huldra, to tap into her strength without letting her out— without letting her tear him to shreds.

"Now it's time for me to teach you a lesson, Sam. Can I call you Sam?" I spoke slowly as I stalked toward him.

I unzipped my leather jacket so my M&P .40 peeked out to say hello.

Samuel turned and bolted.

I hesitated before loping along at an easy pace after him. Huldra are fast runners. We climb and jump through trees, strengthening our already powerful legs. He wouldn't outrun me. I kept an arm's length behind him; no sense in finishing my workout before building up a sweat. My prey flung open a metal door to the dark, rainy outside. He scrambled down the cement steps cascading down Seattle's hilled streets, two at a time, toward the waterfront.

He swung right, slipped into an alley, and wove around huge trash bins. Thankfully, the street lights didn't reach between the squat buildings. Samuel's human eyes could not see in the dark. But mine could.

An elderly man sleeping against the brick wall had his legs sprawled out into the alley. Samuel tripped over the man's shoe and toppled to the wet cement.

The homeless man awoke with a gasp and pulled his legs into his chest.

I lunged at Samuel.

"Lesson one," I said as I slammed his shoulders into a dirty puddle and straddled him. "You're a fucked-up person who does fucked-up things to good people."

"Lesson two," I said as I punched him in the face. His head cracked against the cement a little more than I had intended. "The only people you'll be teaching are your cell mates, who I'm sure will be eager to learn new ways of making you scream."

"And lesson three," I said as I turned him over and pulled his hands behind his back. His dislocated finger flopped around, which made me smile. I grabbed zip-tie handcuffs from my jacket pocket. "This is a citizen's arrest for jumping bail."

A small amount of blood matted Samuel's hair. He swayed when I hauled him to his feet.

I flashed the homeless man a smile. "He's just a little dizzy," I said.

"Or drunk," the man said with a cackle.

With one hand I kept Samuel from falling over. With the other, I reached into my back pocket. I pulled out a Subway gift card—which I carried just for these occasions—and handed it to the man.

"Thanks for helping me catch this guy," I said.

"Happy to help," he replied, examining his new acquisition.

Taking the empty side streets, I walked the dazed and confused skip to the parking lot where I'd parked my new car.

Did I really want Samuel's stink in it? I wished I could walk him all the way to the jail to save my leather seats from his blood. But seeing as the Snohomish County jail was a forty-two minute drive from Seattle, making it roughly a nine hour walk, I decided to just pick up a bottle of leather cleaner on my way home. That's why I'd chosen a car with easy-to-clean seats. Cloth would have meant being stuck with a man-scented vehicle. Tempting my inner huldra too much wasn't a good idea. What I did—the way I walked the line of using my huldra hunting prowess—was already dangerous.

"Strong women are a turnoff," Samuel grumbled.

I tightened my grip on his arm until my nails bit in deep. "Shut it."

Samuel had no clue it was a huldra who pushed him toward her car. Outside of the Hunters and the Wilds, no one knew of my supernatural existence. And if they did, I'd have hell to pay. Today I was the predator, but if I failed my monthly inspection at the Hunter complex, I'd quickly become their prey.

The Hunters were a secret sect started in the early days of the Catholic Church to turn the humans against Wild Women—huldra, rusalki, mermaids, harpies, succubi, and species I'd never heard of. Once, people revered our otherworldly gifts, but then the Hunters showed up and soon villagers were demonizing the Wilds. After hate came forgetfulness. Through the ages, humans turned our existence into folklore and myths.

I not-so-gently placed Samuel in the backseat of my car and attached his cuffed hands to a stainless steel chain in the seat.

"Wherrrr we goin'?" Samuel slurred.

I buckled his seat belt and slammed the door shut with a bang. He winced.

I slid into the front seat and roared the engine to life.

"I thought we'd pay a visit to my friend." And the object of many steamy dreams, dreams that had nothing to do with what my huldra wanted with men and everything to do with what the woman in me wanted. Just thinking of his name made me smile. "Officer Marcus Garcia." Putting it to voice made things tingle all over in anticipation.

TWO

I PERFORMED a quick bark check after I parked in the unloading area behind the jail. It was a precaution I took after each hunt. Huldra are connected to nature, the forest, the trees. Our original Scandinavian foremothers could change their skin to mimic the bark of a tree to blend in and keep from being detected. But they were wild and powerful, and I was not. None of us were anymore. Rigid self-control came at a cost. My coterie believed that cost to be worthy. I wasn't so sure.

A small bark patch whispered of my ancestors along my lower back. If it ever became more than a whisper—a dark, raised declaration of my huldra lineage—I'd have more pressing matters than the perverted bail-jumper sitting behind me in a daze. I swept my hand over the barely there patch and sighed with relief. Now on to more...enjoyable matters.

Police Officer Marcus Garcia. My newest eye candy and the reason I preferred to take only the cases that required a visit to the Snohomish County Jail. All six-foot, two-inches of him were hot as hell, with dark hair cut short on the sides and left a little longer up top. Long enough to pull, I imagined.

"Officer Marcus," I said, trying to appear professional, but still using his first name to show a personal connection. Yes, I was flirting.

He stood and smiled. "Bail Enforcement Agent Faline," he responded, mocking my semi-professional salutation with one of his own. "I heard you were bringing in a bail skipper."

"Yup. I've got a kidnapper here for you this evening," I said. I shoved Samuel forward. He hit the front desk, folding over it, landing on a stack of community service flyers. I handed Samuel's bail piece—paperwork indicating that he was a fugitive—to Marcus.

"Those are your favorites," Marcus joked.

"He's Samuel Woodry—jumped bail a month ago and has been hiding out in Seattle ever since," I continued.

He typed a few things into the computer and then made a quick phone call, ordering a guard to bring out a wheelchair. "Looks like he'll need a doctor, too."

"Really?" I feigned surprise.

"Do you wait 'til they're near death before you decide to bring them in?" he asked. His brown eyes sparkled. Yeah, Officer Marcus was flirting with me too.

"No, they just put up a fight and get all tuckered out." I flashed an innocent smile.

"You always choose the fighters," Marcus said.

So he'd been keeping tabs on me, huh?

Marcus made his way from the desk to the steel door separating civilians like me from "official police business." I couldn't see him for a second as he pinned in the key code to open the door.

"I'd like to think that they choose me," I said.

Marcus propped the door open and I pulled Samuel from resting on the front desk and shuffled him toward the younger officer behind the door, waiting with the wheelchair. "Either way," he said. "The people of Snohomish County thank you. You've removed one more bad guy from the streets."

I scoffed. "Yeah, but each time I remove one, ten more animals are let out on bail when they should be locked up in keyless cells."

"Innocent until proven guilty," he reminded.

"I'm not a cop; I don't have to toe the party line like *some* people."

When did the conversation take a turn from the direction of hey-let's-maybe-get-naked-sometime to criminal justice policies? For all the skips I catch, many more are let out, or aren't caught in the first place. But I continued hunting them down because someone needed to make sure the victims got their chance at justice, and because I had bills that couldn't pay themselves.

"Our list of legal obligations runs a lot longer than yours," Marcus said.

"We're on the same side." I tried to smooth the little wave of building tension between us.

"Very true." When the younger officer wheeled Samuel through a set of doors and out of view, Marcus spoke. "I'd like to be on the opposite side of you."

I raised an eyebrow.

"With a table for two in between us," he continued. "Maybe some wine and your favorite dinner, a juicy rare steak."

Okay, so we talked a lot when I dropped off skips. It was hard not to; he was so damn hot and he asked questions like he'd actually listen and remember the answers. My kind didn't have romantic relationships. For huldra, falling in love and exposing a human to our kind was too risky. But relationships and amazing sex were two very different things. And I'd found that a man who could listen tended to be pretty great in bed.

"Officer Marcus, are you asking me out on a date?" I tilted my head and gave a half-smile.

He gave one nod. "Officer Marcus isn't, because he's on the clock, but civilian Marcus definitely *is* asking you out on a date. At Emory's on Silver Lake, at eight o'clock tonight?"

I pulled my phone from my pocket and glanced at the time. The screen reminded me that I had a check-in at the Hunters' complex tonight. And I was running late.

"I have somewhere to be; it's a personal thing that I shouldn't miss. But I can meet you at Emory's a little after eight o'clock, if that works." I hadn't been with a man in over a year, and more than anything, I wanted Marcus to be the one to break my dry spell.

"Sure. Meet you there at 8:15?" Marcus asked.

"Works for me."

I went over the logistics in my head as I unlocked my car. Check-in was in Arlington, I lived in Granite Falls, and my date with Marcus would be in Everett. I didn't have time to attend check-in and then run home and back to Everett. And I didn't want to wear my work clothes tonight. I needed something more feminine, more enticing. A short black skirt and high heels, perhaps. I sent my sister Shawna a text, and asked her to bring me a change of clothes.

* * *

From Everett, I took Interstate Five to Arlington where the Hunter compound nestled deep into a wooded plot of land. I turned down a gravel road, passed an open iron fence, and parked in front of the training building in a "Reserved" spot beside Shawna's empty Subaru. I was late. Again. I emptied my gun holster and sprang from my car making a mental note to add "buy leather cleaner" to my list of things to do tomorrow.

The Hunter complex consisted of multiple buildings sprawled across private acreage, but the large training building interrupted my view of any other structures behind it. The moment I stepped through the open double doors of the oversized one-story pole barn, a Hunter in all black closed the doors to shut out the rain. The entrance had been made narrow by gates leading me through a metal detector. In a hurry to join my coterie, I walked through the arch and was repaid by a blaring mechanical screech. I backed up and shot my arms in the air before four Hunters ran to my front and back and patted me down.

"In my boots," I yelled over the hustle. "I just came from work and forgot. They're in my boots."

A large Hunter (they were all large to varying degrees) in black cargo pants and a long sleeved black shirt elbowed my stomach, knocking me onto my butt. He and another went to work yanking my boots off. Two daggers clanged onto the cement floor.

"Sorry," I added. "I was in a hurry and forgot they were there."

The elbowing Hunter met my eyes with the frigidness of the North Pole. "No. Weapons. Allowed."

My gaze shot to his own crossbones-decorated dagger holstered at his right hip and then bounced back to look him in the face. "It won't happen again," I said coldly.

"It'd better not," he grumbled under his breath as he stood and placed my daggers into a plastic container and secured the container in a locked cabinet.

I didn't need to be escorted to the small room off to the right of the training area, but two Hunters took it upon themselves to make sure I made it there nonetheless. Aunt Renee paced one side of the wall while my other two aunts and three sisters each sat behind a long table, staring forward at a blank white board. The Hunters called this the school room. I called it the huldra indoctrination room, a phrase my mother had coined during her post-check-in rants, which usually took place while she scrubbed dishes and grumbled under her breath.

Hunters and huldra went way back, though huldra weren't always the ones being schooled. Hunters thought of themselves as a "religious" group, but not even the pope was privy to their existence. They used to be called The Blessed Ones. The males had been born with supernatural strength that they claimed was a gift from God to his favorite believer—one of the chosen at the Council of Nicaea— their forefather. The Hunters' emblem, found on their daggers, their jewelry, and all over their complex, was a cross made from bones with a ruby at its center. But don't ask me the meaning behind anything they do or say. When it came to Hunters, explanations were few and far between. I only knew bits and pieces of their history and abilities through stories passed down from elder huldra.

My ancestors saw the crossed bones of Hunters' dagger hilts often, I'd imagine. According to my mother, back then Hunters deemed huldra—and others like us—evil, and as such, a threat to humanity and to ourselves. My kind held strong until the many long years of Inquisitions. In those days, Hunters posed as human men—as judges, knights, and priests. And as such they profited with money and prestige, setting their secret group in a place of power. After that, it all went downhill for my ancestors. Hunters maneuvered politically, and before long the different groups turned on one another. The harpies hated the succubi who hated the mermaids, and so on. To bring order to the chaos they'd created, Hunters governed all the groups—kept us a secret to the world and safe from each other. Of course, that's not exactly how they tell it. They insist on a rendition in which they're our saviors.

Aunt Renee paused her pacing when I entered the school room. The Hunter shut the door behind me, leaving me alone with my coterie. "You can't just bring weapons here," Aunt Renee said through gritted teeth.

"Like I'm sure you heard me tell them, I forgot."

"Forgetfulness is not an excuse. If we want to get respect from them, we need to give it." Aunt Renee's black ponytail covered the bottom half of the poster tacked to the wall behind her. There were a few "educational" posters sprinkled throughout the room, warnings of how to spot a succubus and what made them so dangerous—they stole their enemy's life force and saw everyone as their enemy. Succubi were the closest supernatural group to us. They lived in Portland, Oregon. But huldras had a fantastic sense of smell. I was sure my nose would tip me off to a nearby succubus long before my eyes.

I ignored my anxious aunt and sat in the empty chair beside Shawna. My partner sister greeted me with a warm smile and a head shake.

Huldra prefer an even number of coterie members, since we don't marry or have long-term relationships. The even number gives us each a same-age life partner in our sister. It's not as difficult an aspiration as one might think. When my aunts and mother were ready to bring the next generation of huldra into the world, they timed their daughters' conception to make sure two of us were born in the same year. Celeste and Olivia were born twenty-five years ago, and Shawna and I are twenty-four. Aunt Renee is a nurse and Aunt Patricia is an acupuncturist. Between the two of them, they planned conceptions based on menses, body temperatures, and moon cycles with the help of herbal tinctures.

I opened my mouth to ask Shawna if she'd brought me a date outfit, when a Hunter entered the room.

"Good evening, ladies." All six feet, seven inches of John stood in front of the white board. His newly shaven face held a grin. His grey hair, cut into a high and tight, didn't fool me. As the leader of Washington's Hunter complex, John was strong.

Unlike my sisters and aunts, I didn't trust the Hunters. They stank of contempt for my kind. John just stank a little less.

John wrote a list on the whiteboard, adhering to this month's topic of proper human interaction. Our check-ins were monthly and the training topics were cyclical. They consisted of a handful of lessons—how to fit in among humans, huldra history, huldra medicine, and ways to avoid and detect our enemies: mermaids, succubi, harpies, and rusalki.

Once John finished his little lecture, complete with tips to prevent physical interaction with injured humans—a possible huldra trigger—he motioned toward the back corner of the room. On his signal, the four Hunters standing outside the door entered the room and switched on the ultra-bright lamp that reminded me of a surgical lamp you'd see in an OR.

John never conducted the screenings; he only stood back with his arms folded over his chest. I liked to think he stayed to make sure the younger Hunters weren't too rough with their screening process.

My aunts, sisters, and I stood in a line, with my Aunt Patricia first up. A blond Hunter wearing latex gloves motioned to Aunt Patricia. She pulled the right side of her long skirt high enough to expose the number tattooed on her upper thigh. The blond Hunter positioned the lamp to illuminate the numbers, read them off to the brunette Hunter, who typed the code into a laptop attached to a cart.

"Nine. Two. Zero. Five. One," the brunette announced and he pressed the mouse pad. "Present and accounted for." In their database we didn't have names, but rather numbers given to us at birth. It helped to maintain a shred of privacy and squashed any risk of our names being leaked and our existence being known to the humans.

"Thank you," the blond said to the brunette. They never wore name tags and rarely used their names in front of us. Possibly for the same reason.

He motioned to my aunt's shirt. She let the hem of her skirt fall to her feet and turned so that her back faced the blond Hunter. She pulled up her flowy shirt and shifted to aim her back into the bright light. The blond ran a gloved finger over my aunt's small bark patch and nodded. "She's clear." He looked up. "Next."

I was last in line, a position I took every month. I had a tendency of leaving the screening Hunter irritated and chose not to allow another member of my coterie to be on the receiving end of that irritation. The blond repositioned the lamp three times after I pulled down the right side of my black fitted jeans. I knew I'd pass. I hadn't killed a guy in the last hour since I'd checked my bark. Not that I'd ever killed anyone.

"Every fucking time we have to play Where's Waldo to find her identification number," the blond grumbled under his breath as he scooted closer to my thigh in an effort to locate my numbers.

"Language," John chastised.

The blond studied the center of the tattoo, filled with vines and trees and branches, and muttered something under his breath. The first time I showed up for a screening with my new tattoo the Hunter threatened to force me to undergo laser removal. But he couldn't do much more than threaten because, according to the original pact between the Wilds and the Hunters, adorning our bodies with art was a Wild right. After all, our priestess foremothers covered themselves with sacred tattoos. I loved trees; they were sacred to me. I liked tattoos. And I hated screenings. The math was simple.

"Okay, I think I've got it," he said in record time. Normally it took him longer. "Eight. Two. Zero. One. And I think that looks like a three."

Damn, it might be time to add another couple branches to that tattoo. I buttoned my jeans and turned, raising my cami to expose my bark.

THREE

SHAWNA RAN to grab the bag of clothing from her car after the double doors to the training complex were shut and locked behind us. The rest of our coterie filed into my aunt's crossover and drove for their homes as I stuffed the reminder card for next month's screening into my back pocket and unlocked my car for my partner sister and me. Each mother and daughter pair in our coterie occupied a modest little house built high in a tree—where huldra felt more comfortable and safe. But the homes were located on the same property, so carpooling was a convenient form of transportation.

I tidied up the files filled with police records, credit card receipts, and photos strewn across my front passenger seat. While staking out Samuel the bondsman I work for, Dale, sent me information for my next hunt, a woman with a knack for hiding.

Shawna's deep brown dreads barely moved as she closed the door to her Subaru and rushed to slide into my front passenger seat. "This bag contains the magic potion to break your dry spell," she said with a dead-serious voice. She couldn't keep a straight face and laughed.

Her smile fell when she spotted a mugshot atop the pile of bail-jumper paperwork that I'd set on my dashboard. "You don't usually go after women."

"I do if they've skipped bail after being charged with human trafficking." I'd been watching this case since newspaper headlines first announced the success of Seattle PD's sting operation in unearthing the city's underground trafficking ring. Dale's call assigning me to the skip was a welcomed one.

"You sure you should take this one?" Shawna was asking if a case involving the disappearance of grown women would stir up old hurts. She hadn't been the one to lose her mother, so I didn't blame her for not knowing that the hurt never feels old; it lingers at the surface fresh as the day it was made. Before my mother's murder, four huldra ran our little coterie—my mother and my three aunts, though my aunts and I aren't related by blood. Almost twenty years later, it was just my aunts. Thinking about it tore the wounds back open.

Some part of me welcomed the pain. It made me a better bounty hunter and ensured my mother's memory would never dull. Plus, this case was no different than the others I'd taken involving abducted victims.

I flipped the photo over—out of sight, out of mind—and reached for the bag she held. "Little black dress and black heels?" I peeked inside.

She nodded. "Unlike your car, your closet is incredibly disorganized," she said. "A pile here, a pile there. If that dress wasn't hanging up, I wouldn't have known if it was dirty or clean."

"One good whiff and you'd have figured it out, I'm sure." I winked at her.

"By the way, it smells like blood in here. Nasty," she added.

I rolled my eyes. "I know. Cleaning is on the top of my To Do list."

I rummaged through the bag. "Oh, yes, thank you!" I'd forgotten to ask for perfume, and Shawna had thought to bring it. I pulled the glass bottle from the bag.

Shawna threw her hand up to stop me. "Ack! Not in here. I don't want to be tasting eau de Faline for the rest of the night."

"What? So eau de dog is better?" I asked, sniffing her and then pretending to be repulsed.

"Please," she said, waving me away. "I smell good."

"Sure," I joked and then asked more seriously, "catch any dogs today?" The scent of dog treats wafted from one of the many pockets along the legs of her beige cargo pants.

Shawna worked at her dream job—an animal rescue sanctuary. Her heightened sense of smell, hearing, and sight helped her to catch skittish dogs that either ran away or were dumped in the woods by their owners. When we were teens she volunteered at the local animal shelter and hasn't stopped helping animals since.

"Yeah. An Akita living in the woods on someone's property. Poor thing was starving, eating the man's chickens. Thankfully he called us before she got sick or something." She shook her head. "You have a date to get to. In short, yes I caught a dog today. It will be helped and fed and rehabilitated. It was a good day. Now go knock him dead and break that dry spell."

She slammed the door behind her and then turned to give my car window a big, wet kiss.

"You're cleaning that!" I yelled through the window as she turned and got into her green Subaru.

She waved and gave me an innocent smile before leaving the Hunter complex. I pulled out too, set on changing my clothes anywhere but here.

* * *

Marcus was already waiting at our table for two when I entered the restaurant. If I thought he looked amazing in a police uniform—which I most certainly did—then he looked out-fucking-standing in dark jeans and a heather grey Polo shirt.

I passed the host with a mumble about my party already waiting for me as I made my way to Marcus. He stood and only sat when I did.

"Nice view," I said, appreciating the dark expanse of the lake outside and the way it reflected the patio twinkle lights. I also spotted my own reflection, my lean physique, high cheekbones, and deep red hair cascading down my bare shoulders.

"What I'm seeing looks even better," he said, his eyes focusing solely on me.

A smile lifted my lips. Yes, this would be a fun night. "You shine up pretty well yourself, Officer Marcus Garcia." His clean, warm scent did things to my body—happy, tingly things.

"I don't think I've ever seen you with your hair down. It's beautiful."

I'd let him run his fingers through my hair later, if he wanted.

"Thanks. I only put it up for work." I took a sip of lemon water and glanced at the menu.

My phone buzzed in my little purse and I pulled it out to glance at the screen while Marcus studied his menu. My sister Olivia, a novelist, texted that she'd just started editing a book about a sexy, tall, buff, and handsome cop and would probably need my expertise on the subject sometime soon. I rolled my eyes. Word got around quick in my coterie. She'd been talking to Shawna, which meant she'd be at my house bright and early tomorrow for every detail.

After the waitress took our order—I got the steak, rare, with potatoes and Marcus got the halibut with rice and mango salsa—Marcus leaned forward and stared at me.

The single votive candle in the center of our small table sparkled in his chestnut brown eyes.

When he didn't return my smile I asked, "What? I can see the wheels spinning."

He settled into his chair. "Why bounty hunting?"

"Why not?" I asked, deflecting his question. Of course, I couldn't exactly tell him that I'd wanted to be a detective, but that John thought it wouldn't be safe for me working alongside government agents while tempting my inner huldra on a daily basis. One wrong decision witnessed by another detective and not only would my kind and my coterie be outed, but they may even force us into invasive testing. John hadn't been keen on my current line of work either, but it was a good compromise, so he signed off on it.

When Marcus didn't give in to my deflection, I gave a half answer. "I don't think our society understands the repercussions of rape and abuse. The way a society's laws and leaders react to such offenses says a lot about who they view as important and who they view as inferior."

"Okay. But what does that have to do with your decision to hunt down bail-jumpers? Why not make a difference as a therapist or lawyer?"

I didn't enjoy bringing up old wounds, but I found myself short of deflecting answers. "My mother went missing when I was little. After a long investigation with no leads, they—" I had to swallow hard as I thought the rest of that sentence—the Hunters. Gathering myself, I went on, "Pronounced her dead. Not a day goes by that I don't wonder about her last days, what happened to her, if her death was painful. I guess that motherless little girl inside of me is trying to bring fairness to unfair situations by catching skips. I bet having the defendant there to stand trial helps give at least a tiny bit of closure to the victims and their families."

Marcus's brows furrowed. "I'm so sorry for your loss."

I shrugged off the discomfort of revealing my wound. "It was a long time ago."

The server swung by our table to drop off a cutting board of warm bread with a tiny bowl of garlic butter. I cut a piece of bread and slathered it with creamy goodness.

"There's a question I ask every cop," Marcus said, reaching for the bread knife.

"Not a cop," I said. I took a bite of bread.

"You're more of a cop than a few people I know on the force," Marcus said, disregarding my lack of a badge. "Who's your favorite super hero?"

I took a sip of water. "Are we talking about comic books or cartoons or movies?" I asked.

"Anything." Marcus took a bite and waited.

"Oh, that's easy, then. The female Thor, after the male version fell and lost his hammer. Pre-patriarchal goddesses weren't just worshipped for fertility, home, and hearth. Some, like Freyja, were warriors. Maybe it's wishful thinking, but I imagine the authors wrote Thor, Goddess of Thunder based on those warrior goddesses."

Marcus's eyes lit up. "So then you're into comic books?"

"I wasn't really until I saw the first issue in the store front window, with the new Thor's red lips, crazy blonde hair, and armor covering her head and chest. I had to check it out. Loved it so much that I subscribed to get the latest issues," I said.

"So, not Wonder Woman and her lasso of truth?"

"She makes the list, but if I were to have a second favorite super hero it'd be Seattle's own Poison Ivy."

Marcus laughed. "Poison Ivy? She's not a hero, she's a villain."

To some, huldra were folkloric villains too—deadly, evil villains. Supernatural creatures who lured men to their graves. So I associated with Poison Ivy. Sue me.

I spread butter across another piece of freshly cut, warm bread. "So you're into comic books then?" I threw his exact same question back at him.

"More like super heroes," he answered. "If I find them in comic books, great; if not, that's okay too. When I was a boy I had a thing for good versus evil, where's the line, what happens if it's blurred, stuff like that. I don't wonder about that line so much anymore, but I still like a great hero story. Seriously, though, Poison Ivy's been Batman's nemesis more than once."

"Her and Batman were on the same side when an earthquake rocked Gotham City, and the two of them worked together to take Karlo down," I reminded him. "But who says Batman is the ruler by which we measure who's good and who's bad? Poison Ivy's focus is protecting nature despite who she has to align with or fight. That's a true hero—someone who doesn't let others get in their way of doing what's right. So then who's your favorite hero?" I sunk my teeth into the now semi-warm bread and flashed Marcus a closed-mouth smile.

"Superman," he said with a decisive nod. "I always liked how he discovered his true origins and abilities as a young person and then used them for good."

"Don't laugh, but I went through a phase where I binge-watched Smallville," I said.

"Me too." Marcus laughed.

The server interrupted with our food.

Three bites of steak and two swigs of wine later, I asked a run-of-the-mill first date question. "So have you always lived in this area of Washington?"

Marcus wiped his mouth with a napkin. "No, not originally. I was born in Spain, but shortly after my mother left us, so my father moved us here to be closer to his family."

"So you and him are close?"

"No. I think we'd both like to be closer, but we're just too different. Every time we tried to spend time together, we butted heads. Eventually we stopped trying. What about you? You from here?" He took a bite and watched me intently. The way he leaned forward told me he was interested.

"I am," I said. "I live in the same house I was born in, just over in Granite Falls, out in the woods."

"Ah, so you're a woodsy woman?"

I laughed. "I haven't heard that one before."

"You haven't?" He seemed to consider his use of words. "I guess it's the same as woodsman, but with my spin on it, being that you're a woman. I'm asking if you're a nature lover."

"One of the most intense nature lovers that's ever lived."

"Oh really? I doubt that. You're staring at him." Marcus narrowed his eyes. "Pop quiz, where's the best place to hike?"

"Um, besides my property?"

"Damn. Okay, other than your property. Have you hiked Mt. Rainier?" His eyebrows rose.

"More than once. Yes."

"Have you stayed in those cabins sprinkled near the mountain? The secluded ones with a hot tub? Nature lover's paradise?" he asked.

"I had no idea they existed." I tended to hike like a true huldra, by jumping from tree to tree. We also slept in the branches when in need of a nap.

"Yeah, I've always wanted to stay in one in particular. It's private and it's right beside a river." Marcus sat his fork down and placed his napkin on the empty plate in front of him. He leaned back and sipped his red wine.

A musky hint of arousal mingled with Marcus's scent. He was thinking of what he'd enjoy doing with me at that cabin. I couldn't read minds but I didn't have to. It was written all over his face. And now I was thinking it too.

My fingers running through his thick, brown hair. His body so close to mine that our scents mixed and I wouldn't be able to tell one from the other. His bare chest. Oh, I couldn't wait to see him shirtless. And pant-less too, for that matter.

"Are you ready to get out of here?" I asked, motioning to our finished meals and empty wine bottle.

"Yeah." He glanced at the table. "What did you think about the wine?"

"I'm more of a blend woman, but those Oregonians know how to make pinot noir. Thanks for having me try it," I said.

"I have another bottle waiting at my apartment, just sitting there. It deserves to be shared." His eyes darkened.

It seemed Marcus and I were on the same page.

"I'd love to," I said with a smile.

"Perfect."

FOUR

MY HULDRA FOREMOTHERS had sat at the edge of the European forests, beckoning lone warriors seeking rest. The man, once intrigued, would come closer until he followed the huldra woman deep into the woods, until the two of them were completely alone. She'd shed her dress and the man would be so in awe of her nakedness that he'd fail to notice the patch of bark at the small of her back.

They'd have sex, right there in the woods. And if his love-making abilities pleased her, she would allow him to return safely to the place he came from. If he was a selfish or lazy lover, however, the huldra would take her owed pleasure in another, more violent form. She'd kill him, one bite at a time.

Some parts of that folktale were true events. Some weren't.

Marcus drove us to his apartment. It was a swanky building decorated with bold reds and blues that looked like it belonged along the waterfront in Seattle, not Everett, Washington,

"Welcome to Casa de Marcus," he said, flicking on lights as we walked into the open floor plan living room, dining area, and kitchen. A black leather couch and dark coffee table faced a flat screen TV mounted above a fireplace. If I kept walking past the couch, I'd end up on a balcony overlooking the Puget Sound.

Cops didn't make enough to afford this type of home. Maybe he came from money.

This realization intensified my attraction to Marcus. The job was far from easy. Marcus must have really wanted to help people if he chose this career despite his family's wealth. His childhood fascination with heroes made sense.

Marcus uncorked the wine and grabbed two glasses.

"No family photos?"

"My dad isn't the only family member I butt heads with," was all he said. "Here, have a seat."

I didn't want to pry. If I did, he may pry about my family, and I wasn't about to explain the workings of a huldra coterie. Instead, I joined him on the couch.

"Can I ask you a question?" He leaned toward me.

His face neared mine and my skin buzzed. "It depends."

"Do you mind if I kiss you?" he asked.

I opened my mouth to tell him that I wished he would skip the asking nonsense and kiss me already, but before words had the chance to fall from my mouth, his lips were on mine.

And they felt fantastic.

At first it was soft and sweet, until it wasn't. Until it transformed into something deeper. I wanted more.

I had to have more.

My fingers found the flesh beside his spine and pressed into him. His thick bands of muscle tightened under my touch, creating a frenzy within me. My fingers climbed to his hair and ran through it. They inched down to his sides, searching for the hem of his shirt. I pulled the fabric over his head and flung the thing onto the floor.

Apparently, he had been waiting for me to give the green light. Within a breath, my dress was somewhere on the ground. He spared a moment to drag his lips across my chest as he unclasped my bra. With his lips trailing and kissing my chest, he lowered me until my bare back connected to his leather couch. I reached to help him remove his jeans, but he batted my hands away.

The scent of his need wafted around the two of us, drawing us in together, tying our bodies as though our arms and legs were the string and our lips the knot.

Hunger growled within me as I took the sight of him in. Dark ink cascaded across the tops of both of his perfect shoulders. A filled-in cross stretched between his pecs over the center of his chest. What looked like old world symbols and ancient letters of a foreign language inched down the inner sides of his biceps. They had been completely covered under his shirt, but now it was as though I were getting a private viewing to a very exclusive art show.

Marcus's tongue drew circles around my belly button before traveling south. When I reached to unbutton his jeans a second time, he removed my hand. Apparently, the man sought to make the night about me. I silently promised to return the favor another time.

The whole point of sex is pleasure.

So I leaned back and let Marcus get me to the point. More than once.

Marcus's arm wrapped around me as we lay on a thick red and brown rug in between his couch and blazing fireplace. He trailed his pointer finger over my right hip and thigh in a circle, thankfully staying clear of my lower back, an area I allowed no one to touch and no human to see in the light of day.

"Hey," I said, my voice throatier than usual. "This won't make things weird on a professional level, right?" I probably should have asked the question before we took each other's clothes off, but I doubted we'd have given honest answers at that point.

"Yeah, of course, it won't be weird," he said, the base of his voice rumbling against my cheek.

I took a cleansing breath and smiled to myself.

"You have interesting tattoos." He drew invisible circles around the very tattoo I'd revealed hours earlier to a frustrated Hunter. "Is this a tree within a woman?" he said, gaze fixed on my thigh.

"Yes it is. I'm impressed. She's grounded, rooted to who she is. It's a good reminder for me to do the same."

"As wise as the trees and as beautiful as all of nature combined," Marcus said under his breath.

I tilted my head up to look into his eyes. "Yes. Exactly that."

Marcus took the opportunity to lean in and kiss me. And I was thankful for the interruption. His deeper understanding of my own thoughts made my heart thrum and we couldn't have that.

When he pulled away, I asked, "What about yours? Any significance?"

He licked his bottom lip. "Yeah, I guess you could say it's a manly tradition in my family. My uncles and dad all have similar tattoos, though I think my dad's may extend past his shirt sleeve by now. I don't know, I haven't seen him in over a year."

I propped myself up on my elbow to look into Marcus's eyes. The fire Marcus had lit after we'd transferred from the couch to the ground now warmed my backside. Orange hues danced across his face and glowed along his skin. Marcus ran his hand through his hair, clearly uncomfortable talking about his family.

Now it was my turn to draw shapes along his ink. "Which ones have the most significance to you?" I asked, against my better judgment.

"This one right here." He touched his left pec, right over his heart.

"It looks a lot like a tree," I said, shocked that I hadn't noticed it earlier. But when a sexy man is naked in front of you, you don't examine and critique his body art. You just see his whole body as art.

"It is," he said with a smile. "A tree without leaves or roots."

"It's hard to have one without the other," I mused.

"Well it's not done yet." He kissed me. "So," he said, changing the subject. "Does this mean I can tell everyone at work that the hard-ass bounty hunter is my girlfriend?" Laughter rolled from his smile.

I pretended to shove him. "Ha! Well, that'd be difficult seeing as I don't do relationships."

"Do you do second dates, then?" he asked.

"I guess it depends what the second date is, and with whom." I gave him a wry smile. "And how the first date ended."

"A buddy of mine from a precinct in Mill Creek was promoted, so he's throwing a party at some swanky hotel in Bellevue. Do you want to be my plus one?" he asked.

The idea of a date in front of a bunch of people I dealt with on a professional level did not excite me. But another date with Marcus did.

Plus, networking with cops who could possibly do me a solid down the road wasn't a bad idea. And I still hadn't gotten Marcus's jeans off, so technically my dry spell had yet to be broken.

"Okay," I said, hesitating a little.

"Really?" he asked, surprised. "You'll go with me?"

With one simple nod I broke a cardinal huldra rule. No second dates.

FIVE

THE ELEVATOR from the Westin Bellevue Hotel's parking garage emptied me out into the front lobby where Marcus sat, waiting.

"Swanky is one word for it." I referred to the hotel decor as he kissed my forehead.

Marcus wore black slacks and a fitted charcoal striped button-up dress shirt. I smiled inside, picturing the slew of sexy tattoos hidden beneath the layers. Was it me or did he look a little more pumped up than the night before? Swollen, like he'd just finished an intense workout enhanced by a magic protein shake.

He pressed his hand to the small of my back and I pulled away to loop my arm through his. Male fingers across my bark brought up images of an operating room lamp and Hunters checking my patch with gloved hands—pretty much the opposite of what I wanted to experience tonight.

"Another gorgeous view tonight," Marcus said, eyeing me from my head to my feet and up again.

When I'd gotten ready for tonight I had wished I hadn't worn my little black dress the night before. I'd used up my wild card outfit. Thankfully, I had three sisters and three aunts with full closets and little dresses of their own. I didn't fit into Shawna's petite sizes, but

Olivia's clothing worked just fine. Tonight I wore her black dress complete with black, muted sequins sewn into the skirt. This dress always made me laugh with irony. The sequins reminded me of a mermaid. Not that I'd met a mermaid.

"Thanks," I said. "You're looking on point tonight as well."

He lifted one eyebrow, probably over my word choice.

"You just come from the gym?" I said.

He shook his head. "No. Why do you ask? Do I stink?"

"No. You just look...swollen. The good kind of swollen."

"I wish I had. Maybe then I'd know why I'm so damn sore." He winced as he turned toward the ballroom where the event was being held. "I was this close to smelling like Icy Hot tonight."

A low stage had been set up at the front of the ballroom, and out-of-uniform police chatted while holding little plates of appetizers and long-stemmed wine glasses or short, thick whiskey glasses.

I'd come into contact with more than a few cops in attendance while dropping off skips, though I doubted they'd recognize me with my hair down and in high heels. Marcus veered us toward the white linen-covered table of finger foods.

"Sorry, I don't see steak bites," he joked.

"That's it," I responded. "This party is officially over. I'm going home." I pretended to turn and walk away, but Marcus grabbed me by my waist and wrapped his arms around me. Okay, so Marcus had no issues with PDA. I, on the other hand, did.

I gently pulled from his embrace and pretended to be overly interested in the display of food. "No caviar either," I said, keeping up with the game.

"Oh well, I guess we'll have to slum it. Abbey Smoked Brie, hardened sourdough, and red wine it is."

I let out a laugh as Marcus grabbed one plate for each of us and used tongs too little for his hands to place cheese and bread onto our plates.

"Can I ask you a serious question, Faline?"

"It depends," I said with a serious tone.

"What are you looking for?" Marcus turned and our gazes connected.

"Bad guys?" I said.

"No, I mean with us, with this." He motioned to the two of us. "Long term, short term... I know last night you mentioned your aversion to relationships, so..."

"That's a really random question."

"Is it? I've been thinking about it since your comment." He took a bite of bread with brie.

I couldn't help but watch his jaw move—the light stubble of beard threatening to grow. I thought I'd been pretty clear as to what I was looking for tonight: round two, to return the favor. Even if I wanted more than that, it was not an option. I had rules for a reason, least of all to avoid broken hearts, most of all to avoid outing the existence of my kind and getting Marcus killed in the process. The no-dating rule was for his safety as much as it was for mine.

"Maybe it is a random question," he said after he swallowed his food. "But I don't just leap into bed with any woman. There's something here, and before it moves any further, I need to know your feelings."

I took my time. My tongue played with my teeth to keep from speaking. I didn't want to answer him. I didn't want to stop seeing him yet. But I also didn't want a relationship. I couldn't have a relationship. It would never work.

"Honestly?" I bought one more second. "I understand what you're saying. I feel it too, a connection. And I'd really like to get a room and see where that connection leads us tonight. But I'm not at a place in my life where anything beyond that is feasible. So seeing where it takes us long term isn't an option."

I placed my hand on Marcus's arm. His jaw clenched.

"Yeah, I kind of thought that's what you meant last night, but I needed to make sure." He pulled his arm from under my hand. "The problem is, you don't want anything serious, just a casual sexual relationship. Which I'm not saying there's anything wrong with that. But, personally, I don't have sex with a woman unless we're in a serious relationship."

"Is there a particular reason for that?" I asked, a little dismayed.

"Is there a particular reason you can't be in a committed relationship?"

Yes, but nothing I could share with him.

We stood beside the food table in an awkward standoff.

And this is why huldra don't go on second dates, I could imagine Shawna saying.

Marcus's cell phone buzzed from his pocket, breaking the silence between us. He slid it out to check the screen. "I've got to take this. It's work."

I gave a nod and thanked the universe for the distraction.

He answered the phone without saying anything. I used my heightened hearing to listen to the man's voice mumble something about his father on the other end of the line and then hang up. Marcus slid his phone into his pocket.

"I've got to go," was all he said before setting the plate on the tall circular table and turning to leave.

"Wait," I said. "So this, today, it's done?" When he kept walking, I quickly caught up. "*You* brought *me* here."

"It's nothing personal, I swear. There's a work emergency I have to deal with. Stay, enjoy the party. I've just... I've got to go. We'll talk later?"

I took a breath and reminded myself that neither he nor I had a nine-to-five job. "Yeah," I said. "I understand."

He paused long enough to give me a quick hug, before leaving the ballroom. I didn't even have time to stiffen up in his arms.

I headed toward the white ornate doors to leave, but realized I still held the appetizer plate and doubled back.

"Hey, don't I know you?" a man asked as I passed him. He stood at the table nearest the doors. He looked to be in his forties and wore khaki slacks and a blue button-up dress shirt with an ugly tie. His shirt's buttons pulled taught around his belly. Silver strands sprinkled his hair at the temples.

"You probably do," I said, looking for another, less occupied, table to leave my plate and get out of there.

"I've got it! You work for Dale, don't you?"

I paused long enough to give the man a double-take. "Yes. You're the private investigator Dale uses every now and again, aren't you?" I left off the part where Dale vowed to never use the man's services again after a botched job left us without a skip by the trial date.

"I am," he said, straightening his tie. "Though, I dropped the ball on the last job I worked for him. Feel real bad about that. Not sure if he mentioned it."

His name came back to me. "Yeah, Brian, it put Dale in a tight place. Lost him a lot of money, too." Dale had entertained the idea that Brian had been paid by someone else to *not* find the skip. I looked around the room of police officers. "What are you doing here, though?" Brian wasn't known as the most professional PI. It had a lot to do with his willingness to stoop below the law to get what he needed. I'd also recently heard rumors that he'd started working for unsavory clients, locating people whose safety would be jeopardized if they were found.

"Ah, well Rod and I go way back. Wanted to wish him well with his big promotion."

A uniformed police captain stood on stage and spoke into the microphone, calling the room to a toast.

Brian grabbed two glasses of champagne from a waiter who walked the area offering drinks from a silver platter. I eyed my escape as the room quieted.

"Here," he said. I turned to an outstretched glass of champagne. "They're about to make the toast and give a speech."

"No, I'm fine, thanks. I was just leaving."

"Well, I'm glad I ran into you then. Like I said, I feel really bad about how I dropped the ball with Dale and I was hoping to make it up to him." Brian still held the drink toward me.

I didn't take it.

"Make it up to him?" I asked. "How?"

"You heard about the sting operation on that underground human trafficking ring?"

"Yes."

Brian leaned in and lowered his voice. "I work for a client who wants to see your skip found just as much as you do."

I accepted the glass of champagne.

"We can't talk about it here, of course," he said, eyeing the crowd of law enforcement.

The police captain onstage called for a toast and I joined the others in the room with a raise of my glass. I gulped down its contents and returned the empty glass to the table.

"Obviously," I said, eager to hear any juicy details Brian could provide. Of course, he and I both knew nothing he could say would make up for the many thousands of dollars Dale lost from trusting Brian. Which is why I wouldn't trust him either. But a tip was a tip.

"I got a room up on the third floor. You know how police parties can get a little rowdy." Brian took two steps from the table and waited for me to follow.

I followed him from the ballroom, but made my intentions known in the hall. "Here's fine," I said, peering around the empty walkway. But rather than the white walls and bright paintings I'd noticed earlier, my vision faded as though darkly tinted windows encased me from behind and muted out the world.

"You sure?" Brian asked. "You look like you could lie down. You okay?"

I barely heard him. My head swam. I tried to speak, but my tongue felt too big to push words past. "Yessss," I slurred. "I'm perfffectly—"

* * *

My head pounded. I reached my hand up to rub my temple, but my muscles shook and my arm fell to the ground.

In a haze, I blinked my eyes open to see what held my arms down.

I cleared my throat and licked my lips. An odd taste...like pennies.

I worked at sitting up. The room spun around me. Light from outside street lamps trickled through openings in the thick floor-to-ceiling drapes. A large white duvet-covered bed took up most of the room. A suitcase stand stood beside a flat screen TV.

A suitcase stand?

A hotel room. I was in a hotel room, on the floor between the foot of the bed and the TV cabinet. I blinked again. Oh crap. The light scent of testosterone played with my nose. Was there a man in the bed, sleeping? Had Marcus returned and changed his mind? Why couldn't I remember?

If it was Marcus lying on that bed, I was in no shape to have breakfast and converse with him. I not-so-silently stood to gather my things and tiptoe out of the room. My legs ached like I'd returned from a hard-core gym day. I peered down to see why. Black sequins littered the hotel room floor. The bottom of my dress was frayed and one shoulder strap had been completely ripped off.

I spotted my little black clutch on the TV stand and grabbed it.

"Marcus?" I whispered, hoping and praying it was Marcus who I'd allowed to ruin Olivia's dress and not some guy I'd just met in the fog of...whatever fog I'd been in last night. I didn't know why it mattered to me, but it did. Except, I didn't remember getting drunk last night. And if I had, I'd never been so drunk that I'd blacked out. I didn't think huldra were capable of that—alcohol didn't last long in our systems.

When no one answered my whisper, I crept toward the door. I'd figure it all out later, after a shower and a gallon of coffee. As I tiptoed past the queen-size bed, an out of place shape caught my eye. It was wedged between the bed and the wall, up near the nightstand separating the two.

I gasped and flung my hand over my mouth.

Blood. Lots and lots of blood pooled around a man who lay face down. I wouldn't have known his pants were khaki if I hadn't met him earlier. The shirt he'd worn, the blue button-up, now looked more mauve with strips of fabric missing from his shoulder blades to his belt. I bent closer to his body. Where fabric should have been, three craters dipped into his back. Blood matted his brown and silver hair.

Instinctively, I reached up to touch my own hair. My fingers caught in the sticky tangled mess. His blood. It was in my hair. But how? My spinning head cleared. The penny taste wasn't pennies.

I had to find answers, and fast.

My gaze quickly shifted around the room. No suitcase. No keys. Nothing to suggest Brian had been staying here tonight. Except, of course, for Brian's body facedown beside the bed. Shit. As unlikable as the guy was, he didn't deserve to die.

I thought to call the police, to call Marcus, but I knew what would come next. Creatures like me don't go to jail. The Hunters intervene and exact their own brand of justice that no human court would sanction.

I hurried for the door, but stopped short when I passed the bathroom. A long full-length mirror stared at me through the open bathroom door. It looked like someone had dipped a sponge in brownish red paint and painted me with it. Dried blood cracked around my knees.

With hesitance, I set my purse onto the marble bathroom counter and padded on bare feet across the tile. I swiped my fingers across my lower back and gasped. Tears escaped my eyes and cleared a path down my cheek. With a shaky breath I lifted my dress and twisted my body to view my back in the mirror.

A wide patch of russet brown bark extended from my tailbone and up my spine, six inches wide from one side of my back to the other. My stomach turned in disgust and my heart jumped in excitement.

My huldra.

I had let her out. And now it'd be impossible to get her back in.

SIX

AFTER COVERING my head with the largest towel I could find in the bathroom, and then hurrying out of the hotel, I sped along the empty freeway heading northbound toward home. The blue digital numbers on my dashboard said it was two o'clock in the morning. Mist fell from the sky and every few seconds my wipers swept the damp haze from my windshield.

As hard as I tried, memories of walking to the hotel room or killing the man refused to show themselves. The only possible explanation was that he'd put some sort of drug in my champagne. But huldra don't succumb to Rohypnol like humans. And why would Brian want to drug me?

"Call Shawna," I commanded to the Bluetooth in my car.

It took five rings for a tired Shawna to pick up. "Faline?" she asked with a raspy voice.

"I'm on my way home. I need you to wake everyone up and have them meet me in the common house." I took my exit and continued driving over the speed limit, my car hugging the curves of the winding country roads. Evergreens loomed on each side, blocking what little moonlight sifted through the clouds.

"What's going on?" Shawna asked through a yawn.

Shawna's voice broke the damn and I answered in between sobs. "I killed. A man. Shawna. I don't know how. Or why. I. Killed him." Shivers ran down my body and the hair on my arms stood.

I pictured Brian lying in a pool of his own blood and my shrill of excitement made me want to vomit in disgust. My huldra wanted more.

I gripped the steering wheel, and my hands shook with strength.

I didn't pull my car behind the common house where our four homes hid high up in the evergreens. I threw it into park as soon as I neared the front door of the common house and jumped out.

"How could you?" Aunt Renee yelled the moment I swung the front door open. She paced along the length of the couch in the living room, just past the slate tile entry.

"How could I what? I don't remember doing it!" I shot back.

Huldra groups do not have leaders. We all lead and we all follow. So Renee's parental attitude this evening was not appreciated or accepted.

Shawna sat on the couch and patted the cushion beside her.

"No, I'm sorry, but you cannot sit on the furniture in a blood-soaked dress," Renee chirped, shaking her head. She wore a long, white robe tied around her waist. It almost glowed against her dark hair and skin.

The scent of male blood wouldn't be the best addition to a huldra home. I pulled the dress up over my head, but my unexpected strength tore the thing in two. I peered up at my coterie as I gripped two handfuls of black fabric.

My sister Olivia laughed and quickly put a hand over her mouth. "Sorry, it's not funny. It shouldn't be funny," she mumbled through her fingers.

I padded to the kitchen, tossed the two pieces of the dress into the trash, tied the bag, and placed it beside the side door leading to the patio. I thought better, and opened the glass double doors to place it outside the house, onto the patio. I returned to the living room and stood beside the couch, beside my partner sister.

Celeste lifted her nose. "You smell delicious," she said before licking her lips. She took a hesitant step toward me.

"It's in my hair," I said with a groan. "His blood."

"I'm well aware," Aunt Patricia answered. She stepped between Celeste and me.

Aunt Renee threw her hands into the air. "This is just... I can't..."

"Tell us what happened, Faline," Shawna spoke up, diffusing the tension in the room. "From the beginning."

"Okay." I thought about sitting on the couch, but still didn't want my bloody, matted hair to touch the fabric. I opted to stand.

When I finished sharing what little I remembered of the night, Aunt Patricia rubbed Celeste's arm and walked toward me. "Do you think he was working for someone else?"

"What? Brian. Definitely. He's never *not* working for someone."

Shawna chewed her lip. "He said he was working for someone on the human trafficking case. Could that person have hired him to kidnap you?"

"Maybe, but I don't see why." A cloud of fuzziness moved and recollection hit me. "The papers I have mention a whole ring of people involved, but nothing of any evidence found and the skip is the only name given. They only brought up charges against one woman, which is weird that one woman would take the fall for a whole operation. Still, I don't see how that has anything to do with me."

"He didn't drug you," Aunt Patricia said solemnly.

Aunt Renee nodded. "Drugs don't affect us that way."

"Then how did he get me back to the room?" I asked.

"It's got to be the succubi." Aunt Renee glared out the sliding glass door. She shot a glance to her sisters. "They're getting revenge."

Aunt Abigale sucked in a breath.

"Wait," I said with hands in the air. "They've already gotten their revenge. I have a missing mother to prove it."

"Marcus isn't from Oregon, is he?" Shawna asked, worry etched in her brow.

"No, I made sure to ask before anything happened between us." I thought to comfort my sister with a touch, but didn't want to soil her sleeping shirt. "But Brian travels." I corrected myself. "Traveled, all over the west coast. He could have met the succubi and agreed to work a job for them."

The succubi were a territorial group. Even in the old country they'd war with the huldra over who had claim to which village. Both groups preyed on men and neither wanted to share.

Patricia shook her head. "He wouldn't need to agree to anything. They make men do their bidding and leave the men with not even a memory of what they'd done. Just like you haven't any memories of what you've done."

"But they can't cross state lines," Celeste said.

"Haven't they before?" Renee reminded us of my mother's abduction.

Except, they hadn't abducted me. They'd gotten a man to do it for them. I still wasn't sure how he was able to cause me to black out, to let my huldra free.

My huldra.

They hadn't anticipated that she'd be so close to the surface, excited from hunting skips, scratching to be released. When I blacked out, my huldra broke free.

I swallowed the lump forming in my throat. I had not made the same mistake my mother had. I did not choose to mate with a succubus's man. "They have no reason to target me."

"You are the daughter of their enemy. The offspring of their human male whom they believed betrayed them for a huldra. You are the third point in their triangle of revenge." Patricia brought her hand to her mouth and tapped her teeth. "But why now?"

"At least one succubus has to be up here, pulling the puppet strings," Aunt Renee argued. "Every hotel has cameras. A security guard monitoring the camera system would have spotted you leaving looking the way you do and called the cops. Do you hear any sirens? Because I don't. Only a succubus would be able to wipe the memories of any witnesses and cause security tapes to disappear."

My scalp itched. I reached up and sticky flakes of dried blood greeted my fingers. I quickly dropped my hand to my side.

"Is it weird that I want to lick her?" Celeste said, still eyeing me. The dampness of the ground had moistened my feet on my way in, but now it dried and blood cracked around my toes. My arms didn't look much better.

"Keep your head about you," Patricia, Celeste's mother, scolded.

"You and your sisters will be on your own, leading this coterie someday; these are the types of things you'll have to deal with."

"I think it's time we taught the succubi a lesson," Aunt Renee interrupted. She stopped pacing and stared at me with what looked like complete control and confidence. "We should plan an attack."

"Attack on what?" I asked, exasperated. "Their home? Do you realize how insane that sounds?"

"They won't stop until you've suffered your mother's fate." Aunt Renee sat on the couch as though she were about to serve tea and cookies. Her sudden extreme calm unnerved me.

"It'll be a bloodbath. No. I won't agree to it. And you've forgotten the Hunters. They have rules against this. We can't cross state lines." I scratched a patch of dried blood from my right arm. Tiny bits of red fell onto the wood floor. "I'll clean that up later."

Patricia nodded. "Let's focus on the here and now," she said. "Since we think we know how this happened, we need to figure out how it will affect Faline. I see from your movements, that you've gained speed? And strength too?"

I nodded. I opened my mouth to add that I could also now feel my huldra right under my skin, vibrating, yearning for more strength. But I bit my lip instead. Their heavy minds didn't need more troubles added to the heap.

"Then I suppose the next step is to watch you closely," Aunt Patricia said.

Renee scoffed. "And just wait for them to try again? What if Faline's strength wears off? She's stronger, faster; it's time to strike now."

"Sister," Patricia said. "There's no telling what Faline's body is going through. Huldra haven't killed for centuries."

I cringed.

"Faline, we can reconvene to discuss every symptom you're experiencing." Patricia nodded to Renee. "And we'll conduct a full physical, once you're cleaned and the scent you're wearing isn't so... so...tempting."

"Yeah," I said as I made my way through the living room toward the back door that led to the four tree homes, antsy to leave the confines of walls.

Shawna gasped. I froze in place and closed my eyes. I'd completely forgotten.

"Your bark," Shawna whispered.

I inhaled and tears filled my eyes. Frustration and anger washed away, leaving me raw and vulnerable—the two feelings I hated most.

"The Hunters will be screening us in less than a month," said my partner sister.

"I know."

"What are we going to do?" Celeste asked.

No one answered.

I reached my hand in front of my face and spread my fingers apart. In one second, with just the thought of creating bark across my skin, russet colored ridges sprang up where knuckles belonged.

"It's growing!" Olivia shrieked. "Across your back!"

I didn't turn around. I didn't want to see their faces. I thought of bark covering my whole body and instantly pinpricks tingled from my back and stretched to my legs and arms. I bolted from the common house, ran past our tree homes, and sped deep into the forest. My huldra wanted out.

SEVEN

MY FOREMOTHERS USED to live in woods much like those I crouched within. Dark, emerald, fuzzy moss clung to the russet tree trunks, and sage green, porous moss hung from the branches. Ferns sprouted up like mini bushes, blotting shades of green along the dark brown dirt. To keep my inner huldra at bay, I ran across my property so quickly my feet barely touched the ground.

My foremothers. This was normal to them, natural. Bark façade covering their skin. Naked among the evergreens and the alders. Wildness was their nature. So why did it feel so wrong for me? I flung myself at an evergreen and dug my fingers into its soft outer layer, pulling myself up the trunk until I jumped, feet first, onto a branch. Higher. I needed to go higher.

Moonlight filtered through clouds and pine needles. Rain sprinkled down my scalp in a much needed shower. My tangle of matted red hair calmed until it hung straight. Water mixed with blood as it dripped from the strands and wound down my butt and legs.

I fought the embarrassment crashing inside, the ache to run away from my coterie and never return. I'd be protecting those that I loved if I just left tonight. I could live deep in the forests like my foremothers had. My foremothers. Wild Women. Had they struggled with the shame of their existence? Huldra history lessons taught by the Hunters said yes. But my mother's whispered bedtime stories had once led me to believe otherwise.

"Long ago, men and women lived equally in peaceful farming lands and cities built on the belief of cooperation," she'd tell me monthly, each night she returned from her Hunter check-in, as she tucked me into bed. "These areas thrived. But people from another land with different beliefs, who sought to take the success of others for their own, took over. They had no interest in cooperation or equality, and soon they established a hierarchy in these once peaceful cities based on gender and wealth. In time they condemned the original goddesses and gods of the land, and claimed their own gods to be the true rulers of heaven and earth. They even ruined the goddess temples.

"The goddesses knew their worship would soon fade into forgotten history. In one last act of protection for those who lived by their teachings, the goddesses bestowed upon their highest priestesses their own supernatural abilities. Each goddess had a different skillset of abilities."

"That's when Freyja made us," I'd say each time she told the story.

"Yes," she'd answer, "and when Lilith created the succubi, and when Atargatis created the mermaids... That's how all the Wild Women were created."

It'd been easy for my mother to speak of huldra and succubi as one, as Wilds, before they'd killed her. Now, because of that thinking, she couldn't speak at all.

"And where were the Hunters with all their promised protection when the life-suckers took my mother?" I muttered into the night. Mist formed around my warm breath in the cold air.

"They joined forces with the Oregon Hunters to get her back." Shawna answered.

Shocked, I scanned the ground and then the other trees, but didn't see Shawna. Out of all of us, she threw her voice the best. Within a few breaths, Shawna stood at the base of the tree whose branches I sought refuge within.

I lay my stomach onto the branch and peered down at my partner sister. "But they didn't return with her."

"At least they tried," Shawna said.

But it was too late for me. I'd traveled past the point for Hunter protection—if there ever was such a thing—and crossed the line from their charge to their enemy. They just hadn't realized it yet.

I stood and walked toward the trunk of the tree. I jumped to the lower branch, and the next lower, until the balls of my feet hit the moist dirt with a thud.

Shawna inhaled deeply. "You smell like...squirrel?"

I nodded. Thankfully, the ingestion of animal DNA had no effect on my bark patch or huldra abilities, because while I've been told other Wilds practice veganism, I've never heard of even a vegetarian huldra. "I needed to hunt. It crossed my path." I ran my fingers through my wet hair. "Were you sent to come get me?"

"Yes." Shawna cocked her head. "I also wanted to make sure you didn't try to fall on your proverbial sword and leave us." She turned, without waiting for my response, toward the front of our property where our tree homes stood. I followed.

"So what'd they say?" I asked when Shawna walked in silence for a few minutes too long. She was much better than me at keeping her thoughts to herself. And it drove me up the wall.

"Aunt Renee wants to discuss it with you," Shawna answered. "But I can't stick around for what I'm sure will be a...lively discussion... because I need to try to get another couple hours of sleep. Tonight's the benefit for the animal sanctuary."

My hand dropped to my side and I turned to look at Shawna. "That's right. Do you need help with setup or anything? The least I can do is buy you a pint of coffee." My poor sister would have to run a whole event after the night's drama. I suddenly felt guilty for an entirely different reason.

"I may take you up on that. But seriously, it's hard to think about that when we have your check-in to worry about," she said.

I grabbed her hand. "Well don't. Worry about me, I mean. Check-in isn't for another month. That gives us a lot of time to figure things out."

A slow smile worked its way onto my partner sister's face. I hated that it took so long to get there, that I had caused her this anxiety. "Okay. But you're still coming, right?"

I wove my fingers through hers like I had when we were little girls running through the forest together. "I wouldn't miss it."

* * *

I carpooled to the benefit with my two other sisters and three aunts. Celeste and Olivia sat in the last row in my aunt's crossover. The two partner sisters chatted quietly. Whereas Olivia's dark features looked more Hispanic, Celeste's most resembled those of Vietnamese women. Huldra don't track their human lineage, so I couldn't say for sure.

I stared out at the night sky from a middle-row seat and shuffled through the evening's early events. When I'd woken from my post-shower nap, I saw that I'd missed two calls from Marcus and he'd left a message. I still hadn't listened to the voicemail.

Marcus and I hadn't finished our last conversation, let alone agreed to separate on any sort of terms—good or bad. But to be alone with him again, with succubi after me, had the potential to end tragically. I refused to put him at risk. When I returned to work I'd try to pick the skips from different cities so I wouldn't have to drop them off at Everett Municipal—wouldn't have to see Marcus.

"You sure it's safe for you to be around humans?" a voice asked from the front seat.

"I am fine," I said for the one-hundredth time.

"Because if you're not, that's okay too." It was my Aunt Renee talking, though she didn't turn to look at me. She got carsick easily.

I almost repeated my new phrase for the one hundred and first time, but Patricia reminded her sister of the coterie's agreed plan—which was basically to do nothing but wait. Considering our next check-in, we had a little more than three weeks to decide on our next move. Since I'd agreed to wait, Renee had been goading me to change my mind.

We reached the great double doors of the event center—a sprawling building in the country. Bright lights and the scent of fresh-baked bread flooded out from the entry. We walked across the stone tiled foyer where a modest bar stood, covered mostly with wine bottles. A tall, handsome bartender quickly served his customers full glasses of reds, whites, and some cocktails, keeping the long line moving.

"Hello, welcome, thanks so much for coming." A woman in black dress slacks and a royal blue, silk top greeted us as we entered the dining hall. She eyed our invitations with a quick glance and escorted us to a large round table with seating for ten.

The benefit for rescued animals was being held at a ranch-style community center in Arlington on a five-acre plot of land. The many floor-to-ceiling windows gave way to views of mountains in the distance and horse pastures lining the square lot.

"Shawna puts on the best galas," Aunt Abigale said with motherly pride as she sat and folded a white fabric napkin across her lap.

Aunt Patricia nodded. "I look forward to this every year."

Posters propped on easels lined the dining hall, and an ongoing video of dogs playing with ropes and chew toys projected onto a white curtain at the front of the room.

Servers in black slacks and white button-up tops breezed through the room leaving warm bread on each table. I reached for the sweating glass pitcher of ice water with lemon wedges, and poured myself a drink, then offered to fill the empty glasses belonging to my coterie.

The large potted plants in each corner had to have been Shawna's decision. Greenery and trees are to huldra what name brand clothes are to high schoolers.

My three aunts served themselves bread smeared with butter, and then passed the food to Olivia, Celeste, and me.

I was slathering soft butter onto my chunk of pre-cut bread, when Renee spoke past the bread in her mouth. "You sure you're not feeling your huldra, being around so many human males?"

"Aunt Renee," I scolded. I peered around the room. My warning gaze came to rest on her. "Not here. People can hear you."

She lowered her voice to hide her words from those outside the huldra persuasion. "I think we should attack, that's all I'm saying."

We had to have looked odd, women sitting at a table with lips moving like a regular conversation, but void of audible sound. But nowadays, with Bluetooth earbuds in everyone's ears, it wasn't like they were going to notice.

"I don't want to start a war we can't finish," Celeste added. "Plus, we've got time. Using a male didn't work, so even if they aren't going to quit, they have to regroup before trying again."

"Thank you," I said, nodding toward my sister.

I picked up Shawna's scent before the other members of my group seemed to realize she was headed to our table. My sense of smell must have gotten stronger. I turned to look for her among the people mulling about. She cut through the crowd and stood behind her mother, Aunt Abigale. They both had mocha skin and black hair, though Abigale didn't style hers in dreads.

"Oops, I almost sloshed my drink on you," Shawna said, wiping her mother's shoulder. "I can't talk long, but I wanted to come and say hi."

"It's lovely." Aunt Abigale held her daughter's hand on her shoulder and gave it a squeeze.

Olivia lifted her nose and inhaled. "Is that an alcoholic drink?"

Shawna laughed. "Yes, long island iced tea." She shimmied the tall clear goblet-looking glass. "If I'm going to present a touching, heartfelt speech that'll give people the urge to open their wallets and write checks, I'll need this elixir to turn down my anxiety a few notches." Shawna had an insatiable love for animals, not so much for people, and certainly not for public speaking. "Did you see the bar when you came in?"

I nodded. I'd hoped to get myself a glass of wine before Aunt Renee started in.

Shawna continued, "The bartender showed up late." She gave a cleansing breath. "But he's here now, so the festivities can begin." She took a swig of her drink. "Oh, and yes this table will be full, so when the others come please be gracious and act human."

"We'll be perfectly polite," Aunt Renee assured her.

"You have nothing to worry about. You outdo yourself every year, and I'm sure this year will be no different," Aunt Abigale boasted on her daughter's behalf.

A young man in black slacks and a white button-up shirt hurried over to my sister and tapped her on the shoulder. "Excuse me, Shawna.

I'm sorry to interrupt," he said to my aunt then turned toward Shawna. "The bartender is saying he ran out of vodka."

Shawna's eyes widened and she pointed to her drink before she turned around to address the young man. "There's more in the storage unit outside. I'll go grab it." She turned to us. "If I'm not back before the event begins, enjoy."

She didn't return to our table. The humans she mentioned, however, did. We offered the obligatory smiles and then kept mainly to ourselves. Thankfully, the awkwardness didn't last long.

The woman who had greeted us at the dining room entrance made her way to the front of the room with a microphone clutched in her right hand. Each soft fold of her dark blue silk top shimmered. "Welcome to our annual benefit," she said to the crowd. "Where we endeavor to give back to those animals who've given us so very much."

The room filled with applause and she stood beaming while a video of animals from their rescue center played across the screen behind her. "Our four-legged friends are among our most precious natural resources. It means a lot to the staff at Northwest Animal Rescue that you made it out tonight, but most of all, it means a lot to our four-legged friends. It means another year of meals, of proper bedding, of unconditional love, and of medical care. Hopefully your presence also means these amazing animals will have a second chance at happiness."

She paused for the crowd to applaud.

"Allow me to introduce Shawna Frey, our valued and hardworking director, without whom this night, and most of our rescue center, wouldn't have been possible. Shawna?" The woman in the blue top scanned the room for my sister. "Shawna? Where'd you go?" she said with the timid laugh of someone who was ready to hand over the microphone and retreat from the limelight.

People from the audience looked around the room as though they'd know my sister when they saw her. I scanned the room, searching each table, each face, but Shawna was nowhere to be seen.

"She's probably busy making sure tonight runs smoothly," the woman up front said with a nervous laugh. She motioned to a staff member standing near the entrance to the dining hall, who quickly slipped out the double doors to find my sister.

Minutes ticked by and still no trace of Shawna. With the passing of each one a very bad feeling started to settle in my gut. For Shawna's sake, I stayed put as long as I could. When the staff member didn't return five minutes later, I stood.

"What are you doing?" Aunt Patricia said from the side of her mouth. She smiled to the humans at our table.

I leaned down to whisper in her ear. "Something isn't right. Shawna is too on-the-ball to miss that cue. I'm going to go make sure everything's okay."

"I'll go with you," Olivia said as she stood and folded her napkin to place on her empty plate.

The remaining members of my coterie couldn't join us; they'd risk causing a scene. I was beyond the point of caring about such things. Something was wrong. I could feel it down deep. My huldra screamed at me to act, and with each passing minute, I grew more and more powerless to resist.

EIGHT

"Let's rule out the bathroom first," I spoke under my breath to Olivia as we exited the dining hall.

Olivia and I briskly walked into the women's restroom and checked the stalls. No one. I left and popped my head into the men's bathroom, but only smelled the presence of males, which in this case, wasn't pleasant. We stood in the restroom alcove between the men's and women's bathrooms. "You think she got locked in the shed?" Olivia offered.

"Let me ask the bartender if she ever returned with the vodka." We headed toward the makeshift bar.

A disorganized line of ten people stood near the bar chatting in aggravated tones, texting, looking about, and even tapping a foot in one case. No one stood behind the bar.

"Do you know where the bartender is?" I asked a woman who shifted from one high-heeled boot to the other, holding an empty white wine glass.

"Well, he said he had to grab more wine from storage, but that was a while ago, and now I'm missing the event," she complained. "I don't know why he thought he needed more bottles." She pointed to a row of varying types of corked wine along the bar.

Olivia and I only shared a look before running from the building. The entrance patio was inlaid with stones that reminded me of European cobblestone streets. No storage buildings sat within view.

"Around back," was all I said before taking off at a run. Olivia followed close behind.

"You've gotten faster," she said, trying to catch up.

I didn't need to think about that right now. Every moment I didn't find Shawna my huldra rose closer to the surface, protective of her partner sister. Was that a scream I heard? I paused, going very still.

"Wait, did you just hear that?" I said, with the storage shed in my line of sight.

I bolted for the driveway. My sister's faint screams didn't come from the shed, but from the black Bentley tearing out of the gravel driveway. I knocked my heels off and chased after her, pushing myself harder than I ever had before.

Shawna cried out again in a muffled slur as the car left the driveway and sped away, down the road and into darkness. Still, I pursued my sister and her abductors despite the increasing distance between the car and me. My bare feet smacked the wet pavement as I willed them to push me faster than possible, even for a huldra, fast enough to reach the car that now sped out of sight. I stopped short at the street and smacked at the air in front of me. My lungs worked to draw in more air. Everything in me wanted to keep running, but there was no way I could outrun a speeding car.

"Did you catch the license plate?" Olivia asked between gasps of air after she caught up to me.

"It was covered." Angry tears filled the corners of my eyes.

My aunt's grey four-door crossover screeched to a halt beside me on the empty, dark road and the passenger doors flung open. Olivia and I jumped in.

"I'll kill them. I'll kill all of them," Aunt Renee hissed as she slammed her foot on the gas. We peeled out. The car fishtailed before it found its traction and raced in the direction our sister had been taken.

Aunt Abigale sat in the second row of seats, rubbing her arms and rocking. Her eyes glazed over. It would have been easier if Shawna's mother were filled with rage like her sisters—anger was an emotion one could work with, use to fuel their fight—but only fear shone in her eyes. It took the rising tension in the car to a whole other level, a new level of discomfort.

"All they had to do was control another unsuspecting male. Get him to try again." Aunt Renee smacked the steering wheel. "Where the hell is that damn car?"

"We've lost them. We've lost her," Aunt Abigale whispered from behind us.

Rain pelted the windshield. The wipers worked at full speed. Silent tears fell from Celeste's eyes. Aunt Renee pulled the car to the side of the road.

I sat in the front passenger seat and turned to the others. "Why would they take her, though? It's not like they mistook her for me. We look nothing alike."

"We have no car tracks to follow. We should be smart about this— go home, gather what we need, and then go get her. Tonight." Renee eyed Patricia in the rearview mirror. "The succubi are no doubt en route to Oregon. We'll dig up the weapons and go."

Patricia nodded. "Yes, we'd be smart to recover those, but attacking tonight would be unwise. If we're heading home, we should stay the night and leave in the morning, well rested and with a plan."

"We have weapons?" I asked, surprised. Everything they'd taught my sisters and me revolved around keeping our heads down and maintaining peace, following the rules. Soon after I became a bounty hunter they'd requested that I keep my gun in my tree home, or my car, because it made them uneasy.

"Of course we have weapons," Aunt Renee spat. "We knew there'd be another Wild Woman war one of these days. It was only a matter of time." She quieted for a moment as though her statement brought new ideas to mind. "If it's a war they want, it'd be dumb for us to pursue them without weapons of our own." She pulled from the side of the road, using her SUV's four-wheel-drive to release us from the mud with ease, and made a U-turn toward home.

Aunt Patricia rested a hand on my shoulder from the second row of seats. "What my sister is trying to say is the peace your mother dreamed of between every group of Wild Women was a lofty goal, but nothing more than a dream. We've never been at peace with the other groups, least of all the succubi. We have a stash hidden for such a time as this."

"According to her stories, all our kinds got along at one point," I said. I'd mentioned her stories when I was a child and received a scolding for it, so it wasn't a topic I brought up lightly or often.

"Fairytales," Renee said matter-of-factly without taking her eyes from the road.

"But you've placed so much trust in the Hunters. Why assume you'll one day have to protect yourselves?" I said. It made no sense.

"Forced trust is just a more palatable expression of obedience," Renee spat. "Where are they now? Where is your mother? Where were they last night?"

"John is different," Celeste reminded us of the local Hunter complex's leader, who'd moved to his post long after my mother's disappearance.

"Yes, John is different." Aunt Patricia's methodical mind spun as she spoke calmly. Though I would not mistake her calm for not caring. She possessed the peace of a tiger stalking its prey—a calculated calm. "And while Faline could not go to him for help about last night, without revealing what she'd done, there is no harm in reporting Shawna's abduction. That should be our first stop before an illegal trip to Oregon."

"Is that our plan?" Olivia spoke up from the third row of the crossover.

My two aunts nodded. Shawna's mother stared ahead with tears in her eyes while Celeste sat beside her, rubbing her shoulders.

Aunt Renee turned into our long and winding driveway. It stretched through trees to keep our homes hidden.

"I'll go to the complex and talk to John alone," I announced. "The succubi took her because of me. She's my partner sister. And if our whole coterie descends on the Hunter complex, unscheduled, it may cause more problems than we're capable of handling at this point."

"That's not a good idea," Celeste said. "What if they do an on-the-spot check-in examination? They'll never let you leave the complex."

I eyed my aunts for confirmation as I spoke. "I don't think they're allowed to administer an exam without at least a twelve-hour notice, right?"

"According to the agreement between the Wild Women and the Hunters, yes," Patricia said, meeting my gaze. "Best not to mention your hotel mishap, though. I'm sure there's some sort of fine print to this rule that we aren't aware of. Those in charge do love their loopholes. Plus, John is still a Hunter and part of his job is to make sure we don't do what you did that night."

I nodded. I had no intention of reliving that blood-filled night. Not even through words.

"And if John does nothing?" Renee asked as she parked her car in front of the common house. "Like the Hunter complex leader before him did nothing when *my* sister went missing?"

Abigale shuddered and I spoke more to comfort her than to answer Renee. "Shawna is my sister. There's nothing I won't do to get her back."

Renee shot me a look of offense.

I hadn't meant to offend her, but assuring her of this was the least of my worries. I reached an arm behind my back and ran my fingers across the bark ridges beneath my shirt. Yes, my aunts had done everything in their power to find my mother, their sister, all those years ago. But the huldra in me, now awake and growing in strength, gave me a power my aunts hadn't dreamed of possessing. Hopefully, it was enough to save my sister, but not so much that a Hunter could sense a difference in me without the bright surgical light, without pulling up my shirt for examination.

I met the eyes of every woman in the car and gave an unwavering nod of confidence that I desperately wished I felt. Before the invention of lights and routine check-ins, Hunters could sense the depth of wildness inside a Wild Woman just by being near her. I didn't know how they did this, but for the sake of my sister and my own safety, I wished I did.

NINE

I INCHED my car toward the security camera and speaker box and stopped. I'd never just "dropped in" on the Hunters. And while I knew I wouldn't be met with tea and cakes, I hoped I'd get a welcome that didn't include a locked gate or guns pointed at my car. I glanced into my backseat to double-check that my jacket was still thrown over my suitcase, hoping the security camera didn't get a glimpse and scolding myself for not storing it in the trunk. Shawna knew me better than anyone, and the other night in the woods she'd hit the nail on the head. My proverbial sword had been drawn. And I was waiting to see whether or not I'd have to fall on it.

With my huldra released and now threatening to take over whenever she liked, and a growing bark patch to show for it, I was a liability. And without my partner sister to stick around for, there was little reason to put my coterie in that predicament with the Hunters. So, I'd talk to John. If he didn't offer help, I'd drive to Oregon and face the succubi. The rest of my plan depended on whether or not Shawna was with them and still living. My coterie knew I might drive across state lines without Hunter approval. My next check-in exam would reveal that I'd killed a human, so breaking their rule prohibiting Wild Woman traveling outside our area seemed trivial. They didn't, however, know that even if I survived a run-in with the succubi, for the safety of my coterie, I may not come back.

I pressed the red button on the speaker box. "Um, I'm here to see John." I didn't know his last name and I didn't care, truth be told. He may be the kindest Hunter I'd encountered, but he was still a Hunter.

"Who is this?" asked a man over the speaker. The security camera shifted to point at my driver's side window.

"My name is Fa—" They knew my identification number, not my name. I rattled off my number. A mistake like that wasn't like me. I couldn't help it. I was barely holding it together.

I waited five long minutes for a response, getting antsier by the second. By the time the iron doors opened and I parked in my regular "Reserved" spot, I was ready to explode. I hopped from my car and almost ran into John's barrel chest.

"How can I help?" he asked. His scent did not match his relaxed appearance, but the strong cologne he wore kept me from identifying what exactly he was feeling.

"My sister has been abducted. I saw the car of the person who took her." I kept to the side of my car, allowing John to tower over me from the curb.

John nodded, a little too unconcerned. "Did you get the plates?" he asked.

"No, but I know who took her. The succubi." I spoke quickly. Time was of the essence.

John, however, did not seem so rushed. "It's not uncommon for different Wild Women groups to reach out and remind the others who's top dog every so often."

I wondered if he referred to my mother's disappearance. If he knew that it was likely caused by a dispute over succubi territory—a man visiting from Oregon who'd shared his bed with my mother. Unbeknownst to my mother, the man had already been claimed by a succubus.

He continued, "And I have a hard time believing a human could overpower a huldra in such a way as to abduct her. Hmm, well that poses a few problems for us."

"Okay?" I asked to get him to speed it along.

"First, the complex in Oregon would have forewarned us if they'd given sanction for any succubus to travel across state lines into our territory."

"They could have enthralled human males to come up here to do their bidding," I reminded. If that were the case, it still wouldn't account for my blackout, but I couldn't tell that to a Hunter.

"Still," he said, kicking a pebble. "The succubi aren't charges of the Washington complex."

"They're dangerous!" Anger flashed through John's eyes, so I lowered my tone. "You've taught us about them plenty of times. Warned us. And they have my sister."

John's words were short and crisp with a hard edge, unlike any I'd ever heard from his mouth. "Look, I understand why you'd think they're the reason your sister is missing. I tend to agree with you; in terms of location, they're the nearest group of Wild Women, not to mention they're highly temperamental. I also know they're dangerous, and that's why I'm not sending my men after them." He gave me a long, hard look, clearly trying to get me to look away, to back down. I didn't.

Finally, he went on. "My men are trained to handle huldra, not succubi. I will not send them into a succubi lair, which in Oregon happens to be an apartment building full of life-sucking creatures. They're probably halfway to Portland right now, anyway. I'll make a call to the Oregon complex and have them summon the succubi's leader." He turned to head back into the training building. "That's all I can do."

My huldra seethed inside me. I closed my eyes to calm her. "You're supposed to protect us," I said, unable to believe what was happening.

He didn't turn around or stop walking to respond. "And we do. We protect you from yourselves."

* * *

Three long hours into the drive, locked in my confining car with nothing but my racing thoughts of what-ifs regarding Shawna, my phone rang. I jumped at the sound and hastily searched the front passenger seat for my cell. My eyes glued to the freeway, my hand patted and shoved aside the reusable grocery bag of snacks Celeste had packed for me. Eating hadn't entered my mind. I remembered my new car possessed Bluetooth and pressed the button on my steering wheel to answer the call.

"What did you get?" I asked. Shortly after pulling myself away from the complex—when I wanted to chase after John and force him to do his job—I'd called Olivia with bits of information John hadn't realized he'd given me. The succubi group lived in Portland, filling a whole apartment building. Being that Olivia was a research guru, she got right on it.

"Okay, so I searched through county records to find any apartment buildings sold to a private organization or person and not rented to the public after the sale of the property. It was a bitch cross referencing everything, but I found one, built in the twenties, bought in the forties, and never rented out. I looked it up on Google Earth. I don't know what a succubi lair is supposed to look like, but this is white brick in the heart of downtown Portland. Didn't they say succubi need to live near lots of people like an overly extroverted person, but one who's demented?"

By "they" she meant the Hunters. Not a group I trusted at the moment. But telling her what John said about protecting us from ourselves was another conversation for another time.

"Yes," I answered, flipping through the "facts" the Hunters had taught us over the years about succubi. "They absorb the energy of humans, so they have to live near them."

"I wonder why the Hunters let them live," Olivia said.

"Maybe they're only allowed to absorb a certain amount." I got back on track. "Text me the address so I can copy it into my GPS."

"Doing that right now."

My cell vibrated with a new text.

"And Faline?"

"Yeah?"

"Try not to get your life sucked out of you," Olivia said. "Who knows what they could do with a huldra's energy."

I shuddered at the thought. But right now, I was more worried about what I was going to do to them.

* * *

A few hours later I parked my car across the street from a three-story white brick building with black trim in the heart of downtown Portland. Shockingly, no vandalism or trash littered the exterior. The whole drive here I'd thought of the best way to approach their lair. Going over it again and again was all that had kept me sane and able to drive slowly enough to stay off police radar. Parking down the street and hiding in the shadows wouldn't work if they were anything like huldra. They'd sense my presence on their property—either my energy, my scent, or both. And if they did have Shawna, I'd need my car close by in case she wasn't up to running. Plus, she was only the bait, right? I was who they wanted. So I'd give myself over, whether it be just a way to get in the door and grab my sister, or in exchange for her.

I turned off my engine and finished the apple I'd forced myself to eat. The food sat heavy in my stomach, but I figured I'd need the energy it provided. My car's interior light beamed bright, threating to give me away, so I quickly locked my doors and it faded into darkness.

It was three o'clock in the morning. The sun would be up, with humans walking the street, in three or four hours. The street was empty, but that didn't mean I wasn't being watched. I tapped each boot leg, making sure my daggers were in position, and opened my jacket to unlatch the safety from my holster.

I eased the car door shut behind me and ran to the right front corner of the building. I sniffed the air and didn't smell urine, which surprised me seeing that I was standing in an alley in the downtown area of a city. A single streetlight glowed yellow and lit the early morning mist.

"You shouldn't be scared," said a female voice from behind me.

I turned and spoke into the night. "I'm not scared."

"Fine. If you want to split hairs. You shouldn't be anxious."

I spun around. I was alone. But clearly I wasn't.

"We'll talk to you if that's what you want, as long as you refrain from flipping your shit when they come to escort you in."

"What the hell?" I said under my breath. "When who escorts me?" I hadn't even made it to their front stoop.

"This is a limited time offer. The answer is yes or no," she said. It sounded like a threat except her words were void of any emotion.

I listened closer, closing my eyes to feel from which direction the words came. I jerked my head up and to the right and saw a window slam shut.

Crap. Had I just ruined my chances for a negotiation?

"Yes!" I yelled up toward the window in the most confident voice I could muster, considering what I was agreeing to. I wasn't sure if succubi had super hearing or not, so I erred on the side of caution.

"Come with us, huldra." Two succubi stood at the corner of the building; no human had the capacity to appear out of the blue without my knowing they were coming. They looked me up and down for all of one second before turning to walk in step toward the stoop. I figured they'd come out of the building while I yelled and hadn't just appeared out of thin air. At least I hoped as much.

I kept their pace, walking behind them. The one on the right had short, dark spiky hair and wore a fitted t-shirt and ripped jeans. The female on my left also wore ripped jeans and a fitted t-shirt, but she wore her hair in a bob cut, right below her ears.

"So, how many of your kind live here?" I asked, when all I wanted to do was scream for them to hand over my sister.

Neither female answered. In fact, they showed no indication that they'd heard me.

We stood on the front stoop until someone buzzed us in. The door shut behind us and we waited in the tiled entryway. Stairs with an ornate dark wooden banister stretched up, then twisted, and then stretched again before us.

I followed them up to the first level and passed a line of three doors. A succubus with dark brown skin leaned on the banister. A lollipop stick protruded from between her lips. Only her eyes moved on her blank face as she watched us pass. She brushed her many beautiful braids to the side, revealing a snake tattoo extending from her ear, down her neck, and hiding under her shirt. She pushed herself from the railing and trailed us, still sucking on her lollipop.

When we reached the third floor, another row of doors greeted us, along with a blonde, pale-skinned succubus. Golden hair spilled over her left shoulder. The right side of her head had been shaved with only the fuzz of blonde remaining. A snake tattoo wound from her forehead hairline, around her ear, and down her neck.

John's concern for his men played through my mind.

The blonde joined the lollipop-sucking female, following behind us. When we reached the last door, on the last floor, the spiky-haired succubus knocked. A tongue-clicking sound responded from the other side, and she pushed the door open.

If I thought I had an entourage behind and around me, I had been mistaken. Nine succubi, sitting and standing, dwarfed the apartment's living room. And they all focused on me.

As I'd done on every floor, I sniffed the air for Shawna's scent but only smelled succubi and human.

"Your need emanates from you, huldra," said a Filipino-looking woman lying on a red velvet couch. Hers had been the voice I'd heard from the alley. A man in only a pair of navy blue silk boxers lay on the other side of the couch, resting his head on the armrest. "What is your name?" she asked me.

The female's red silk thigh-length robe hung open, exposing her naked body. Long inky black hair cascaded down her full breasts. A tribal tattoo wrapped around each of her thighs like belts. A pink lotus flower tattoo acted as the buckle on her left thigh. Another belt-type tattoo wrapped around her rib cage, outlining the lower portion of her breasts, with an image of the goddess Lilith in its center.

"My name is Faline and I come on behalf of my coterie." My hand hovered over my gun, hiding behind the front of my jacket. "We also reside in the Pacific Northwest." I pulled from my bounty hunting skillset. I'd negotiated with family members of skips to turn their loved one over to me. This time it was my loved one that I wanted, which upped my anxiety and the ante.

"Ah," she said, brushing aside her hair to reveal a breast. "The Washington coterie."

"The only huldra coterie in the country," I said. Did she not know, or was she playing mind games with me?

"Fascinating," she said, tilting her chin up and narrowing her dark brown eyes. "You are not ugly."

"Thank you?"

The mostly naked man lying on the other side of the couch stirred and let out a moan.

She laughed. "I don't mean to offend. It's just, I've heard your skin is covered in bark and your eyebrows hang like moss from its host tree."

Now I knew she was playing games. Human folklore spoke of the huldra's beauty...except for the rare stories of huldra becoming grotesquely ugly after marriage which, since we never married, was absurd. I assumed the Oregon Hunters taught about huldra in the same way the Washington Hunters taught us about succubi—using human folklore as though much of it were fact. I clenched my fists.

"Oh." The woman giggled and leaned back. "I've made the huldra angry. Maybe now we'll get to see her bark."

"Why are you discussing these things in front of a human male?" I said through clenched teeth, no longer able to suppress the question. Humans should not know the existence of our kind.

"Did you know your anger floats from you, red as blood and fire?" She licked her lips. "I would love to taste it, let it sizzle within my muscles. I've never tasted huldra energy." Her smile grew. "Oh, wait. Yes, I have. She's beautiful, isn't she, darling?" The woman slid over to sit on the man's lap as he woke. She brushed her hand along his five o'clock shadow.

He stared at me and nodded.

"Would you like to share both of us? Would that be fun for you?" the woman asked the man.

His grin grew.

"Well you can't have her! You're mine, not hers. Do you understand me? Mine!"

The man shrank into the couch and said, "I'm sorry, Marie. I only agreed because I thought it was what you wanted."

Marie lowered her voice to barely audible so that the human couldn't hear her. "He's full of shit."

"Are you the leader?" I asked, ready to move this along and get my sister back.

"I am." Marie stood to tie her robe.

"As you've probably guessed, I've come to discuss a possible trade." My gaze flickered to the man. "Is there somewhere we can talk without your...partner?" She may be comfortable exposing her sisters to a human, but I wasn't.

She laughed and brushed her hair behind her ear. "Him? My partner? No, when he wakes up in his bed tomorrow morning, he'll think this was all a faded wet dream. He'll have no idea where he's been all night or who he's been with. He'll just know it was the best fucking dream of his life. Literally and figuratively."

Just like I'd woken on the hotel floor with no memory of releasing my huldra. Except I knew my nightmare had been real. My jaw clenched.

Marie snapped her finger and the succubus with dreadlocks placed her hand on the man's forehead. He closed his eyes and slumped back, laying his head on the armrest.

"Enough pleasantries." Marie shot me an ice cold glare. "You are a Wild Woman, a huldra no less, in the home of my sisters and me. I should drain you of every emotion skittering through that wooden body of yours."

I hitched in a sharp breath and gritted my teeth.

"You'd better watch where you direct that anger of yours," she seethed. "You flesh eaters don't belong here, and I can make it like you never came."

"And I can throw you out the window so quickly you wouldn't see it coming," I said, unable to hold my tongue any longer. "I. Want. My. Sister!"

Five succubi turned to face me, like a military unit changing marching directions. Without so much as a finger placed on me, my muscles gave in to absolute exhaustion. My legs felt like fern leaves, bending outward, threatening to collapse. I searched deep within myself, begging my huldra to fight them off, to hold me up, to keep me standing.

And I did stand...for all of two seconds.

Like the heavy burden of hail on a fern leaf, my legs gave in and I crumbled to the floor.

TEN

My muscles ached with heaviness. A red sheer swath of fabric hung above me, pinned to the ceiling. Something invisible held my arms and legs, stretched out across a bed as though they'd each been tied to a post. Only, they hadn't.

Five succubi stood at the foot of the bed, expressionless, staring at me, no doubt concentrating on keeping me restrained. My knees throbbed from the fall.

It looked as though I'd stepped from a regular apartment living room in downtown Portland to a mini version of an ancient sex temple. Orange and red sheer scarves hung over lamps. Red wallpaper with gold embossing covered the walls. A carved shelf took up one wall and was filled with incense, crystals, smudging sticks, a vined plant, and statues of Lilith. Lilith created the first succubi from her most trusted temple priestesses thousands of years ago, according to my mother's bedtime stories.

"You, a huldra, enter my home, the home of my sisters, claiming that *I* took your huldra?" Marie spat the words.

I jolted in place, unable to move.

She sat on a lounge chair in the corner.

"I—"

"Silence!" she demanded.

My lips stilled against my will.

"A huldra cannot be trusted. Your kind is sneaky. You hide in the forests and pretend not to exist, blending in with the trees, growing your vines to snatch humans for dinner like a spider plants her web. How do I know you haven't also learned to blend in with your lies, learned to omit the energy of truth as lies spew from your mouth?" She stood and paced the bedroom.

"All of you other Wild Women are liars. Only the succubi stand for who they are despite the ridicule. Only we are picked off because we do not hide like huldra, like foxes." Her dark eyes lit up and her tone changed. "Foxes. That reminds me. I've heard stories that your kind has fox tails. I'd like to see yours."

Without my consent, my arms flattened against my sides and my body rolled over onto my stomach. My lips worked again, but a little too late. "We don't have tails," I said into the deep orange blanket threaded with gold as Marie lifted my shirt enough to reveal my lower back and the lack of tail lump beneath my jeans. How the hell were these succubi able to physically dominate me in such a way? If they had monthly check-ins like the rest of us, how were they able to use their succubi power without being caught?

"You're far more boring than I had been led to believe," she said in a pouty voice before her tone changed. "But, she *does* have bark."

I wasn't sure if I'd ever get used to the fact that a person no longer needed a high-powered lamp to see my bark. I also refused to be a spectacle. The humiliation of it allowed me to burn through their control. I shoved my arms beneath me and pushed my torso from the comforter but was quickly thrust into the mattress. They must have turned up the intensity on whatever they used to control my body.

"Are you like a chameleon? If I bring a lighter shade of wood near you, will your bark change to match it?" she asked with wonder in her voice.

Her childish bullshit grated on my last nerve. Too bad there wasn't a damn thing I could do about it. I gritted my teeth and accidentally let out a low growl.

Marie gasped and jumped away, letting my shirt fall into place.

"You're working with the mermaids, aren't you?" Marie shouted. "You've come to scout us out, so you can destroy us and claim our territory."

"You're fucking crazy," my words muffled into the blanket.

"Let me see her," Marie said.

They used my own energy against me, manipulating my limbs from afar. I was turned onto my back and made to sit up against the dark headboard with such control that none of me bobbed in place. Marie cautiously lowered herself onto the chase lounge in the corner, eyeing me as though I could disappear at any moment.

I cleared the growl from my throat. I was done playing nice, done placating the evil Wild. "You took my sister. Just like you had me attacked, for what my mother did years ago. As though killing her back then wasn't revenge enough. She had no idea you'd already claimed the visitor from Oregon."

Marie jumped from the lounge and leaned over me. Her breath warmed my cheek. "I did no such thing."

My head throbbed and my vision blurred as I pushed against her power. I gained control of the tips of my fingers and dug them into the comforter.

Marie gasped at my movement. "I did no such thing!" Her words pulsed through my head, the pain threatening to split my brain open. "We are not monsters! You are the monsters, you and the mermaids, killing humans at your whim, biting into their flesh like they are nothing more to you than a steak. We may play with humans, give them a dreamy night of pleasure, but we'd never hurt one, never kill one."

The honesty in her tone shocked me. Was it possible they truly weren't behind my mother's abduction like we'd thought all those years? It made me think back to the way John had acted. Was it possible the Hunters planted lies about her disappearance to make us think the succubi did it?

She spun from the bed. She faced the line of succubi who held me in place with the powers of their mind. Their foreheads glistened with sweat. At least I was making them work to keep me down. "Get her out. Now. I want her out of my home. We were fools for even entertaining the idea of a civilized conversation with such a foul creature."

My body flung from the bed and hovered over the wooden floor. "Wait!" I yelled. "Please. I need to find my sister. If you didn't take her, if you didn't order the attack on me, then who did?"

Marie snapped her fingers and I dropped to the floor. I quickly stood of my own accord, ignoring my throbbing knee. "I was attacked, night before last." If they hadn't taken Shawna—which explained why I couldn't pick up her scent—then I needed whatever information they could supply. And to get information, you've got to give it. "I blacked out and when I woke up, I'd killed my attacker, a human male. Whoever was behind my attack must have come back and taken my sister instead."

"You're suggesting your attacker was enthralled then?"

"Or for hire, but that wouldn't explain how I blacked out. I assumed it was succubi magic," I said.

"We can put you to sleep, cause you to forget what you've done, but we would never force you to kill a man." She nodded to the row of succubi, who relaxed under her gaze. "We don't condone hurting others. Goddess knows we have enough to deal with, unintentionally absorbing the energy of the hurting humans every day. We wouldn't cause such pain."

"Killing my mother caused pain. A lot of it," I said in a cold tone.

"Your mother was that huldra, huh?" Marie sniffed the air. "I thought I remembered a scent similar to yours. She'd mated with a male from our territory. A male with whom our leader, at the time, enjoyed nighttime visits. When he returned to Portland, he stunk of huldra and when questioned, spoke of the love of his life. Our leader was irate. But she did not act on her anger, outside of breaking a china cabinet full of dishware."

"I don't understand," I said. My head swam with questions. Marie's heartbeat hadn't sped when she spoke of her leader's innocence. Her scent hadn't changed. She'd been telling the truth. "Who else would have cause to end her?"

"Your mother or your sister?" Marie asked.

Could two similar instances have been ordered by two different parties? Not likely. "You're suggesting one group or person is behind my mother's murder, my attack, and my sister's abduction?"

"I'm suggesting nothing," Marie said. "I am offering a deal, however."

Now she wanted to negotiate.

"Six days ago a sister of ours left without so much as a goodbye letter. She emptied her drawers, told her roommate she was doing laundry in the basement, walked out the front door, and hasn't returned." Her throat didn't catch. Tears didn't fill her eyes. I wondered how often sisters left the succubi galere.

"And her clothes aren't in the laundry machine?" I asked.

"No. They were in the laundry bag she had slung over her shoulder when she left."

"So then what's the deal?" I said.

Marie sat on the edge of the bed. "I will give you information that could help get your sister back and answer your questions. In exchange, you follow up on my information where you will most likely find our sister and get word to her."

"Deal."

Marie spoke to the other females in the room. "Do you agree she tells the truth?"

They nodded.

Marie spoke to the tan succubus with dreadlocks. "Return the man to his home. We are finished with him for the night. Remember to place an empty bottle of whatever alcohol is in his cupboard near his bedside." The tan succubus nodded and left the room.

"I lead this galere, but I do not speak for them," Marie said to me. "You and I can discuss the possible deal, but until I get agreement from every member present, nothing is settled. Do you understand?"

"Very much so," I said. My coterie always had to meet, discuss, and agree upon any action we took as a group. Not that we'd had a lot of action.

Marie led me into the main area of the apartment, now brimming with succubi ranging from late teens to late fifties. "She has agreed to strike a deal. We will trade our information for her agreement to locate our sister's whereabouts and relay a message to her. Do you support this deal?"

A resounding "Yay" filled the room along with yips and tongue-clicking.

Marie stood beside her older sisters as she spoke to me. "Our scouts have reported news of the mermaids building an army. Within their ranks are humans and creatures alike. Our informants tell us the mermaids cut all ties to the Hunters many years ago, that they've been in hiding. We believe the army they are building may be to oppose the Hunters. And we fear our sister has run off to join their ranks."

A rash of cries, tongue clicks, and yips forced her to pause. She gave the other women a harsh look and they swiftly fell silent. The pain of loss in their eyes was so familiar it pinched at my heart.

"If she does not show up before our next check-in, she will be a fugitive and hunted down. If she's made it to the mermaids already, we need to know that she's safe. Our informants cannot make contact with the mermaids as they are not Wild nor human—"

I interrupted her. "Not Wild nor human? Then what are they?" Not one lesson from the Hunters included a being similar to Marie's informants. Well, other than Hunters themselves—they weren't Wild or human. But there was no way Marie's informants were Hunters.

Marie ignored my question and continued, "And as you know, the Hunters won't let us cross state lines without prior approval, which they won't give. But, seeing as you're here, you obviously can."

More soft comments interrupted her, this time words of distrust and suspicion. She held up a hand until they fell silent again. "When you arrive, they'll accept you as another member of their army. The mermaids must know more than us if they are preparing to wage war. They may have the answers you seek."

A grey-haired succubus added, "We need our sister to contact us so that we can warn her, one last time. Standing against the Hunters will only end in her death."

Bark tingled along my lower back. To be an enemy of the Hunters was not safe.

"How did the mermaids break from the Hunters?" I asked. "And why would they build an army against them?"

"That is not a part of our deal. Do you still accept?" Marie said.

I had no choice but to move forward with my search. "I agree to your terms."

Marie moved a strand of hair from my shoulder. "If you'd like, we can return to my bedroom before you leave. I've never been with a huldra." Excitement twinkled in her eyes.

"I'll pass, thank you."

"Maybe some other time, then," she said, licking her lips. I thought she intended to shake my hand, so I took hers. But she drew me into an embrace. Warmth flowed into me as though I were soaking in a deep, jetted tub. My muscles unwound. The exhaustion headache eased away.

She whispered into my ear, "First, allow me to heal your exhaustion and muscle fatigue, restore your energy, and then we will supply you with everything you'll need to locate our sister."

Succubi healing abilities were the stuff of many a lesson at the Hunter compound, except they hadn't been called "healing" so much as bewitching. I figured, though, even if it came through bewitching, I could use all the energy I could get. I happily melted into Marie's arms and accepted the energy healing. I did not black out. I did not lose control. I only felt light as a snowflake and as bright as one too. Images of my mother and Shawna flickered behind my eyes.

"Please," I mumbled. "Don't heal me of my anger. I need it."

Marie giggled along with a few other succubi. "You aren't the first to believe that, but I'll leave it if you like."

"I'm heading to California," I said into my Bluetooth as I sped up to enter the morning commute of traffic heading southbound on I5. I explained the plan, the deal I'd struck, and how the mermaids were rumored to be building an army.

"Do you think the mermaids could have taken Shawna?" Aunt Patricia's voice boomed through my speakers. I turned the volume lower.

"Possible. I don't know how probable, though. But they can cross state lines and don't have Hunter check-ins. Who knows how powerful they are. And Marie seems to think that they'd at least be able to give me information to help me find her."

I was on speaker phone. Olivia spoke up. "Faline, you think maybe they *wanted* you to kill your attacker? What if they sent him, knew he'd cause you to unleash your huldra? If they're building an army, wouldn't they want an unbridled huldra? And then they took Shawna on accident instead of you? We didn't see who was in the car. It could have been mermaids."

She had good points. "Except, I'm not sure how they'd get the two of us confused," I said.

The road blurred before my tired eyes for at least the thousandth time. Not even talking to my coterie was helping any more. I saw a sign for upcoming lodging and food. Though it killed me to do it, I flicked my turn signal on and got over to the slow lane. If I didn't get sleep soon I'd end up a smear on the highway and do Shawna more harm than good. I was to that exhausted point where not even stress would keep me awake much longer.

"I've been thinking since you told us about your discussion with John," Aunt Patricia said with a frustrated sigh. "What if the Hunters know more about this than they're leading on?"

I exhaled loudly. "I know. It's been nagging me too." I hoped we were wrong.

"Text us the mermaids' address, please, once you stop. Just in case," Olivia said.

"Olivia wants to see what their place looks like," added Celeste.

"It's not an address," I answered, still feeling the dread from when Maria explained their location. "It's an island. San Miguel Island, off the coast of Southern California. I'm supposed to charter a boat to get there. And their house is off the grid, undetectable by plane or satellite images. So you won't see it anyways."

"Are you serious?" Celeste spoke up. "You're going to an island...out in the middle of the ocean?" A huldra away from mountains and trees was like a fish, or a mermaid, out of water.

We said our goodbyes as I parked outside the Marriott's entrance. As I grabbed my wallet an idea occurred to me. The succubi assumed their sister ran off to join the mermaids. But they couldn't know for sure that their informants were correct about the mermaid army, if their informants were even trustworthy. How much of their assumption was planted on false hope? Of course I'd visit the mermaids. If they had any information about Shawna, it was worth the trip. But I'd be a fool if I spent time chasing a succubus on the grounds of hearsay from an unknown scout. When looking for a missing person, you always start at the morgue. And seeing as I didn't have contacts at any Oregon morgues, there was only one person I could call.

My stomach rolled in on itself. With how many times I'd had to swallow my pride in the last twenty-four hours you'd think my stomach would be full.

I dug my phone out of my pocket and walked into the Marriott. I pressed on his contact information with shaky fingers.

"Hello?"

"Hi, Marcus." I said. "It's Faline."

ELEVEN

I STOPPED at the hotel's front desk and waited behind a sharp-looking business woman to check in. I blamed my jitters on lack of sleep and not nerves.

"I've been trying to get a hold of you," Marcus said, his voice made up of only maybe a quarter of irritancy, which was good, I thought. "It's like you fell off the face of the earth."

I pulled my phone away from my ear to look at the date and time. "It's only Monday afternoon," I said. "It's not like I've been avoiding you for a month or anything."

"So then you were avoiding me."

"Not exactly... I need to ask a favor." If I weren't in public I'd have face-palmed for such an ineloquent delivery.

The woman ahead of me in a black pencil skirt took her key card and made her way through the lobby. The concierge smiled and greeted me, fully expecting me to step up to the counter and check in. He did a quick sweep of my attire: jeans, calf-covering black boots, and a leather bomber jacket. I zipped my jacket to hide my holster and its contents.

I decided to finish the call with Marcus before checking in. I turned on my heel and walked past the counter, past the floor-to-ceiling rock fireplace, past the stand of ice water, tea, and coffee, and found a seat on a plush brown couch. I could stretch out and sleep right then and there.

"So you ignore my calls and then a day later you're asking for my help?" Marcus asked. "I'm not giving you a hard time. Just trying to make sure I've got it straight." He laughed.

"Sure you are," I said, feigning annoyance with my voice, but glad he wasn't mad.

"Excuse me, ma'am." The man from the front desk walked toward me. "If you're waiting for one of our guests I'd be glad to notify them that you're here."

I shook my head and let out a groan. He wanted me to check in or leave, not crash on their couch. I covered the receiver of the phone and answered the male whose square gold name badge identified him as "Luke." "Thanks, but no need, Luke. I'm checking in, but I need to finish this business call first."

"Fair enough," Luke said, nodding and backing away like we'd just had a standoff and I'd won.

"Check in?" Marcus asked. "Are you traveling?"

"That's a lot of questions for someone who wants nothing to do with me unless we're in a serious committed relationship," I quipped, pulling from his comment the last time we talked at the party.

"Hey, I'm calling you, aren't I? And I never said I wanted nothing to do with you. If it were up to me I'd have everything to do with you." Marcus went silent.

Yeah, that was awkward for the both of us, and he knew it.

I blew out an exhale. "I'm in Oregon. Working on a missing person case," I said.

"Oregon is outside of your jurisdiction," the cop in Marcus responded.

"I'm not in law enforcement, not technically, so nothing is outside my jurisdiction. Plus," I added, "it's for an acquaintance." I struggled to say that last part. An acquaintance who used her Jedi mind tricks to steal my energy until I was a pile of slop on the floor and then pinned me to her bed. Marie did return my energy to me and then some, so I figured it was a wash.

"You're conducting your own civilian investigation."

"Oh, come on, Marcus, don't say civilian with so much indignation in your voice. Civilians are people too," I joked. I eyed the coffee dispenser to my left but remembered that after the phone call came nap time. No coffee for me.

Marcus didn't laugh. "Clearly I can't change your mind on this vigilante thing you're doing. So what help did you need from me?"

"It's not illegal to ask questions, to look around," I reminded him.

"Faline, we both know you're not going to stop at the asking questions part," he said.

"I need to know if any females between the ages of eighteen and twenty-five have turned up in any Oregon morgues recently." I got up and poured ice water with lemon wedges into a clear plastic cup before sitting down on the couch. According to Marie, my missing succubus had a love of body ink. "The female I'm looking for has a slew of tattoos; one in particular is of a snake."

"No," was all he said.

"Come on, seriously? You're going to say no?" I moaned inwardly. If I was going to fast-track this search, I needed that information.

"Do you have any legal documents giving you clearance, as a bounty hunter, to look into this exact case?" he asked.

"No."

"Then it'd be illegal for me to share anything I found. I won't do it."

"Think of it as a favor," I said. "For leaving me early Saturday night."

"Yeah, I left early, and I'm sorry. I told you it couldn't be helped. But that's not a fair trade. I left early, you probably did too, and you probably went out and did something else equally as fun. Not a huge inconvenience." Someone else's voice called for Marcus through the receiver. He had no idea how wrong he was. And the fact that he hadn't brought up the dead guy found at the same hotel as the party spoke volumes. Whoever orchestrated my attack had wiped up their tracks and mine.

"Are you at work?" I asked.

"Yeah," he said.

I didn't have all day to convince him. Any minute he'd be pulled away for some task or another. I pursed my lips. If the Hunters had allowed me to be a detective, I would already have had access to these sorts of records. I needed those records. My gut told me that the idea of a young succubus running off to join the mermaids was about as plausible as Shawna deciding to get into an unknown car for a never-ending joy ride. Maybe Olivia was right. Maybe the two disappearances were connected and the mermaids had pulled the strings.

I didn't want to, but I had to do it. "That's not what happened that night," I said. My chest tightened. I'd never allowed outsiders access to my family life. I couldn't stand the vulnerable state it forced us to step into. "I didn't leave right after you. Someone attacked me, but I got away. The next day my sister was abducted. And then today I found out that my acquaintance's family member has gone missing."

"Oh god, I'm so sorry. I didn't know. Why didn't you call me? Why didn't you report it?" Protectiveness rumbled through his voice.

I spoke quickly, before he got any ideas. "Because I think it's personal." I couldn't very well tell a human cop that it was the mermaids' fault.

Marcus whispered into his phone, "You think you're being targeted for putting a skip behind bars?"

I hadn't thought of that angle. "If what happened to my sister and me is completely separate than the Oregon woman's disappearance, then that's a possibility. Which is why I need to know if the Oregon morgues have had any new women brought in."

"You want me to check the Washington morgues, too? Does your sister have any identifying marks?" The cop in Marcus was trying to piece a case together. His movement of the puzzle pieces tore at my very being.

I dropped the empty water cup. My phone slipped, too, before I caught it.

"Faline? You still there?"

It had been an obvious next step to check the morgues for the succubus. But the reality that Shawna could be lying lifeless, on a metal table too...

"I'm here," I barely said.

The line went silent, other than the rustling of precinct business on the other side of the call. Phones rang, computers buzzed, people talked. "I'm sorry," he said in a lowered voice. "That was insensitive."

"No, I... I—" I stuttered.

"Text me your email and I'll send you Oregon's missing persons cases. It may take me a few hours. I'll let you know after I've contacted the morgues."

* * *

I stretched across my queen pillow top bed and grabbed the glass of water from the nightstand. My charging cell phone flashed that I'd received calls, texts, and emails during my restless nap. Reality jolted me from my sleepy haze of where I was and why. I nearly dropped the water in my haste to grab the phone. The fact that I could have slept through that both amazed and horrified me. I must have been more tired than I'd realized.

My heart sank as I scrolled through each one, hoping beyond hope that one would be from Shawna. They weren't. A text from Olivia included screen shots of San Miguel Island from aerial views. No buildings or people had been caught in the pictures. From what she'd gathered, visitors were rarely allowed on the island due to choppy waters around the land and sudden weather changes. I wondered how many boats in that area went missing every year.

Guess I was about to find out; a huldra venturing out onto open water—only for my sister. It felt surreal that I could even think about something so mundane when my sister was missing. But I suppose that was the analytical part of my mind trying to cope. It's what made me a great bounty hunter.

I took a closer look at my inbox. Marcus's name, from what looked like a private email address, caught my eye. He hadn't included any friendly notes to the attached documents. I opened them and scanned the names. Marie hadn't officially reported her sister as missing. So I wouldn't find that name in the missing persons list. I wasn't sure why Marcus had sent it to me. I spent my time searching the list of bodies found, looking for a Jane Doe with a snake tattoo or the succubi identification numbers on her body. My mood lifted a little more each time I swiped to the next page and didn't see a female body with a number tattooed on the thigh.

I glanced from the screen of my phone to the empty wall.

I'd been searching for a Jane Doe mostly, but because Wild Women used portions of their goddess's title as their surname I also searched for a Lilith or, goddess help me, a Frey on the off chance the police had found their ID cards along with their bodies. We used our legal names for our driver's license and our assigned numbers as identification with the Hunters. This way the Hunters knew us only by our numbers and the world knew us only by our names. It kept the two separate, or so the Hunters had assured us.

But procuring our names was as easy as me scanning this list.

Huldra opted for last names having to do with their goddess, Freyja. My coterie had chosen "Frey" as our last name. From meeting with Marie, I knew that succubi used parts of "Lilith" as their surname. If the other Wilds followed suit then the Mermaids used pieces of their goddess' name, Atargatis, the harpies used variations of Innana or Ishtar, and the rusalki used Mokosh. If a Hunter took the time to look, he'd be able to locate every single one of us—where we lived, where we worked, where our annual benefits for our pet rescue centers were held.

Shitfuckdamn.

A knot settled in my stomach. If the Hunters had anything to do with the disappearances, my possible suspect list just grew exponentially. I was fifty steps behind whatever this was and definitely not closing in fast. As much as I wished I could run in ten different directions at once, I had to focus on my next step. One step at a time. If the mermaids really were building an army against the Hunters, they'd have a whole lot more intel on the organization than I had. And right now, I needed information to help me catch up. Shawna's life—hell, all our lives—could depend on it.

TWELVE

I AVOIDED PASSING through the redwood forest on my drive from northern to southern California. Climbing its ancient trees didn't seem right without Shawna. And I didn't want to take the time, not even for that.

I couldn't count how many times I'd listened to the playlist on my phone from Oregon, through Sacramento, past Bakersfield—which lacked trees and greenery in a bad way—and toward Los Angeles. Though, I didn't make it to LA because I cut off onto I-5 and headed west until the Pacific Ocean stopped me. Until I was in Ventura, CA. I'd driven all the way through since my hotel nap, only stopping for gas and food.

I parked at Ventura Harbor and twisted myself in my seat to pull clean underwear and socks from my suitcase and then stuffed the articles of clothing into my purse. I jumped out of the car and speed-walked down the dock to where the charter boats were. It was all I could do not to run. If the mermaids had any information that could lead me to Shawna, I couldn't get to them fast enough. And I had a feeling they did.

"Just a moment," said the captain of the boat Marie had chartered to take me to the island as I stood on the dock, waiting. I had expected a balding older man with a gut and a worn-out fishing hat. What I'd gotten was a Native American man with thick black hair, broad shoulders, and biceps that just wouldn't quit. How could I tell he had such biceps through his sweater and wind-breaker? A woman knows these things.

Very few people milled about in the early morning hours of this weekday. The cries of seagulls and the soft breaking of waves filled the crisp morning ocean air.

The captain disappeared down the stairs below deck.

"All right," he said, poking his head out of the hole that led down below. "Come aboard."

"Can I...can I get a little help?" I asked, reaching my arm out though still standing on the dock. Unease took over with the possibility of being trapped at sea. The waves were my enemy. I preferred the stability of trees. Though, if I thought about it, standing at the highest point of an incredibly tall tree had a waving affect. Especially on windy days. Still, I could always jump down from the branches and plant my feet firmly on the ground. Not so much with ocean travel.

"Sorry, I thought you'd done this before." He leaned toward the dock with an outstretched arm.

I had to do this for Shawna. Freyja only knew what horrors she was enduring right now. I wrapped my fingers in the captain's until he heaved me onto the boat. My huldra responded to his touch by flaring up inside. That was new, and disturbing. The moment I could let go of him, I did. I stood with wobbly feet as the waves beneath us kept the floor moving.

"Here." He handed me an orange life jacket.

I held it for a few minutes, studying the contraption, wondering how to put the damn thing on. I hated how inept I felt.

"I'm Caleb, by the way," he said while turning the motor on and messing with the dials near the steering wheel.

I put the life jacket over my head. "Caleb, um, what do I do next?" I asked.

"Ah! Sorry. I don't normally do this. It's my brother's business. He doesn't go out on weekdays, so he asked me to take you. Just secure the clasps and you're done." I decided to pretend he hadn't just said that he doesn't drive a boat on a regular basis.

Caleb, satisfied with my safely attached orange vest, backed the boat away from the dock and maneuvered it out into the Pacific Ocean. A grey and blue inflatable skiff trailed behind us, attached by a rope. I found a place to sit as far from the edge as I could and prepared for a white-knuckled ride on calm waters.

Not one word passed between Caleb and me during our first hour out on the water. The obligatory conversation starters didn't sound right when I played them out in my head.

Until the tip of an island revealed itself. "So which island is that one?" I asked.

"It's Santa Cruz Island," he responded. "I can't believe someone like you hasn't been out on the water before." He shook his head while keeping his gaze set on the expanse of water in front of us.

"Someone like me?" I asked, confused as to who or what he thought I was.

He eyed me and I cocked my head.

"Oh! You're not—?" He cut himself off.

I didn't answer, but my brows furrowed. Not what?

Caleb spoke a few words that held no meaning to me. The hairs at the base of my skull stood. What did he think I was? What was I walking into?

"What language are you speaking?" I asked, now thoroughly confused.

"Nothing. Never mind."

"What's going on? What did you mean, 'someone like me'?" I pressed.

"Someone from Oregon. That's what I meant," he said, his gaze rested on the water ahead. "Your sister's credit card, the one I ran when she scheduled the trip, the billing address said Portland, Oregon. I have friends up near there," he said.

His accelerated heartrate told me he was lying, but pushing for answers wasn't working. Threatening the only person on the boat who knew how to maneuver the thing wouldn't help my cause. I decided to try a different angle—chat him up and learn whatever I could about anything he'd be willing to share. Something is better than nothing. "Have you gone hiking up there?" I said.

He nodded.

"Then you'll understand when I say that I'd rather spend my time hiking...on soil...with evergreens towering in all directions." Or climb the evergreens, but that was too much information.

"I get where you're coming from, but for me, it's always been the water. Since before my daughter was born, she's been on the water." He stopped and laughed to himself and then shared his little joke, "In the water too."

I smiled. "So you have a family?" I asked.

"Married five years now. We have a two-year-old girl." With one hand he held the wheel, with the other he pulled out his cell phone and showed me a few pictures of his beautiful raven-haired wife holding their chubby-cheeked toddler.

It made me think of my own family, my sister, and all that was at stake. The pain must have showed on my face because Caleb put the phone away with a guilty look. Probably to change the subject, he gave me the history of the islands as we sped past them, some larger than others, all sprinkled with vegetation. I didn't mind. His stories made our trip go by quicker, despite the choppy water. The local islands had been occupied by humans for at least 12,000 years. The island's earliest known residents were the Paleo-Indians, called the Chumash people. Before San Miguel got its current name, the Chumash people called it *Tuguan*.

As Caleb spoke, I wondered if his ancestors had lived on one of the islands we'd passed. I also wondered where the mermaids played into all of this. Their existence on San Miguel Island, or *Tuguan*, wouldn't be in the history books. But had they lived alongside the Chumash people? Had Caleb grown up hearing folk tales of swimming women? How long ago had they liberated themselves from the Hunters and joined the humans? These were things I didn't dare ask him and he didn't offer up.

We neared the island, and Caleb anchored the boat and transferred a bag into the skiff. Despite his offer of help, I walked on my own, down the few steps at the back of the boat, and stepped into the grey and blue inflatable skiff.

Wind beat at us and waves worked to shove us this way and that as the skiff's motor raced us toward the deserted beach. Salty air filled my nostrils, making it hard for me to discern other scents.

I spit my hair from my mouth only to have the wind smack it back at my face. These mermaids had better have information leading to Shawna or I was going to make fertilizer out of some succubi.

"Calm weather they're having today." Caleb gave a laugh and seemed to make the skiff move faster.

He shut the engine off as we neared the crescent-shaped, sandy beach surrounded by cliffs. Patches of green grass clung to the gentle slopes of what looked like wide steps in the otherwise rocky cliff. White sand separated the rocky base from the blue ocean water. Caleb jumped from the skiff and used the rope to pull it to shore. The dry land beckoned me, and before he pulled the inflatable boat completely onto land, I jumped from the skiff. Salt water filled my boots within seconds as I ran through the shallow water. It took willpower to refrain from kissing the sand.

A naked woman ran from a crevice in the cliff. "Ah, Caleb, I haven't seen you in forever!" she said as she wrapped her arms around the man in an embrace. Her skin appeared dark tan until she stood against Caleb's much darker complexion. Her thick, inky black hair draped down past her butt. What looked like deep green scales sparkled in patches on her shoulders and hips and a few spots on her long, lean legs.

He squeezed her tightly, picking her up off the ground in the process.

The woman kissed Caleb on the cheek and took a step back. "Let me see how much she's grown," she said.

He pulled his phone from his jacket pocket and showed her the newest pictures of his daughter. The woman's scales disappeared into her skin as she oohed and aahed at the digital photos. The way her scales melted into tan skin reminded me of my bark.

Caleb finished with the pictures and stuck his phone into his pocket. He glanced at me before leaning in to whisper in the mermaid's ear. "The woman said she was one of you, but she's never been on the water."

"Who said I was one of theirs?" I asked. I couldn't help but stomp toward the two apparent friends; my boots were full of water.

The woman turned to me and smiled. "Welcome. My name is Gabrielle. And you must be Faline." As she closed the gap between us I noticed tiny shells tied into the roots of her hairline part at the top of her head. Small bits of wet seaweed clung to strands of black.

"I'd better go. It was nice to meet you, Faline." Caleb headed for the skiff.

I waved. "Thanks for the ride."

I waited for his skiff to pull away before I got to business. "Clearly, you knew I was coming."

Gabrielle shrugged. "Come on, I'll take you to the house."

"I'm not going with you. Not until I get a few questions answered." I dug my wet boots into the sand.

She took four steps up the path cut into the cliff side before she turned around. Her hands rested on her hips. "If you come with me, I'll explain things on the way. It's a long walk. Normally we swim to get to this side of the island, but asking a huldra to swim in the ocean would just be...ridiculous."

Well, now she was making sense. I took two steps toward her. "If you don't normally walk this way, why is there a footpath? And how do you know I'm huldra?"

"The footpath is older than you or me. It was created by the humans who occupied this island hundreds of years ago. And you smell like soil and trees, that's how I know you're huldra," she said, her voice bouncing on the wind. "I'd take off those boots if I were you. Boots and sand don't play well together. In fact, take everything off if it'd make you more comfortable."

So mermaids could throw their voices too.

I quickly unlaced my boots and pulled them from my feet. I left the daggers hidden inside. That's another reason I opted to stay clothed, to conceal my M&P .40. Didn't want to show my cards too soon. I tied the boot laces together and threw them over my shoulder.

I gladly peeled off my wet socks and wrung them out. My toes wiggled in the sand. Instantly, I felt more grounded as the soles of my feet connected to nature. I let out a sigh of relief I hadn't known I'd been holding and then ran after Gabrielle to catch up.

The moment I walked beside her, she explained, "Caleb is Chumash. That's why his family's touring business is the only one allowed to pull onto this island. They pre-arrange visits so we can make sure to keep hidden. They only bring humans here a few times a year, so it's not a bother. Plus, we help family. If anyone calls requesting a private visit to the island, his family lets us know."

"Wait. You're related to him?" I asked, confused. Huldra only birthed daughters and from what I saw at Marie's, so did succubi. I'd assumed it was a Wild thing.

"I guess we could be in some way. Like half second cousins twice removed or something." She laughed. "To us, the Chumash people are family. Our sisters are family. Our sister's children are family. We don't pay attention to how we're related, just that we are."

"And why is it okay for them to know about you?" I said.

We crested the top of the cliff. Green low-lying bushes covered the flat terrain and blue ocean framed the horizon.

"We've recently started sending out a call to all Wilds. We figure only those answering that call would ask for a private boat ride to a remote island. Plus, Caleb told us the billing address for your sister's credit card and we knew there was a Wild group in that area. Though, I'd expected you to be succubi, not huldra." She brushed her hair from her shoulder, but the wind at our backs proved her effort worthless.

I stopped. "This call you've started sending out. Does it involve attacking and abducting Wilds?"

Lines crinkled Gabrielle's forehead. "We would never."

I peered at her thigh. No tattoo. No numbers.

"Are you building an army against the Hunters?" I hadn't meant to get to business so soon. I'd planned to use a little more finesse, but my concern for my sister grew with each passing moment.

"The Chumash people have always known about us," she continued answering my earlier questions as though I hadn't asked the latter. "They gave us safe haven when the Hunters rounded everybody up and tattooed them with numbers. We agreed to protect their island from those who would try to rape it for profit, and they kept our secret."

"How have you protected it?" I asked.

"Well, technically we don't protect the Chumash people anymore. Their descendants left the island for jobs and the elders died off. But we still look after the island. When rich tycoons came out for a visit, to see how much money they could make from the land, my foremothers created horrid storms to scare them away, made them think the island was unsafe and uninhabitable. Now we only cause the nearby seas to be choppy and the wind fairly extreme to keep tourists from visiting year around."

She started walking again. I kept pace with her.

"And as far as your army question, we can discuss that after you've had a chance to rest."

"So it's true. You don't answer to Hunters?" A week ago the news would have shocked me, and I'd think it sounded nice, but nothing more. Now it had me thinking that there was another way to live.

"That's our house up there." She pointed to what looked like a blurry mirage in the distance. "No we don't answer to them. Not at all. You know, the last Chumash wise woman foretold of your kind," she said matter-of-factly, as if every Wild had a medicine woman giving us our future forecast.

When I didn't answer, she paused to examine me until her gaze rested on my face again. "She'd said a tree woman would find the sea women—us. That the tree woman would begin a war to release our sisters from bondage."

Chills worked their way through me. Huldra may not have a medicine woman foretelling the future, but I knew the sound of prophecy when I heard it. And this prophecy involved me.

THIRTEEN

My LEGS WOBBLED. My stomach grumbled. Travel exhaustion wore me thin. Sleep deprivation, worry, and hours of drive time combined with hours in a boat seemed to do that. And my heart ached a little more with each passing hour that Shawna spent away from our family. The culmination weakened me. So Gabrielle's words didn't have to burrow too deep to hit a nerve.

How could I start a war when the mermaids were the ones building an army? I looked out over the island and saw no signs of Wilds training to fight. I saw no signs of Wilds at all.

"I don't have long to stay," I said, wishing Caleb were still near the shore so I could get my information and leave this oversized bathtub behind. "I need to know if a succubus named Heather came to you, and if so, where I can find her." I had bigger questions too, about the Hunters maybe being involved in taking Wilds, but I had a feeling this woman wasn't the one to ask. Her answer to the easier questions would tell me.

"You look like you could use some rest," Gabrielle offered, evading my questions with the ease of a politician.

Definitely not the one to ask. Fine. I could play games too, but not while running on empty. I ignored her and made my way toward the one building on the island. Gabrielle couldn't be the only mermaid holding the answers to my questions.

There were no paved walkways outside the mermaids' home. No lounge chairs or outdoor fire pits. Not even a potted plant.

"We don't want our residence to be noticed from the sky," she explained as though she knew my thoughts.

"Do mermaids read minds?" I asked. Succubi could read energy, so why not?

"No." She laughed. "You're so tired, I think your poker face fell asleep hours ago."

Great. My poker face. I needed that.

Mirrored glass made up the exterior of Gabrielle's home. Other than seeing my own and Gabrielle's reflection, it looked as though the short green bushes and flat land went on for another few miles. But in reality the house stood only ten feet in front of us, built on the edge of a cliff.

"The roof is a living roof. It's more dirt and grass and bushes. Keeps us hidden," Gabrielle said as she led the way around the side of the house and walked through a floor-to-ceiling opening.

From the outside of the mermaid home, I would have never expected the opulence on the inside. Mermaids lived in excess. It was probably all those treasure ships their foremothers attacked. On a floor-to-ceiling glass shelf sat rows of books. On the middle shelf, in place of books sat a large silver gem-encrusted Faberge egg and a golden crown filled with triangles and circles and crosses.

Early afternoon light streamed in through the windows and lit up the large living room, despite the black granite floor tiles. Everything looked bright, shiny, and new. Two overstuffed white couches beckoned to me, both equally sleep worthy.

"Let me get you a resting tincture," Gabrielle offered. "Some of my sisters are masters with herbal remedies."

"No, thank you," I said before a yawn. So far, everything Gabrielle said rang true to me. It was the tidbits she'd refused to say that left me concerned. No way was I trusting her to give me a sleeping tincture.

"Can I get you a drink, then?" she asked.

A capped bottle of something would ensure it hadn't been

tampered with. "Yeah, do you have any wine or beer?"

"I do. Wait here a moment." Gabrielle's bare feet padded out of the room to what I assumed was the kitchen.

I stretched my hearing to listen to her movement and realized my mistake. If she uncorked and poured the wine in the kitchen she'd still have time to sneak something into my glass. Call me paranoid, but recent experiences had made me wary.

I listened as she opened the fridge. Glass bottles dinged as she moved them to pull one out. But something else caught my audible attention, not in the kitchen but down the long hallway that led off the living room. A female's moaning...combined with a man's.

My coterie didn't bring men to our home for many reasons. We only sought sexual pleasure with humans (never an ongoing romantic relationship) and, when it was time, a mating partner for procreation. Our home was the only place we could truly be ourselves. The presence of a human would ruin that.

The giggling of two females further down the hall pulled me from my thoughts. I missed my sister.

"How many mermaids live here?" I asked as Gabrielle entered the room with a bottle of beer in hand. She offered it to me and I popped the metal top off. It resisted sufficiently for me to believe she hadn't tampered with it.

I took a swig of hoppy liquid as she answered. "Many. This home is much larger than it appears to be from the outside. Optical illusion with the mirrors. We have twenty rooms and in some rooms, more than one sister resides. More than a few are couples, life partners, mates."

"Where are the others?" I had hoped to run across someone else who could give me a little more than island history and a house tour.

"Let me show you to your room." Gabrielle walked down the hallway.

"My room?"

When she didn't respond I figured it couldn't hurt to see what she meant.

Black granite with specks of silver, the same as the living room floor, covered the walls. The hallway ended in floor-to-ceiling glass looking out over the water. Etched within the glass, nearly from floor to ceiling, was their goddess, Atargatis. A flowing veil draped over the top of her head and reached the bottom of the window. The right side of the veil gathered slightly around a knee whereas the left side opened to expose a fish tail. Her torso appeared fully human in its nakedness.

Gabrielle opened the door to the right of us and invited me to enter a bedroom. A white king size four-poster bed with a white comforter and white pillows took up a large portion of the room. White night stands stood on each side of the bed and a white wooden dresser sat against the wall shared with the next room over. It took a moment for my eyes to adjust to the overwhelming amount of white. Two outside bedroom walls of glass offered up a breathtaking view of the sandy beach and gently rolling ocean beyond.

I sat my boots and socks on the floor near the bed and walked to the windowed wall to get a better look.

Gabrielle opened a door near the dresser. "Here's your bathroom. You share it with the room next door, Elaine and Sarah. There's a lock from the inside of the doors for privacy. Make sure to unlock it when you're finished using the facilities. There are towels under the sink and we have no set meal times, so enjoy a shower, a nap, your beer, and we'll see you when we see you."

"Wait." I caught her arm before she left the room. She didn't seem to mind my touch. "I'm not staying. I'm not here to join your cause or your army or whatever, despite what your wise woman said. I just need some information and I'll be on my way."

Gabrielle gave a loaded smile. "Where will you go once you leave our island? Once you've gotten what you came for?"

"Depends on what I learn here," I said. Hopefully my next stop was wherever Shawna was.

"What the mermaids tell you? What I tell you?"

"Yes."

"Then believe me when I say, if you don't rest up for the next part of our journey, you'll be kicking yourself and cursing me. Your strength and performance are critical." She gently pulled her forearm out from under my hand.

"*Our* journey? How's that?"

"All questions will be answered when my sisters are present," she said, turning away from me. Gabrielle's butt cheeks and long hair swayed from the room before the door shut behind her.

I could have knocked her out of the way and bolted down the hall, out of the house to freedom. But then where would I go? Swim to the Californian coast? Not on my life. Let's just say the movie Jaws caused enough damage to keep me from ever wanting to splash around in the ocean which, being huldra, hadn't been a life goal of mine in the first place. Besides, I wasn't going anywhere until I found out something that helped me find Shawna.

I peered around the room, but my eyes wandered to the ocean view in search of the triangular top fin of a great white. I took another sip of beer. It was as though I was in an alternate dimension where the goddess never died. Where my mother's stories were more than just wishful mutterings or whispered ancient history. I felt along my neck for my Freyja charm and grasped it in my fingers.

"Thank you, goddess," I murmured, for keeping me alive so far. "Please do the same for Shawna." I'd survived an energy-wielding succubi den and a three-hour boat ride in the Pacific Ocean. Now, I sat in the bedroom of a mermaid home with a beer in one hand and the emblem of my goddess in the other. But what was any of that compared to what she was going through? I couldn't even imagine. And that was the problem. I didn't know who took her, why, or what they might be doing to her.

Going through this all over again was too much. I felt like I might explode at any moment.

Yes, I appeared to be safe, but much like the mirrored siding of the mermaids' home, appearances only represent what others want you to see. Not necessarily what's hiding beneath the surface. Gabrielle hadn't been as trusting as she'd let on. She'd placed me in the room farthest from the front door. Trapped, in essence. If at least one mermaid lived behind each of the many bedroom doors lining the hallway between my room and the entry way, I'd have a lot of scaly bodies to fight before reaching fresh air. Mermaids were tactical, that much was obvious. I wondered how many watched from the water and cliffs as Gabrielle and I walked to their home.

After locking the bedroom door, I pulled my cell phone from my jacket pocket, but it had no signal. I grabbed my charger from my purse and plugged it into an outlet in the wall anyway.

Being told what to do wasn't on my list of all-time favorites, but I figured taking advantage of the bed and bathroom wasn't a terrible idea. I stared at the bed, and then at the bathroom. Go to sleep or take a shower? I needed both as badly as an evergreen needs rain. I decided to side with the tree and get me some rain—first a shower, then a nap.

* * *

I'd fallen asleep to the music of ocean waves slamming against rocky cliffs and woke up gloriously well rested. It wasn't as amazing as falling asleep to the sound of the breeze flowing through leaves and rain filtering through branches and plunking my roof, but it came in at a close second. And I hadn't slept that good since Shawna's disappearance. I had a feeling the beer I'd downed had a lot to do with that.

I sat up and stretched. As usual, I'd kicked every bedcover, other than the sheet, to the floor. I had to pee so I pulled myself from bed and sauntered sleepily into the bathroom. The outer wall was glass, mirrored on the outside. Both inner walls and the floor were black granite. The granite counter held a large white shell on top as the sink. Well, at least that part fit the mermaid stereotype.

As I lathered the sea salt cleansing bar in my hands, I twisted my torso to study myself. Dark russet bark covered the small of my back. It was a sight of beauty that brought with it the certainty of suffering.

A sound registered at the outskirts of my mind, but didn't tear me away from my reflection. At least not until a mermaid stood in the opening from our shared bathroom to her bedroom.

"Oh, I'm sorry, the door wasn't locked so I didn't realize. I mean, I heard the water running, but that room's been empty for so long I figured the sound came from another bathroom." The red-haired female had strangely tan skin and wore only a shell necklace. She didn't turn around and leave. She didn't come in. She only stood there.

I peeked over her shoulder where another female lay naked on the bed, reading a book. She looked up from the pages and made eye contact with me. I half expected them to be like the succubi and invite me to join their mattress dance later, but they only stared.

"I've never seen an actual tree woman before," the redhead said, ogling my bark. "I'm Sarah, by the way, and that's my mate, Elaine." She pointed to the female on the bed.

I hated that my first reaction was to turn and hide my lower back from her, hide it from the world.

"I want to see her back," exclaimed the brunette female, Elaine. She leapt from the bed to stand beside her partner.

I finished rinsing my hands and turned the faucet off. I considered their request for a quick moment before showing the two Wild strangers my back, the part of me that I loved a little more every day. The part of me that was going to sign my death warrant with the Hunters.

"Can I touch it?" Elaine asked. She gently pushed Sarah's hips aside so she could get through.

"Will you let me feel your scales?" I asked in response. I didn't expect her to say yes.

"Of course." She inhaled sharply and as she exhaled a smile pulled at her lips. Gold and light blue scales rose across her collarbone and trickled down her breasts, stomach, arms, and legs.

"It doesn't cover your face," I said. "Mine doesn't either."

Elaine reached out to run a finger over my back. I fought the urge to pull away. I willed bark façade to the surface of my shoulders, across my chest and down the rest of my skin. She jumped and laughed. "Didn't expect that to happen."

"It's new to me," I said. "Sometimes it pops up right away. Other times, not so much."

I peered at myself in the mirror. I'd never seen my reflection in this state. My skin echoed the tree I connected to the most: an evergreen. Pride filled my heart and threatened to burst it wide open.

Elaine touched my arm and glided her scaled knuckles over my bark. "It's rougher at your lower back than your arm," she said.

"That's because my back is actual bark and this is only façade." I reached out to glide my fingers along her blue scales. They weren't slimy like I'd assumed they'd be. "They're so soft," I remarked.

"Faline." Gabrielle knocked on the bedroom door and the three of us jumped. "If you're ready, my sisters are gathered to hear what you've come to speak to us about."

Her words reminded me of the wise woman and the war I was supposed to start. In a snap my bark façade melted into my skin and I stood in the bathroom in only black panties and a patch of bark on my back, beside a blue scaled brunette and a naked red head. Only in Wilds land.

"Can you let Gabrielle know that Elaine and I will be out in a few minutes?" Sarah asked.

I nodded and left the bathroom, shutting the door behind me. I pulled on my jeans and black cami. I grabbed a dagger from one of the boots and carefully slid it through my jean's belt loop near my lower spine. So what if they caught a glimpse of my weapon. I'd be dumb not to bring it. I had to stay alive for Shawna. I didn't know these mermaids, or really, any mermaids.

I left the room and made my way down the long hallway toward Gabrielle. She wore a flowing linen halter top dress.

"They're waiting down by the water," she said as I neared her.

From the house we took a steep path down a rocky cliff. Salt water slammed into the side and sprayed toward us. "How many are waiting?" I asked.

"Oh, probably around twenty-five. Some are still out hunting."

In the moonlight, females gathered along the sandy beach. Some were talking, others were basking, naked, in the moonlight. Others still, watched the two of us make our way to them. I eyed the sheer number of mermaids before me and racked my brain for what I knew about the way mermaids killed their prey.

We reached the bottom of the cliff. Moist sand squished between my toes. Mermaids drowned their prey in the sea, and as the last breath of life pushed itself from their prey's lungs, the mermaid placed her mouth over her prey's and stole it. I suddenly wished I knew more about my own power and how to use it to defend myself. What was I walking into?

FOURTEEN

I COUNTED twenty-three mermaids lounging and chatting along the shore. Not only was I the only non-mermaid, but I was the only Wild wearing jeans and a dagger.

Their hair colors ranged from blonde to black, but none had my pale skin. And most wore a smattering of scales sparkling along their flesh like jewelry. I walked through the group and scanned the crowd for numbered identification tattoos while pretending to look where I walked. Dozens of smooth bodies glittered with perfection, none marred by Hunter's marks.

Did mermaids have mind numbing abilities? Were they able to make their prey feel at ease? Because while I was so incredibly outnumbered, I didn't feel threatened in the slightest. That in itself made me uneasy.

"None of us lead our shoal," Gabrielle explained as we made our way toward the tide and I found myself moving a little slower to keep from reaching it. "Some are older, and we certainly respect their wisdom, but the younger members get an equal say."

Rather than seeing mermaids of similar age groups, like I would among a huldra coterie, I saw what looked like mermaids from every age—young adult to grey-haired. "You do not control your procreation —regulate and schedule it," I said, not as a question.

Gabrielle laughed and a few snickers joined in. "No, we don't have much in the way of regulations."

Out of my peripheral vision, I noticed Sarah and Elaine walking from the waves onto the beach to join the others.

We stood by the water, out of reach from the rising tide as it strolled up the sand and receded into the waves. An awkward silence hung in the air despite the howling wind. Clouds eased apart to reveal the hint of a full moon. Gabrielle closed her eyes and inhaled as dark emerald scales rose from her tan skin.

When Gabrielle showed me to my room earlier, she'd assured me I'd get my questions answered once she gathered her sisters. Well, the mermaids were gathered. "I would like to begin our discussion now, ask my questions, so that I can be on my way," I said.

"Are you not a Wild Woman?" A grey-haired woman stood from the hushed crowd. She strode over to us as though she walked on wind. She didn't give me time to answer. "Are you not female? Are you not a descendant of a high priestess who had the breath of her goddess breathed into her to enable her daughters and her daughter's daughters?"

I turned to address the older mermaid. Her orange-red scales draped down her body as though she were on fire. Her words burned with familiarity in my mind. "I am, but a lot has changed since those days," I said, wondering why the Hunters hadn't taught that part of our history. I got to the matter at hand. "You've been trying to recruit Wilds for your war, but I wonder if any have answered your call. A succubus in particular."

Everything in me wanted to ask about Shawna. If they had their proverbial fingers on the pulse of everything Wild, there was a chance they'd have heard something about a missing huldra. But I didn't know the mermaids from any other potential Wild enemy, and mentioning my sister, showing my urgency and absolute need to find her, would be like playing a hand of poker with my cards fanned out for the whole table to see.

"We know it will take time for other Wilds to trust us enough to heed our call." The older female quickly introduced herself as Azul and continued, "This is where you come in, huldra." Azul reached toward me and I moved back. Her scales multiplied, growing up her neck and down both her arms.

I put my hand in the air between the two of us. "I'm a little lost here. Marie, leader of the Oregon succubi galere, sent me. Where I come in is to find out if her sister ever made it to this island, to join your army." I paused a moment, unsure as to whether or not it was time to show my cards. Impatience wore down my resolve. If I were looking for a bail-runner, I'd have no problem keeping my cool to play a mind game. But my sister's life hung in the balance, so I got to the point. "And, also, to seek any information you have on who could have taken my own sister." I dug my toes into the moist sand. Eager to don protective bark, my skin prickled from the rising frustration of having to put myself in a place of enough vulnerability to ask strangers for help in finding my own sister.

Gabrielle and Azul took two steps back.

"The point is that you came as the wise woman foretold," Gabrielle said.

"The point is that while you and your sisters moonbathe, other Wilds are disappearing." I swallowed down my urge to blame them for their life of ease and selected my next words carefully.

But when I opened my mouth to speak, Azul cut in. "Your anger is deserved. The rot of garbage that has been covered with sod, with their lies, is now peeking through the surface and its stench is unbearable."

A deep exhale that I had been holding for days left my lungs as the threat of tears blurred my vision. She hadn't given a name to the garbage, the rot, but my intuition knew. Finally, what I'd known, what I feared, was validated.

I'd realized the possibility that night in the Oregon hotel, when I saw how easy Wilds were to locate based off their surnames. But it wasn't possible, was it? Could it be that it wasn't the succubi who took my sister, who ordered my attack? It wasn't the mermaids. It was those who claimed to be our protectors? Those who wore the veneer of security and strength to cover rotten motives.

"Hunters," I breathed into the wind.

"It's happened before," Gabrielle said. "Twenty years ago, Wilds from all over went missing. But seeing that Wilds didn't communicate, they thought their incident was singular to them. We had waited for a huldra to come to us, as was foretold, but she never did. This time, when the disappearances started again, we decided we couldn't stand by and watch any longer. We took matters into our own hands."

"Your Wild army," I said.

"Yes, but the division of Wilds is proving too large an obstacle to overcome." Gabrielle lowered her head.

Azul gently touched Gabrielle's shoulder. "It is still early," she reminded.

Gabrielle peered at the older mermaid. "But we have Faline now. She can unite the Wilds. Our wise woman's words can come to pass."

My gut instincts aside, this made no sense. "Why the Hunters, though? Why not just trap us when we check in? Why covertly abduct us when we have to answer to them anyway?"

Azul answered, "When the Blessed Ones, or as we now know them, the Hunters, first rose in power they saw us as a threat and tried to annihilate all Wilds. But we banded together and fought back. Above all they sought power. And I believe our power impressed them, so much so that they no longer chose to be rid of us, but to rule over us."

"That's a new version of our history," I remarked, remembering how the Hunters insisted we were too wild to control ourselves so they bravely stepped in to do the job for us.

"You've learned *his*tory. Now hear *her*story." Azul continued, "Why does anyone rule over another? Because there's something they want from those they rule over, something of value. The fact that we cannot surmise what it is does not mean it isn't there."

"Again, why not take it by force?" I asked.

"Do you know how the Wilds lost against the Hunters?" Azul asked.

"Through politics, religion, and wealth they separated the different groups. Divide and conquer," I said.

"Precisely. To divide is to conquer. To allow the groups to come together as one would be the Hunters' demise."

"So you're saying that if they took Wilds by force during check-ins they'd be blatantly behaving in a way that would cause us to not only question their motives, but to know their motives. They can't run the risk of us getting fed up enough to revolt." I gazed at the many Wilds on the beach, listening, and returned my attention to Azul and Gabrielle.

Both females nodded.

"And if my sister is being held by the Hunters, then rescuing her would start a war." The pieces fell together in my mind. The mermaids hadn't stacked the deck, hadn't set any of this up. They'd only known how one hand would be dealt—mine. My mind sifted through the new facts presented and began forming a plan. "Shawna, my sister, is probably at the local Hunter complex." Goddess, and here I was hundreds of miles away. I shook my head, wishing I hadn't been so naive. "That's why John met me in their parking lot—walked from the training building at that hour and shut the door behind him. Why he was short with me. Why he acted like there wasn't much he could do to help. Shawna was there, probably in the training building, ten feet away from me."

My legs weakened and I fell to my knees. Moist sand received my forehead as my tears met with the remnants of high tide. I had to think, had to plan. But my mind refused to focus enough to quiet the tornado inside.

Azul stood above me. "My sisters, we have prepared for this day. Our goddess Atargatis has protected us well with the help of our Chumash sisters and brothers. We've grown in numbers and mastered our strengths as well as our weaknesses. Each of us feels Her call in our bones, Her call to join Her sister goddesses, that we may join their daughters. What do you say, my sisters? Shall we help this huldra begin a war to free all American Wilds so that they too may live in their power?"

My huldra responded to her call. Shivers of anticipation replaced sobbing, pulling me to sit up on my knees. Mermaids, tall and short, thick and thin, stood and ululated into the night with arms raised to the moon. Their voices wove into a choir of power with acoustics to challenge any opera hall. A knot formed in my throat as I stood in the presence of solidarity so strong and so giving toward me, toward Shawna and Heather. Like trees swaying together in a storm, sharing the force of the wind so that all would survive.

I raised my own hands toward the sky in abandon, thanking Freyja for sending help, for sending a renewed hope. It would all be okay. Everything would be okay.

Another sound caught my attention. It started out as a quiet hum but quickly grew in intensity. I first looked out over the waves and then searched the night sky.

"A helicopter!" I yelled. "I hear a helicopter!"

I looked toward the sound, but no lights shone down. They didn't want us to know they were here. The mermaids quieted and turned toward the sound. Wind shifted and the hum became deafening.

"Wind, sisters!" Gabrielle called out. "We need wind!"

Other than the sounds of nature and the nearby helicopter, the beach grew silent. Mermaids kept their arms raised and tilted their faces up as though they asked for assistance from the moon. Gusts of wind picked up and whipped my hair into my shoulders and cheeks. Waves crashed violently to the shore and more so against the rocky cliffs.

My huldra shook within me, begged to come out and join the mermaids, to stand in my power alongside them. But I had to control my huldra. Blacking out at such a time would benefit no one.

The helicopter's motor whirred, fighting the wind, and it changed course. I wished I could see the machine work to stay in flight, but the cliff obstructed my view. I hit the cliff base at a dead run, pushing myself to make it up the steep incline. I was halfway when a lightning bolt unfurled from a clustering of clouds and whipped down to the earth, missing the helicopter by what look like mere inches.

The brief snap of light lit the bone dagger painted on the helicopter's side.

"Hunters," I shrieked.

Another crack of light bolted from the heavens, this time hitting its target. Smoke billowed from the machine as it plummeted toward a jagged cliff and exploded on impact.

The mermaids cheered, but not for long.

"They're here, on the island!" Azul called out.

From the side of the cliff, I viewed the others lower their arms and freeze. Gabrielle caught up to me.

"How does she know more are here?" I asked, still trying to listen for and smell their presence. Only salt water filled my nose.

Gabrielle stood as still as a statue as she spoke, her muscular legs planted into the sand. Hair blew into her face, but she did nothing to remove it. "We absorb the water in the air, and while in the sea, we absorb the air in the water. That's how we breathe. It's also how we smell or sense who's nearby. I'd bet if you tried, you could do something similar." She paused in concentration. "The wind is bringing the scent of males to us, large, strong non-human males."

"Hunters," I said again, still in disbelief. There could be only one reason they were here: to end the uprising. Unless, of course, they had come to kidnap more Wild Women. It seemed unlikely they'd do so in an outright attack. If it was them behind the disappearances, then this wasn't their method.

She nodded.

"I thought they didn't know about you, about your home," I yelled over the commotion.

"They didn't."

Goddess, had I somehow led them here?

She closed her eyes and inhaled. Deep green scales multiplied across her body. "They're coming closer. They know we're down here." She opened her chestnut eyes and looked me over.

"How?" I asked, searching the top of the cliff for Hunters.

"They dropped them onto the island before the helicopter went down. They must have infrared goggles." She gestured toward me. "Why aren't you donning your bark?"

"Why would I? There's no trees to hide in." I looked around to make sure I hadn't missed any growing out of the side of a cliff.

"It lowers your body temperature, makes it impossible for them to see your heat signature. The heat signatures of trees are nothing compared to that of a body." Gabrielle ran down to the beach, toward the others. They gathered in a tight circle. Each mermaid wore a different variation of scale color as they glinted in the moon light.

"Faline," she called to me.

I jogged to the circle. I pulled the dagger from my belt loop. "How many of them?"

"Seven, maybe ten?" another female answered.

"What are you doing? Put your bark on," Gabrielle said with urgency. "They're coming."

The Hunters were really here to attack us? This all felt so wrong, so against what I'd grown up knowing. "I can't, not all the way. It may let my huldra out." I glanced behind us and eyed the top of the cliff again. The crashing waves and salt water disorientated my senses.

"Then we will welcome her and be thankful for her help," Gabrielle said. She pivoted into the circle.

Mermaids whispered plans. Some offered to hide in the cliff crevices for surprise attacks. Others offered to swim around to another beach and climb up to ensure the safety of their house.

"What about the children?" I asked, remembering what I'd been told earlier about their odd procreation patterns. I couldn't stand to see a small child taken.

Gabrielle paused from strategizing. "They've been deep in the underground caves with a few elders and a couple of mothers since you arrived." No, the mermaids were not naive.

The females dispersed in different directions. No battle cries rang out, only stealthy movements. Holding my dagger at the ready, I headed toward a cliff path to meet the Hunters head on.

Gabrielle whispered harshly as she joined me, running through sand toward the cliff. "If you don't cover yourself with bark in the next minute, they'll pick you off like a fish in a barrel."

"I can't control my huldra," I said through gritted teeth.

"Then stop trying. Stop working against her like she's your obstacle, and work with her like she's your best asset. Faline, she is your power! Stand in her without apologies."

Gabrielle and I crested the cliff. Two rows of huge Hunters ran toward us. They wore black cargo pants and black fitted sweaters with zippered pockets along their outer biceps. High tech goggles covered their eyes. The first two reached for their guns.

Guns? So they'd already stopped collecting us secretly and now sought to kill us openly?

"There's one!" a Hunter shouted, pointing to me, completely unaware Gabrielle ran at them, ten feet to my left.

I had no choice. If I had led these Hunters to the mermaids' home, I owed it to them to fight. I owed it to Shawna.

A Hunter cocked his gun and pointed it at me as I willed bark to cover my body. Tingles flashed through my pores and my inner huldra vibrated to life.

A shot rang out.

"No!" I yelled, as I instinctively swiveled on the ball of my foot to run away. Searing pain stabbed into my back. I crumbled to the ground.

FIFTEEN

"WHERE'D SHE GO?" a Hunter yelled to the others, scanning the landscape. Gabrielle had been right; my bark blocked my heat signature. The fact that I lay motionless, sprawled across the dirt probably helped too.

"She just vanished!" another answered.

"Wilds aren't invisible," one scolded.

Gabrielle silently ran to me and crouched down. "Where?" she asked as quiet as a soft breeze.

"My back," was all I could say outside of a groan. I pulled my knees up and lay in the fetal position.

With one rip she tore my camisole from the neck line to the waist hem and flung it into the wind. "The bullet didn't pierce you. Your bark is strong, it protected you, but it's cracked, badly."

I reached down to feel the wound as Hunters, only fifteen yards away, yelled at one another for losing me. My fingers traced unnatural cracks that ran sideways along the upright ridges of rough bark.

"How long will it take to heal?" I asked in barely a whisper.

"It depends. How long does it take for you to kill a Hunter?" she answered.

"Seconds," I heard myself say. I'd never so much as slapped a

Hunter. My mind engaged and I answered her more correctly. "I don't think I can."

"Well, that's how long it'll take your wound to heal." Gabrielle stood and reached toward me to help me up. I rolled to my hands and knees and accepted her assistance.

Out of options, I stood on weak legs and summoned my waning strength. Thoughts of Shawna filled my mind—her kind heart, her sharp wit, her hopes and dreams. Resolve surged through me. This would not be our reality, running and hiding in fear. The seed my mother had planted long ago with her stories, sprouted, pushed from the dirt out into the night and shoved me forward.

"You take the one on the left. I'll take the one of the right," I told Gabrielle under my breath. Ignoring the pulsing pain, my toes dug into the dirt with each footfall as I rushed the males.

A growl bellowed deep in my throat. With my strong huldra legs, I sprang at the Hunter, landing on his back and wrapping my legs around his waist. I had to stay present. I couldn't black out this time.

Only, I *was* blacking out. The more excited my huldra became, the more the darkness encased me and threatened to swallow my conscious self. A knowing deep within commanded that I talk to myself, talk to my inner huldra, bridge the gap and connect my two selves that had been forced apart so long ago.

The Hunter reached his arms to the side of his waist and behind himself, but couldn't wrench me off. He grabbed his dagger from his pants and swiped at my legs as I unwrapped them from his waist and hoisted my weight onto his shoulders.

"One's on me!" he yelled to the other Hunter who ran toward his buddy. The Hunter I clung to stabbed his dagger over his shoulder and I ducked out of the way, leaning my weight to one side. He started to fall sideways, but quickly righted himself.

"I can't see it!" his buddy said. "I don't want to stab you."

Stay present. Stay present. Stay present, I repeated.

Gabrielle bolted for the other two Hunters. A male's scream echoed into the night. She worked quickly. I expected her to return, to help me, but she left me to fight alone.

My inner huldra wanted to choke him, to feel the pulse of his life slow to a stop. Not willing to give my huldra complete control, I talked myself through the act. *Just wrap your fingers around his neck*, I told myself. *The way you wrap your fingers around a branch.*

A huldra's hands are strong, our fingers muscular from climbing. I squeezed, my thumbs directly above each main artery in his neck.

The Hunter coughed and leaned forward. "It's...it's...choking. Me."

With unsure hands his buddy grabbed at me. When he made contact he wrapped his forearms around my waist and heaved. I only held tighter, dug my fingers in deeper. I counted to help stay present, to not black out and give my huldra free rein. In less the twenty seconds lack of blood flow to the Hunter's brain would cause him to pass out. Within a minute, he'd be dead.

His buddy pulled harder and I only dug deeper, wrapping my feet around the Hunter's midsection like a leather belt after Thanksgiving dinner. The Hunter fell forward, losing consciousness, but I held tight. His buddy grabbed his dagger and slashed wildly at where he thought he'd find my torso, only grazing my shoulder with the blade.

And the Hunter's blade burned like no other. But I refused to give in to pain. I accepted it, allowed it to hold me in the moment, in my body and mind.

I kept my right hand wrapped around the Hunter's neck, and with my left hand I reached out for his buddy. Now, rather than me guiding my huldra, she guided me. I wasn't sure what my left hand could do against his dagger, but I obeyed my inner knowing.

Branches shot out of my outstretched, bark-covered fingers and plummeted into the man's chest. He screamed and flailed his dagger-clutching hand. Blood spewed from his mouth and dripped from his lips. His eyes widened as I willed my branches to wind through him, to hook around his organs. His mouth opened, twisting his expression in horror.

The heartbeat from the Hunter beneath me slowed until his breathing stopped. I pulled myself from his body and walked toward his buddy, who now had my branches buried in his chest.

He curdled out a bloody scream and worked hard to hack at my branches. With a sharp bite, the dagger made its way through four of my branches. I flicked my wrist to finish the job for him. With the initial throb of what a bone fracture must feel like, my last branch broke free from his chest.

"Which complex are you from?" I yelled, leaning over him. "Did you take a huldra, a couple nights ago? Where did you take her?"

He lifted a shaking hand to give me the finger as he smiled. That smile told me everything I needed to know. The Hunters had taken my sister.

The Hunter spurted out blood as he pushed words from his mouth. "How...did...you? You...shouldn't...be...able—"

Before I could lay another hand on him, the Hunter fell over. My muscles shook and my head spun as I felt my huldra receding from battle. I couldn't pull my eyes from the man on the dirt. Realization over what I'd done barreled through me like a tsunami. I gasped and pivoted in a circle, checked every direction for another Hunter on the warpath. No one else came for me. But Gabrielle crouched twenty-five feet away, watching.

"I didn't know. I, I..." My heart pounded. I closed my eyes to still my shakiness.

Gabrielle gave me my space, and probably for good reason. "You are capable of doing a lot of things," she said. "Don't you know? Before the Hunters split up the Wild Women, turned us against one another, we were united. And the huldra were our protectors."

I absently touched my lower back. The cracks were gone. My bark had grown thicker. The hot burn in my shoulder from the Hunter's dagger cooled and disappeared. "Does my strength grow with each kill?" I asked, staring into the darkness.

"Our power isn't exclusively attached to mayhem," Gabrielle explained as she stood, but still gave me my space. "It's always been in you, but after years of non-use it's gone dormant. And when you're taught that any part of your power is bad, something to be avoided, you push it down, hide it that much more." She gripped my shoulder and looked deep into my eyes. "So to answer your question, no your strength doesn't grow with each kill, it grows with each time you use it."

* * *

The mermaids glowered in the living room of their home. A few older females sat on the couches while the youngest sat on the floor with their mothers protectively hovering. Some paced the hall with hands on their hips. Others grabbed chairs from the kitchen and pulled them into the living room to sit along the mirrored window walls.

The scent of saltwater, seaweed, and scales filled my nose until I could smell nothing else.

From the moment I'd stepped foot on this island and seen Gabrielle, I couldn't understand why I'd been received so well. My coterie would never have trusted a mermaid who came to our property for help. There would be tests first...

Wait.

"If you knew I was coming, then how did you not know the Hunters had found you?" I asked the couch full of grey-haired females.

Azul released her long hair from a knot on her head. "A little birdy informed us about a week ago that the Hunters had locked on to our island. We usually know when we'll get a flyby of the area and we make sure to stay hidden and in full scales to evade the heat sensors. But two weeks ago a sister who'd been out hunting noticed a boat fairly far out with a drone headed to our shores. With technology advancing as rapidly as it is, we knew it'd only be a matter of time before they'd reach us and learn of our existence. That time has come and gone."

"What does this mean for us?" Elaine, the brunette female I'd met in our shared bathroom, asked. She held a five-year-old red-headed girl on her lap with olive skin and dark freckles across her cheeks. The little one looked more like her mate, Sarah. "Are we leaving?"

The older females on the couch shook their heads as if they knew something the rest of the room didn't, and maybe so.

Azul spoke again. "No, we will not have to leave. Not permanently, at least. For the time being we have comfortable accommodations set up in the caves within the cliffs, where the children hid."

That's when my whirring mind slowed long enough to put a couple more puzzle pieces together. "Wait. You weren't hiding your children from me?" A new level of understanding flickered as the words left my mouth. "You knew the Hunters were coming and you were hiding the children because of them. That's why you were kind to me, gave me a place to rest, to prepare and gain my strength."

I looked to Gabrielle, but she only gave a tiny nod and a tight smile.

"You were using me," I said.

"No, we were helping you," Azul answered.

"Um, that's not the help I came to ask for." Irritation shook within me and I pushed off the glass wall I'd been leaning against. My right foot tingled and I peered down to see bark creeping across my toes.

"Now, Faline, calm down." Azul stood and placed her hands out in front of her.

I shook my head. "What if I'd died? What if they'd taken me? Do you realize you put my coterie and my sister at a greater risk?"

"We did not use you to protect us against the Hunters," Gabrielle said with clipped words, as though the thought of it was offensive. "If you'll remember, my sisters took out most of the Hunters, not you."

"Oh, right." I smiled and scanned the room. "So which one of you took two out? All by yourself?" I turned to eye Gabrielle. "While another mermaid watched?" Bark crept up my ankle and under my pant leg. I wondered if branches could extend from my toes too, and in that moment, five grew from my foot.

"You are not thinking clearly," Gabrielle said, again with a clipped voice. Funny. She hadn't shown that side of herself when she'd wanted me to fight for her shoal. "You know I took on two. You were there."

"And then, instead of helping me, you took a breather." I wanted off this island now. They'd lured me in, distributed sage advice as though they'd cared, and then pushed me into a cage fight. Maybe they were as unstable as the succubi, only more cunning.

"No, I was nearby in case you needed me," Gabrielle argued. "But you didn't. Which means we can save your sister. We can save all the missing sisters."

Bark receded down my ankle along with the branches growing from my toes. Shivers replaced the tingling sensation. "You know for sure that others have been taken recently?" I asked. "Not just Heather and my sister?"

Gabrielle lowered her head and Elaine answered. "Wild Women

have gone missing from every group that we know of. But like I said earlier, we don't know why. They want something from us."

Elaine shook her head and held tighter to her and Sarah's little girl.

"Most American Wild Women are cut off from their origins. They do not remember their traditional roles from before we were scattered. Living outside the Hunter's control, our shoal has passed down the stories from generations past. Huldra were the warriors, the protectors, much like their goddess, Freyja. It is time they become that once again."

If huldra had been the protectors, it made sense that we functioned like a military group with rules and partner sisters, unlike the other Wilds I'd met so far.

Azul walked toward me with softness in her step as well as her eyes. "You are the only living huldra we know of who has tapped into her legacy. We had no way of knowing this when you arrived. We only knew you were huldra, a tree woman, who came to us. We were prepared to train you, to help you."

"So then when do we start saving my sister?" I rubbed my temples to loosen my headache's hold. I didn't fully trust the mermaids. They clearly had layers of intentions behind their words and actions. But for the time being, they sought to save all missing sisters, so our goals lined up.

Azul placed a gentle hand on my right arm, though she steered clear of my fingers, probably knowing branches could sprout from my hands at any moment. For the first time, I noticed dried blood-spray across the chest of her capped sleeve dress. Azul took a long breath. "Fear runs deep, like termites. It rots out your good intentions, your abilities, your power. It turns your strengths into your weaknesses."

Her words conjured an understanding buried deep within myself. In a way, I had feared Hunters. It's why I'd complied with their oppressive rules and regulations. Why I believed they were only there to protect us when my gut had always fought that notion. And when I didn't have the choice to comply with the rigid framework they'd set, I'd blacked out and let my huldra take over and woke up to a bloodied body. I feared my huldra. I feared myself.

I closed my eyes for a slow second, took in a cleansing breath, and nodded my head.

"We would like to book you and Gabrielle a flight to the east coast, to meet with the harpies." Azul smiled at Gabrielle, who didn't return the gesture.

"How will this help my sister?" I said, the wheels in my head already spinning. "Wait. Is this about your war on the Hunters? Reaching out to the other Wilds? But you've already sent word."

Azul answered, "No one has responded yet. This method is quicker. And about your sister, the more allies you collect to help retrieve her, the more likely you'll be successful."

I looked at Gabrielle. "But you're not happy about it. Do you know something I don't?"

She sighed. "The harpies have a thing against the huldra. A long time ago our kinds—the harpies and the mermaids—used to work together to take down those we sought."

"Is that a nice way of saying your victims? Sailors?" I asked, remembering the Hunter's history lessons well. Unsuspecting sailors were lured to the depths of the sea by heavenly singing, or their ships crashed against the cliffs due to sudden storms. None ever survived.

"They were hardly victims," another mermaid I hadn't met interrupted. Her long brownish-blonde hair hung tangled from either fighting, or swimming, or both. "Our foremothers only took down those who would do more damage than good—the pirates and slave ships, before they picked up their slaves, of course."

"Anyway," Gabrielle snapped. "They don't despise us as much as they despise you." Either the tension of the evening had gotten to Gabrielle or she really didn't want to visit the harpies.

I assumed the succubi would distrust my kind due to the mere fact that we lived closest to them, so the Oregon Hunters no doubt focused much of their "trainings" around how awful we are. And I'd heard stories from my mother of a negative encounter between a rusalki and a huldra many years ago, but the harpies too? "If huldra used to protect the other Wilds, why the common disdain for us?"

"We can't be sure," Azul answered. "The scorn runs deep and old, but we believe it may be rooted in the time of the Inquisitions, when

Hunters rounded Wilds up for slaughter and huldras stood at the front lines to defend us. Remember, the winners write history. It's likely that the Hunters twisted the bravery of your foremothers into a less than honorable intention."

Everyone hated the huldra, I was learning. Except for the mermaids, of course.

"Fine. If this is going to help me get Shawna back, when do we leave?" I asked, looking around for the next random mermaid to answer my question. I'd call Marie to explain the newest developments once I got to the mainland. After I reported back to my coterie, of course.

"Caleb will be on his way shortly," Azul answered.

Without so much as a head nod, I turned and walked down the long hallway to the room I'd slept in. I hadn't been here a day and I was already on my way out. Good thing I hadn't unpacked my purse. That suited me just fine. The faster I got to Shawna, the better. At least now, I wouldn't have to face the harpies alone. More than anything, I wanted to go straight to the Hunters' complex and start a shit storm. If only it were that easy. They were the most formidable force my kind had known for ages, so as much as I hated it, I gripped what little patience I had left like my weapon of choice. If all went well, I'd have an army of Wilds at my back. If it didn't, Shawna might not be the only one who needed saving.

SIXTEEN

"WHY DO you have handcuffs in here?" Gabrielle asked. She sat, fully clothed for the first time since I'd met her, in the front passenger seat of my car. White zip-tie cuffs dangled from her pointer finger.

I'd driven to the Oxnard airport—only about fifteen minutes from the harbor. The whole drive had been silent, and now, right before I parked my car in long term parking, she'd chosen to rifle through the glove box and door compartment.

I turned into the parking area and searched for a spot. "What, you don't?" I asked, evading the question.

She arched a dark eyebrow. "We both know I don't have a car," she said. "Oh." She nodded as though she'd cracked the code.

"What?" I asked, my curiosity piqued as to what she no doubt wrongly assumed I had cuffs for. I found a parking stall and pulled in.

"It makes sense," she said, putting the cuffs where she'd found them. "Huldra. You guys like it rough, don't you? Like dominatrix rough."

I tilted my head and stared at her. Seriously?

"No judgment," she promised. "Thanks to current media, it's a respected form of sexual pleasure."

I shook my head. "I'm a bounty hunter. I don't need to cuff my lovers for pleasure." I laughed a little to myself. "Or rough them up."

"The bounty hunter thing makes sense, too." Gabrielle opened the car door, grabbed the straps of her bag from the backseat, and struggled to get it unstuck from between the two front seats. I considered reminding her that my car had four doors, not two—she could open the back door to get her bag. But her battle against the seats was half over and she was winning.

When she'd ducked away to throw on "traveling clothes" as the mermaids had called it, I half expected to see her come out of her room in ripped jeans and a fitted t-shirt like a succubus. I don't know why. And now, as I hid a laugh and watched her overcome the evil backseat, I realized how wrong my assumption had been. Her black slacks hung from her waist and stopped where black high heels started. A black jean blazer covered a pastel green, fitted silk shirt and she wore her hair up in a twist to cover the shells woven into her roots along the part in her hair.

We walked into the airport looking like we did not belong together —me with my dirty jeans and her with her...classy mermaid style. We checked in at a kiosk, went through security, and headed to our gate where we found three empty seats, leaving one between us to set our bags.

"What did you mean when you said that it makes sense I'm a bounty hunter?" I asked. None of my coterie members had jobs similar to mine, so her whole huldra-equals-bounty-hunter thing didn't make sense.

My phone rang before she could answer. I had updated my aunts as I left the mermaid's island the moment my phone screen donned the blessed symbol of cell connection—within sight of the mainland. I hadn't cared that Caleb and Gabrielle heard every word from my mouth.

I pulled my phone from my pocket and answered, expecting Olivia to give me the details of the area I was headed. "Hey, what do you got for me?" I asked.

"Where are you at, Faline?"

"Marcus?" I pulled the phone from my face to check the screen.

"I'm sorry I didn't call you back after you sent the email, which was a big help by the way. I've been incredibly busy."

Marcus cleared his throat. "Listen, we need to talk."

"Good thing we're on the phone then," I said. "What's up?"

"No. In person. We need to talk in person." Marcus's tight, serious voice cut through my playfulness.

I had no idea what terms Marcus and I were currently on, but now wasn't the time to figure it out.

Gabrielle had been pretending not to listen to our phone conversation, but now she stared openly. A large plane taxied past the floor-to-ceiling windows my seat pointed toward.

"Where can I meet you?" Marcus asked.

"Why can't you wait till I'm back in town?"

I paused to listen to the woman over the speaker near our gate announcing that our flight from Oxnard, California to Ashville Regional Airport, North Carolina would be boarding in ten minutes.

"North Carolina?" Marcus's tone rose like he'd been caught off guard. "Why? What's going on, Faline?"

"You're asking a lot of questions and answering none," I said. "That's what's going on."

Gabrielle let out a snort. I'd probably never again see a Wild as regal as a mermaid, snort.

"Fine." Marcus exhaled into the phone. "I'm taking a few days off to meet you in North Carolina. I haven't been one hundred percent open with you about...a lot of things. I haven't lied, but I've left out some important truths."

I perked up. Yeah, I could have waited to hear them when I returned to Washington, but my curiosity got the better of me. "What truths?"

"Like where I really went that night at the hotel—" He sighed and I pictured him shaking his head or scratching his face stubble. "I can't explain over the phone. I shouldn't even be telling you."

"I don't understand. Why do you need to fly across the country to come clean now, though? I'm in the middle of trying to get my sister."

Marcus's breathing filled the silence on the other end.

"How about I call you when I'm done?" I said.

"In the last six months, uh...women...all in the same age range, without spouses, living with female family members, have gone missing. Most from fairly remote areas." Marcus cleared his throat again.

From what the mermaids had told me, none of the missing Wilds had been reported. I turned to Gabrielle with wide eyes and spoke to Marcus. My words were direct and crisp. "We'll be heading to Mount Mitchell, but you can probably get a room in the nearest town, Burnsville. Call me as soon as you land."

Marcus ended the call.

Gabrielle's chestnut brown eyes lit with fire. "Who was that?"

"A man I work with on occasion," I said.

"Your body language would suggest he means more than a coworker to you."

"We went on one and a half dates. The half date was on the night I was attacked, the day before my sister was abducted."

She pulled a cell phone from her purse and stood. "Excuse me. I need to make a phone call," she said before she walked toward a book store and around the corner.

So she was all ears during my phone calls, but hers deserved privacy?

When the airline desk attendant announced that our flight was now boarding, Gabrielle rushed to grab her over-priced bag. I held back an eye roll and walked to stand in line.

"What?" she said, catching her breath as she took her place behind me and searched through her designer purse for her boarding pass. "I wasn't being secretive, I promise. I just prefer privacy. I had to call and warn them."

I turned to look at her. "Your shoal?" But Azul already knew the Hunters were up to something. What else was there to warn them about? "Warn them about what?"

"Yes. And Caleb's family," was all she said in reply.

I found the seat letter and number matching my boarding pass. Gabrielle sat beside me, positioning her purse under the chair in front of her and snapping her seatbelt shut. Thank the goddess, Gabrielle was accompanying me because after what she and Azul had said concerning the harpies dislike for huldra, I figured meeting the harpies on their turf without my gun or my boot daggers would be the opposite of my first meeting with the mermaids. Replaying the Wildshate-huldra conversation in my head brought another question to the surface. Everything had happened so quickly, my rational mind was still trying to catch up.

Four Wild groups, not including huldra, live within the United States. I'd met with two already, so there were two left. "So why the harpies first? If we're going to the east coast, why not visit the rusalki first?" I asked.

Gabrielle paused from preparing her items for takeoff. "North Carolina is closer than Maine." Another top-layer answer in the form of a statement.

I wanted the deeper reason. Distance seemed too simple. "Yeah, I guess, but not by a ton. They're both east coast," I pointed out.

Gabrielle sighed and peered around before lowering her voice. "The harpies and mermaids share a connection that is not present with the rusalki. Whether or not they'll honor our connected histories is another matter. It was long ago and time has a way of tainting the past." She grabbed a magazine from the seat pocket of the chair in front of her and leafed through the pages.

I eyed her for a quick second. She looked prim and proper, not ready to fight her distant cousins. Though, she had held her own against the Hunters...and then watched me do most of the fighting.

Trusting anyone other than a huldra sister would be a mistake. I clicked my own buckle in place and positioned a mini version of a pillow behind my head for the long flight. As I closed my eyes I made a decision; I would pick up a weapon or two before heading up the mountain. Before meeting with the winged, sharped-talon harpies.

* * *

My knees ached from my stationary day of sitting in cars, airports, and planes, so I massaged them with my free hand as I drove. At night the little town of Burnsville, North Carolina looked like a ghost town, with shops closed and its inhabitants at home either sitting down to a late supper or already in bed.

We'd left the airport in a little red rental car. Gabrielle had begged for something flashier and offered to foot the bill herself. While I would have gone for something sportier to get this over and done with faster, other than full size models and minivans they were out of anything else. She'd conceded with the compromise that our hotel must be at least four stars. From her repeated groans as we drove through the small town, it was obvious she now realized that she'd lose that one too.

Her complaining grated on my nerves. If I had my way we'd show up, talk to the harpies, and then catch the next flight out. Agreeing to stay in a hotel kept me from Shawna for another night, kept her away from her coterie for another sunrise. Nothing about that sat well with me. But harpies were delicate Wilds, easily spooked. Gabrielle insisted that by staying in town for the night, it would look as though we were making an effort to connect to them rather than use them for information. If they felt a connection, they were more likely to help us. And I had a better chance at saving Shawna if I had the harpies' help. Plus, I'd told Marcus to meet me in town. Imagining what was so important that he had to tell me in person made my stomach fold in on itself more than it already was.

I pulled off the road into the gravel parking area of a one-story brick building lined with white doors.

"It says 'Motel' in red lettering," Gabrielle groaned.

I shot Marcus a quick text with the motel's name before eying Gabrielle's phone. "Have they called you back yet?" I asked, more concerned about getting this over with and finding my sister than Gabrielle's opinions about motels. Gabrielle had called the harpies' contact the moment we passed city lines, as instructed, and left a message. She checked her phone and shook her head.

"According to the Google gods it's the motel in town that's not a bed and breakfast." I answered her earlier comment, resigned to the fact that I was spending the night in harpy country. "B&B's are too quaint, the owners and guests want to know everything about the other guests," I said. "Too personal."

"Maybe I'll just stay with the harpies," she said with a sigh. "They'll have a cliffside mansion, I assume."

Okay, I'd just about had it. "When did you become a snob?" I asked with a noticeable tension in my voice. "When I first met you, you were naked with seaweed in your hair. Roughing it."

"Doing what I was born to do isn't roughing it—it's called living in my bliss. And just because I *can* rough it, doesn't mean I want to." Gabrielle's cell rang and she paused to answer it.

"Okay." Gabrielle tossed her phone into her purse and let down her dark hair, revealing tiny pink and brown shells. "They'll meet us in an hour at some golf club restaurant. Good, I'm starving."

After grudgingly checking into the motel and viewing our two adjoining rooms, I drove us to the restaurant. The building sat on a golf course, near the mountain range, across the street from a wooded area. Eating was the furthest thing from my mind, but on our way into the restaurant I held a longing gaze at the woods.

"It's weird knowing there's no ocean near us," Gabrielle said after she finished her last bite of trout and pushed her plate away from her. "I don't like it." She finished the wine from her glass as though we were two friends out for a relaxing night. We weren't. My barely touched meal proved it.

The restaurant wasn't large, but the floor-to-ceiling windows overlooking the lit golf course made it appear to be more spacious than it was. The dim lighting and candlelit tables helped too.

"Yeah, your island was rough for me," I said with a casual air I did not currently possess. A Wild entered the building and was probably listening to every word we spoke. "The trees weren't climbable."

I leaned in toward Gabrielle who sat opposite me. "Someone here isn't human," I whispered. I trailed my fingers along the closed switch blade in my pocket. I'd picked it up at a little gift shop in town.

"I know," she whispered and then flashed a smile. She pulled a one hundred -dollar bill from her wallet and left it on the table under the stem of her empty wine glass. We hadn't received the tab yet, but the amount Gabrielle set out would more than cover our meals and tip. "Remember what we talked about. Ask about them, sure, but don't push for information. You don't want to risk spooking them."

My lowered eyes shifted toward the Wild. A woman wearing all white with long blonde hair sat at the bar. She had a cocktail in one hand and the bartender's hand in the other. She laughed at a joke he'd told and tossed her head back. As she tucked her golden hair behind her right ear, she tilted her head toward Gabrielle and me. Her eyes found us and, with a smirk, her focus shifted to the man behind the bar.

"You are too sweet," the harpy said before downing her cocktail and standing from the stool. "I look forward to next time." She eased her hand from his and set the empty glass onto the bar.

Her eagle eyes locked onto Gabrielle and me, and we quickly stood from the table. She left the restaurant, knowing full well that we were following her.

SEVENTEEN

WE TURNED the corner toward the side of the building. The tall harpy stood in the shadow, waiting.

"We're up there," she said in a monotone voice.

"My name is Gabrielle, and this is Faline," my mermaid accomplice said, reaching out to shake the harpy's hand.

The harpy only looked at her. "None of us here are human, let's not pretend that we are."

Gabrielle scoffed and pulled her hand away. "I was trying to be polite, civil. Humans aren't the sole beings with those attributes."

The harpy looked toward the mountains and quickly returned her sharp gaze to us. "Ready?"

"Wait," I interjected. "So where are we going? Your home? To talk... about what we came to talk about?"

Her long neck turned and her head snapped toward me. "You're the huldra," she said.

"And you're the harpy," I said. Now that we got that bit of apparent confusion out of the way...

She inhaled and then exhaled loudly. "Are you going to help us or not, huldra?"

I took a step back. "It depends what you're referring to." I knew they were missing a sister and the mermaids had recently reached out to the Wild groups, but maybe there was a door number three I wasn't privy to yet.

"My kind do not enjoy the company of humans, especially males," the female said.

"Okay." I wasn't sure what her statement had to do with my earlier question, but I played along. "But you were just talking it up with the bartender," I reminded her.

"We rarely procreate, so our numbers are low. We see the error of this now. I am currently trying to right this error. I don't care with whom." The female bent down to remove her flats. She stuffed them into a backpack that had been sitting along the wall where we stood. She put the bag over her chest and pulled the straps around her upper arms. She reached behind her hair and unclasped the back of her shirt at the neck. The back portion of the white top fell from her shoulders and draped down, revealing the lean muscles outlining her spine.

"Okay?" I said, still waiting to hear her point but shocked to learn that a group of Wilds refrained from sexual escapades.

"My mother is missing. There was a leak at one of the rentals. She went out to check on it and never came home." To earn an income, they operated a few nearby rental mountain vacation homes.

"How many of you are left, then?" I asked.

"Three of us."

"Oh," Gabrielle said, shaking her head.

"Azul's contact assured us you'd be able to help." The harpy closed her eyes and let out a hard breath. Talons busted from her toes and huge golden wings unfurled from her shoulder blades.

Gabrielle and I both jumped back.

"My wings are strong enough for me to carry you." The harpy reached her hand toward Gabrielle. "You can follow, I assume?" She eyed me.

I nodded, eager to jump through the forest trees and feel the moist earth beneath my feet.

"I won't fly on an airline whose name I've never heard before," Gabrielle said, not giving the female her hand.

I would've laughed if the mermaid and the harpy didn't look so serious.

"Eonza," the harpy said and inched her hand toward Gabrielle a little more.

Gabrielle gnawed her lip and took a step toward Eonza. I didn't envy her—a mermaid going from open sea travel to open air clearly held the same distress as my huldra self on a boat in the Pacific Ocean.

Eonza flapped her wings. Pulses of air blew my hair from my face and pushed my jacket open. I instinctively pressed the open corners of my bomber down in an effort to hide my holster and gun. Then it struck me that I'd taken a plane here and didn't have my usual big-girl weapons to conceal.

Eonza's lithe, long body rose from the ground. Her torso, arms, and legs were covered with white clothing, but little golden feathers poked out from her V-neck top, revealing sparse patches like a molting baby chick.

She reached for Gabrielle again. "Will you join me or not?" she asked.

Gabrielle squeezed her eyes shut and closed the gap between the two of them. Eonza swept around behind the mermaid, tucked her arms under Gabrielle's armpits, and lifted the mermaid from the ground. Gabrielle let out a little shriek before Eonza shushed her.

"Follow me and do try to keep up," Eonza said as she took off through the night sky toward the mountain.

Gladly.

I rushed to remove my socks and boots, and tied the laces together to hang them around my neck. The boots dangled against the front of my chest as I tore through the golf course and ran toward the wooded area.

Few lights from the small town lit the sky. Human eyes would fail to see flying women. Or a shoeless tree woman, for that matter.

I cleared the empty golf course and entered the forest. Dead pine needles and rotting leaves enriched the earth beneath my feet. I gave a sigh as I ran; the cool dirt reminded me of home. As much as I enjoyed the soil, though, tree-jumping was a quicker mode of transportation, and more fun too.

I bounded for an old fir and leaped for its strongest branch. The poor branch buckled under my weight. It snapped seconds after I jumped to another tree. Energy surged through me, and for fun's sake I changed my skin to bark façade. I willed thick vines to grow from my hands and used them to rope myself from one tree to the next, barely setting foot on a fir's branch before flying through the air again. This time I didn't have to fear my huldra taking over.

Strength vibrated through my body and rang in my ears. I couldn't wait to show Shawna one day, to help her to find her power and tree-jump as our foremothers must have. By the time I reached the top of Mt. Mitchell and allowed my bark to fade into my skin, my cheeks were rosy with exertion and my muscles ached for more.

Gabrielle stood beside a motionless Eonza as she smoothed down her slacks and blazer and ran her fingers through her long hair.

"You missed this," I said, pulling a tiny golden feather from Gabrielle's black hair. "You could make a necklace or earing from it." I faked a smile, hoping the harpy would see me as nonthreatening.

Gabrielle scrunched her face. "That's gross."

I shot a glance to Eonza who wore feather earrings and a feather necklace.

Eonza didn't seem offended. She watched us with a blank face. Her talons eased into her bare toes, which now looked like normal feet. And her feathers retreated into her pores as her wings bound themselves and hid under her skin behind her shoulder blades.

When Gabrielle finished grooming herself she canvased the area. "Oh! Is that a pool? Is it salt water or chlorine?"

She ran to a long infinity pool at the top of the mountain. Its edge ended where the mountain cliff dropped off.

I inhaled and smelled salt water. She probably sensed it too, because she plummeted both arms into the liquid, blazer and all.

"You didn't notice it when you two flew in?" I asked, pivoting on the ball of my foot to take the area in, as though I were interested in the harpies and where they called home rather than the potential information they held.

"My eyes were shut the whole time, and I wasn't paying attention with my other senses either." Gabrielle lay on the cement surrounding the pool, belly down, and hung her arms in the water. "I was trying to pretend I wasn't up in the air—the opposite of taking it all in."

"Eonza, I don't see your house." I peered up into the tree tops, assuming harpies' homes perched within the branches, but only a few small birds' nests resided among the leaves.

"This is our home." She motioned her head toward the pool and Gabrielle's face lit up. Eonza pointed to a narrow opening of cement stairs. "That way. In the mountainside, under the pool."

Gabrielle sighed as she pulled herself from the water and followed Eonza and me. She peeled her drenched blazer from her arms and wrung it out over her head, dripping salt water down her face and back. The open-air staircase led to a large wooden door on the left and only a cement wall on the right.

Eonza opened the door to reveal a narrow sitting room. Every chair pointed toward the main attraction, a thick wall made of glass, overlooking the outdoors. The home had been cut into the cliff and the glass was the cliff's opening. Owl and cat figurines sat along scattered, wall-mounted bookshelves. A large, life-sized carving of their goddess, Inanna, had been engraved into the cement wall. She stood naked holding two circular symbols with wings unfurled. Cats and owls sat at her feet.

"I feel nauseous," Gabrielle said, taking a seat and staring out at the forest below.

"Why? Your house looks over a cliff too," I said, appreciating the view.

"Yes," Gabrielle said. "Over the ocean where the water is always moving. Everything is so still here. The view is too motionless."

"Welcome." Two harpies descended the dark wooden stairs inside the house, from the upper level rooms. The first one spoke to Gabrielle. "You'll get plenty of a view with movement from the bedroom. I'm sure you'll be comfortable here."

Gabrielle shot up and stood beside me.

All three harpies were tall and lean with pale skin and light eyes. They looked related, which I hadn't seen among Wilds during my recent travels.

"Hello, I'm Salis and my sister here is Lapis."

"Your mother have a thing for crystals?" I asked. Being that my Aunt Patricia is an acupuncturist, crystals and their healing benefits had been a topic of discussion in my coterie on more than one occasion.

Salis cocked her head and her tawny hair brushed against her right shoulder. The few feathers tied into the bottoms of a handful of tiny braids blended with her hair color.

"Yes, and also Lapis's wings are blue," Eonza said matter-of-factly.

The three harpies stared at me with unblinking eyes like three birds perched on a branch. Obviously, humor is lost on harpies.

"Our mother is Rose. Her wings are the color of rose quartz," Lapis said.

"And she's mother to all of you?" I asked, just to clarify.

"Well, she couldn't name Salis Smokey Quartz and Eonza Gold," Lapis joked.

It took me a of couple seconds of staring blankly to understand that she'd been referring to their wing colors and crystals, not answering my question. I'd witnessed harpy humor—a little late to the punch and dry as vermouth

"No, that's not what I meant," I said. My mind had already moved past that topic and on to learning more about the harpy group. "So what about your mother's sisters? Where are they?"

"She had none," Eonza answered.

I hoped she'd explain further but no such luck. Instead of answers, all three sets of harpy eyes focused on me.

My cell phone rang and they jumped back. Two blue feathers grew from Lapis' arm.

I answered the phone, a little surprised I had cell service all the way out here. "You in town?"

"I'm at your motel, but you're not," Marcus replied.

"No, I'm not, but if you're willing to wait, I'll be there in thirty minutes." I needed to pick up the rental car at the golf club restaurant on my way back.

"Fine, but hurry up." Marcus ended the call.

What was his issue lately? I was the one with a missing sister. Where did he get off acting like that? Well, I was about to find out.

"I have to go. Gabrielle, you're staying here, aren't you?" I asked, knowing full well Gabrielle yearned for another dip in the salt water pool.

"You're more than welcome to stay with us," Lapis said. "Our mother's bed is empty. You could use that. If you don't mind that we all share a room. Our roof is the bottom of the pool, so you'll be able to watch the water tonight." She smiled as though she understood Gabrielle's needs perfectly, and I remembered that the mermaids and the harpies had a bond. Their foremothers used to wreck ships together.

"Was that your male on the phone?" Eonza asked.

Unsure how to answer, I said, "Uh, not really. No."

Eonza grinned. "Then he can stay in our empty rental house and I will visit him later tonight."

Eonza's coldly formal idea of getting pregnant was none of my business. But Marcus was entirely my business. He wasn't my boyfriend, and would never be, but the idea of him getting it on with Eonza boiled my blood a little.

"Sorry, Eonza," I said. "This male has a Wilds hands-off policy on him." Placed there by me. Also, I wasn't his pimp.

Her smile faded and she tossed her hair. "I'll show you to our room," she told Gabrielle, completely ignoring my presence. "And then we can go for a swim."

Gabrielle nodded excitedly. "Perfect. I'm so dehydrated since the flight."

I gawked at Gabrielle's vacation-mode attitude. But of course, it wasn't her sister being held captive. "All right then," I said, showing myself out as the mermaid and the harpies made their way up to the room on the higher level of the home. "I'll be back later." Though, I doubted anyone was listening.

* * *

I pulled the rental car into a parking spot directly in front of my white hotel room door. Marcus stood on the welcome mat, glaring at me.

Between him and the harpies, I'd had my fair share of staring contests for the day.

I swallowed the lump in my throat and prepared for awkwardness to ensue.

We didn't speak. Not when I exited the car. Not when I walked toward him. Not when I unlocked my room door. Not when we walked in, and not after I shut and locked the door behind us.

I sat on the floral-patterned bed comforter for all of one second before I jumped up and walked to sit on one of the two chairs at the table near the closed curtains—which, by the way, matched the comforter.

Marcus only observed me. I examined him, too. He looked...bigger. His broad shoulders seemed a little broader. His thick, muscular forearms seemed a little more muscular. His five o'clock shadow looked as though it had peaked a day ago. He wore a baseball cap over his normally well-styled hair. Worry lines creased his forehead.

I couldn't take the silence any longer, the sizing one another up.

"Something's wrong," I said.

Marcus considered me for a few moments. He set a manila envelope on the table, but I refused to remove my gaze from his.

"What? Is it Shawna? Did you find something?" I asked.

Marcus bit the inside of his lower lip and looked away. When he turned back, his eyes spoke of betrayal and loss. He jammed his hands into his jean pockets and shook his head. "You're a Wild Woman," was all he said.

I jumped up.

"How do you know what that is?" I demanded.

Marcus looked up at the ceiling and then at the ground. "They're in trouble, the Wild Women, your kind...you're in trouble. It's not just the huldra, it's all of you. You need to act and you need to act fast."

My insides vibrated and I had to blink away tears of frustration. Not even folkloric scholars knew the phrase "Wild Women." They thought each group was a completely separate being of myth. They had no clue as to our connected creation. "You keep saying those words. What do they mean to you, Marcus?" How long had he known? Who'd told him? Had he noticed the bark on my lower back the night we were together? Had I slipped up and said something revealing?

He shook his head, but wouldn't meet my eyes.

I moved toward him. "Marcus!" Despite my better judgement I took his face in my hands and forced him to look at me. His short whiskers pricked my palms. "How do you know those words? How do you know about...me?" Fear flushed through me and my eyes watered.

"Because, I'm sorry. I'm so sorry, Faline," he spoke through a hoarse throat. "But I'm a Hunter."

EIGHTEEN

MARCUS PULLED out of my grasp. And I was glad he did.

I bit the inside of my cheek and stared at my boots. "Fuck it," I said as I tore them off my feet and chucked them across the room. They hit the framed painting of a mountain and sent it crashing to the floor. I thought to grab my switchblade, but my protective huldra instincts responded quicker than my hand. Bark crept along my skin before I had the chance to reach into my pocket for a weapon.

My stomach knotted and my huldra growled to be set free—to somehow hurt the Hunter who not only lied to me, but whose utter betrayal now tore my heart in two. How could he? My thoughts spun with questions about his motives for befriending me, for asking me on a date, for declaring his need for a committed relationship. Marcus of all men.

"Please tell me you didn't set me up at the hotel the night we were supposed to have our second date." My voice broke and I had to take another breath before continuing. "Tell me you were called away on police business, that you weren't lying about that." I'd been physically hurt by Hunters, but I refused to let one make me cry. I fought the tears threatening to spill over and replaced them with hot anger. Bark ridges popped up on the tops of my feet and trailed to my leg like a run in pantyhose.

Marcus's widened eyes shot to mine. "No, I didn't set you up. I'd never do that. Not to you, not to anyone." For the first time, I hated the sincerity in his eyes. "But yes, I did lie about the phone call; it was from the brotherhood."

I took a step back and shook my head.

Marcus spoke quicker. "We both know I couldn't have told you who really called. I hadn't heard from them in a long time. But they said it was an emergency, so I assumed it was about my father. I went straight to his house, but when I got there everything was fine."

I couldn't control it any longer. I had to hurt him the way his words were hurting me. I knocked Marcus onto the bed and straddled him, but once I had the opportunity to harm him, my anger fizzled and I froze, not sure what to do or how to feel. Within seconds he whipped me around and pinned me on my back.

Marcus sighed. "I didn't come to fight. I came to help."

I considered throwing him off of me, but couldn't fully commit to leaving our entanglement. Not with his intoxicating scent so close. His nearness soothed my distress, enabling me to reorganize my thoughts. Whether he really flew all this way to tell me the truth, to aide me or not, I had to hear him out. He might know something about Shawna's disappearance.

He finished explaining as he released me and sat beside me on the bed. "They lured me away from you with a fake call. I didn't know you were a huldra then, but I still wouldn't have let them near you."

I sat up. "But you know now. Why do you want to help me? A Wild."

"Because I've had a thing for you since the day you brought in your first skip and he tried to kick you in the shin, and you took him to his knees for it. The first time I met you." Marcus huffed and straightened his disheveled shirt.

I'd never been in a romantic relationship, so before this moment I hadn't understood the notion of wanting to hug and hit a person at the same time. "I'm so pissed off at you right now... And at myself." I huffed. "That first night we went out, I was trying to bed a Hunter." I'd tried to sleep with the enemy. To save face, I preferred to cover my embarrassment with frustration. Bark grew across my skin in response, but slower than usual. He knew what I was. He knew who I was. And I'd been oblivious the whole time.

I started to ask when he realized I was a Wild Woman, how long had he known, but he interrupted me. "Don't do that," Marcus said in a flat, controlled voice.

"Do what?" I asked defensively.

"That bark thing. Your knuckles." He ground out the words as though it hurt to talk. "Being around a Wild Woman is hard for me— sets my muscles in motion, makes them grow stronger. When you start to change like that...it sets off alarms...that I've never practiced controlling."

So that's why he seemed bigger. Why he'd seemed swollen and complained of his muscles feeling sore the day we went to the police event...after our first date. My line of thought left me with images of Marcus, sans shirt, the first night we went out. I'd just practically scolded myself for trying to bed a Hunter and here I was thinking of trying again. I spoke to fill the lingering silence. "That tattoo on your shoulders, the one you didn't want to talk about the night we went back to your place, is that a Hunter tattoo?"

Marcus nodded and absently touched his chest. "I had the ink done before I left the brotherhood. I haven't been to the complex in years. Not since I found out that my mother didn't leave of her own volition. That's just the story I tell because it's the story I've been told. She couldn't agree to the domination and deceit of the Hunter lifestyle, and once she made that clear, my father wouldn't let her leave with me and he wouldn't let her stay either. The day I learned that truth, I handed in my dagger and didn't look back. You know I've told you that I don't talk to my father much. That's true. Everything I said was true." Marcus ran his fingers through his messy hair. His ball cap must have fallen off during our bed-pinning tussle.

I read Marcus's body language, contemplated his words, weighed them against the many conversations we'd had at the jail's intake desk, our dinner out, and our evening together afterwards.

My feet tingled as though someone ran a feather along my skin. I looked down to see why. My bark receded, faded into my pores. It crawled down to my toes and left smooth skin in its wake.

Was that another secret Wild ability? The ability to intuitively detect truth from lies? Because it seemed that my body believed him before my mind decided on a verdict.

"Your skin's changing," Marcus said in awe.

I nodded. "I trust you."

I started to get up from the bed when he grabbed my hand and locked eyes with me. "Your bark is beautiful. I don't care what it does to me. I shouldn't have told you to stop it from spreading. I'm sorry."

I bit my lip to keep from tearing up. This Hunter was taught to find my wildness repulsive and instead he admired it. I stood, my hand still wrapped securely in his, and walked to the table with him close behind. With my free hand I ran my fingers along the envelope. "What will I find in here?" I asked.

Marcus released my hand, but didn't part from me. His breath on my neck sent shivers through every nerve and muscle. I closed my eyes and swallowed my biological response to feeling him so close, to inhaling his scent.

"When you called from Oregon and asked me to access the missing persons reports, you mentioned a missing friend between the ages of eighteen and mid-twenties with a large snake tattoo. Not many young women have that kind of body ink, but succubi are known for it."

He paused and gave me a look. It felt strange to hear him talk about a Wild Woman as though it were an everyday thing to him. Yesterday he had been only Marcus the Police Officer to me. Today he was someone entirely new.

He went on. "And you were in their region at the time. But I figured it had to be a coincidence. There was no way a huldra was helping a succubus. Still, I needed to be sure. So I pulled up your most recent skip arrest and your last name stood out to me. Faline Frey, as in the Norse goddess Freyja. I kept telling myself it was all a coincidence, but I had to follow my hunch. After I gathered those reports for you, I dug deeper and eventually found what's in that envelope."

"Is it information on Shawna?" I prayed to Freyja there wasn't a coroner's report in that envelope.

He moved to stand beside me. "No."

I released a deep exhale. No coroner's report. I still had time.

"And for the record," he continued, "it's not why I distanced myself either." His tired eyes locked on mine. "I had to think about what I wanted to do. Not to decide what to do, because from the moment I suspected who you were I wanted to help. I had to take a step back, because that decision couldn't be entered into lightly. If I help you, I'd be doing much more than putting my job on the line."

"So then what's in this envelope can get you fired?" I asked, still clinging to the odds that my sister was alive.

Unsure about the inner workings of the Hunter society, I appreciated that whatever risk he took in coming here, he took it for me. It used every ounce of my restraint not wrap my arms around him.

"It's one thing to leave the Hunter complex and refuse to take orders from them. But to be born a Hunter and betray their secrets, help a Wild Woman by exposing their core? They'd kill me if they found out." He tapped a finger on the envelope. "And once this is opened, what comes next *will* lead to them finding out."

I brushed my hand down his arm, suddenly unsure about reading the hidden contents on the table. Was I ready for what came next? For information so detrimental to the Hunters that they'd kill their own flesh and blood for leaking it? I wanted to know. I needed to know. But one question nagged at my mind.

"Why are you doing this?" I asked. "Putting yourself in danger like this."

Marcus pulled my hand from his arm to his lips and kissed my knuckles. And for the first time I noticed how heavy his reality weighed on him. In the slight slump of his shoulders, the concern in his eyes. "I've had a cop mentality since before I joined the police force. For as long as I can remember I've wanted to do what's right and stop others from doing what's wrong. As an officer, I function within legal limits. As a person, I function within ethical limits. And as someone with Hunter abilities, non-human strength, and a worldwide brotherhood at my back, the responsibility is tenfold." Marcus dropped my hand and tucked a stray hair behind my ear. "I'm doing this because I've realized that your kind is in the right. And my brotherhood is in the wrong."

"You're referring to the papers you brought me, what you found? That's how you realized we were in the right?" I asked.

Marcus nodded. He pulled out a chair and motioned for me to sit. He sat across the table from me and pushed the manila envelope in my direction.

I couldn't remember the last time I felt timid, but now as I peeled back the flap and pulled a pile of papers from their container, my fingers shook. At first I only saw the printed files he'd already sent me. I flipped through and paused when the font changed to what looked like letters and dates created by a typewriter.

My throat tightened and I coughed to get a breath.

The form I stared at was my mother's missing person report, dated twenty years prior. Marcus left the table and brought back two glasses of water. His movement pulled me from my daze and I set my mother's report aside, set my sadness aside. There were more reports from the other Wilds' regions, dated the same year, each victim whose surname derived from the title of a goddess.

"They were taking Wilds from every region," I said, setting the loose stack down. I took a sip of water, using the seconds to bridle my racing thoughts.

Marcus neatened the pile of paperwork. "Maybe it was the shock, or maybe I just wanted him to know I knew. But I called my dad after I found this, asked if he knew that Hunters across the nation were abducting Wild Women twenty years ago. He denied it of course, denied all of it. Since I left the brotherhood I'm not privy to their secrets. But I can tell when he's lying."

I rubbed my eyes and leaned into the chair.

"I think what's going on right now with the missing Wild Women is something they tried twenty years ago. But back then they didn't bury the missing person reports very well, probably didn't think they had to because most people didn't have the full-access type of technology we have today." He paused and eyed the papers. "Most criminals have a pattern, especially those who prey on others. My guess is the Hunters have been doing this every twenty years; that'd be their pattern. Either that or whatever they tried to do twenty years ago failed and they've decided to try it again with a new approach. It's hard to tell—I couldn't find any reports similar to these from forty years ago to substantiate my pattern theory. But that's not to say it didn't happen."

The possibility of hidden or destroyed evidence didn't shock me, not since my illuminating time spent with the mermaids. "The Hunters have a way of hiding things they'd like to pretend don't exist," I said, thinking of our false history lessons. I picked up the one report I'd touched more than any of the others. My mother's name wasn't in bold font, but it looked like it was to me. Those letters seemed larger and darker than the rest in the whole pile: Naomi Frey. According to the report, she'd never been found—her case went cold.

"If they'd killed her, would there be a Jane Doe report or some way we'd know?" I asked.

"Not necessarily, but I wouldn't assume she's gone."

"Why's that?" I said.

"Hunters aren't dumb," he answered. "They have a calculated reason for everything they do. If they're taking Wilds every twenty years, there's a reason for it, a plan behind it. But I highly doubt they'd keep her at the complex in Washington. If she's alive and still in their custody, odds are they've been moving her around, as a precautionary measure. The Wild Women most recently taken, they probably haven't gotten that far yet—to move them around." He paused. "I wonder if they're all alive, everyone on these files from twenty years ago. They've got their people in all the right places to *happen* upon a woman's body in the woods and confirm the body belongs to one of these missing women. To close these cases for good. But they don't for some reason."

I imagined he referred to Hunters in coroner positions, signing off on the causes of death as suicides or animal attacks. His response sparked a new question. "The Hunters helped you get your job, right?" I asked.

Marcus nodded.

"So is it plausible to say a Hunter who's also a cop could have handled my mom's case?"

"That's why I brought the reports. Every male born into the

Hunter line is given a biblical first name and carries the last name of a historical pope."

"Similar to how we choose our names," I stated. And yet neither of our two groups fathomed that the other would have such a similar tradition.

"Every cop who closed the missing persons cases twenty years ago, stating insufficient evidence and the probability that the woman chose to run away, had a biblical first name and the last name of a pope." Marcus's eyes held mine, and when I didn't respond, couldn't respond, he continued. "When you're in the brotherhood, they hook you up with the job that best suits their purpose and they control everything you do in that job. So that when they have to do something highly illegal, they have the people in place to cover it up. And when they need to create propaganda, they've got their own people in place to make sure that gets done, too. Where do you think the witch burnings came from? And the twists on the original Wild Women folklore? Why do you think villagers went from seeking the healing of succubi to calling them brides of Satan? They don't get rid of documents and history; they create new ones—documents and histories that push their purpose. This is what they've been doing to your kind for hundreds of years."

"And what's their purpose, then?" I asked.

"Simple. Control through fear." He took a sip of water and I wondered if this topic of conversation was giving him a dry throat, too. "Their tactics change with the culture, but their foundation is always the same: dominate, particularly from behind the scenes. And they like it that way. Because you can't fight what you can't see coming. If you don't know who's pulling the strings, then it's harder for you to cut them. Humans aren't the reason Wilds have to hide what they are. Hunters are the reason."

"Then why come after us?" I asked. "We're not in power. No one knows about us."

Marcus reached across the table and touched my hand. "I've asked myself this a thousand times in the last few days. I grew up with their bullshit about how Wild Women are evil and Hunters are the blessed ones, so it's our duty to suppress the evil. But we both know that's not true. If the simplest explanation is usually the correct one, I'd say they maintain their dominance over your kind because both the Hunters and the Wild Women are more powerful than humans. To them, someone's got to be above the humans and they want to stay on top. I'm sure there's more to it, but I doubt even John is privy to that information."

I still clung to my mother's report. Marcus had mentioned earlier that he'd realized the truth behind his mother's leaving him and in this moment I felt a deeper connection to him because of it. We'd both been lied to by the Hunters. For him the lies were about his mother, created so he'd believe she'd birthed him and not cared enough to stick around. For me the lies concerned who and what I was as a huldra. And according to my mother's closed missing person report, they'd lied about her too. "How did you find the truth about your mother?" I asked.

"I let them think that me becoming a cop was their idea, and technically it was, though I'd always wanted to be a police officer. They're strategic and like to have members in every government agency, anything with power."

"I'd suspected as much," I said.

"Yeah. After I finished my academy training and came home to work for the Everett police, on my days off the higher ups at my Hunter complex assigned me to reorganize their filing room and input the older files and paperwork into the computer. Eventually they had me transfer it all to an encrypted file that only the man in charge could access. They probably figured I wouldn't mention any of the illegal shit I saw because they'd gotten me my job with the precinct and they could take it away—ruin me." He went a little pale as he paused.

I touched his arm. "They'd do that to their own?"

He nodded. "There's this story I heard as a kid about a Hunter who betrayed his brotherhood and ended up serving time in prison because he was set up for a crime he didn't commit. I'm not sure if it was based on facts or a warning from our leaders to stay in line. Either way, I wasn't going to chance it. They had me by the balls; I was still a member of the brotherhood and had to follow orders. The complex leader at the time said that spending my days off working for the brotherhood was a part of my Hunter training." Marcus scoffed. "They give every inexperienced Hunter that line to get free labor out of them. And I ate it up, too."

"What'd you find in the room?" I asked.

"A type of case file they'd made for my mother. It had a copy of her birth certificate and driver's license, but not a marriage certificate. Turns out she was never married to my father. She wasn't from the area of Spain where we'd lived when I was born." His brows furrowed. "And included in the file was an execution order—dated before I was born and ordered to be carried out directly following my birth."

I gasped. Everything Marcus explained made perfect sense, fit like puzzle pieces. And yet it was all so senseless.

"The report was simple and concise. It had the order at the top, and underneath it was the date it'd been drawn up with the execution date two boxes below that. The box labeled 'execution uncompleted' had been checked and someone wrote a little note beside it stating that they couldn't find her. Which is probably why I can't either. I waited until after I left the brotherhood to start looking. She clearly wants to stay hidden for her own safety. Makes sense." I was pretty sure I caught Marcus's hands shake around the glass of water. Just barely.

For Marcus's sake, I wanted to change the subject. I understood the hole that losing a parent creates. But I had a feeling he'd trudge through the details whether I prodded or not. So I prodded. "Do you have *any* type of relationship with your father or have you sworn him off?"

"Both and neither," he said, inserting the stack of papers into the manila envelope. "We don't have much of a relationship, but seeing as he visits my police chief every once in a while, we do talk in passing. Hunter males are the head of their household, making all the familial decisions. He's decided I'm a bad influence and won't let his new wife and children around me."

The pain in his eyes made me ache. I wanted to comfort him, but I had no idea what to say. Before I could figure it out, he went on. "To my face he uses the polite term for someone who abandons the brotherhood—says I've 'gone soft.' But I know how they talk about men like me, deserters. I'd heard about men leaving when I was a gung-ho Hunter. They'd tell us stories about the men being lured away by rebellious women, too weak to break free of her, and drawn away from his brothers because of it. When I left, I hadn't been dating anyone, but I bet that's what they told the Hunters in training. I couldn't have left such a righteous cause and close-knit brotherhood on my own accord. I had to have been pussy-whipped. It was a warning to the younger Hunters: never get involved with a strong woman."

I laughed to break the tension weighing Marcus down. "Pussy-whipped is such a ridiculous term. You know, it's only used by men who aren't getting any."

Marcus grinned. "There's probably a scientific study out there proving that exact phenomenon."

I stood, my mother's missing person report gripped tightly in my hand. "So this just got bigger. Did you know it all started with me thinking the succubi took Shawna? I even went to your...I mean...the Hunter complex for help."

If my little slip-up referring to the complex as his upset Marcus, he didn't show it.

"I figured the succubi would be blamed. That group is usually the go-to for finger pointing," he said.

"And then it turned into my helping them to get word to their sister, Heather," I said. "In a deal we made, which is when I called you. And then the mermaids had this wise woman who told them a huldra would start a war one day, so they turned this whole thing into me starting a war. And the harpies are missing a mother and think I'm here to help them. And now you." I shook my head and let out a sigh. "I just want Shawna." I looked at the paper I held. "And to know what really happened to my mother." For most of my life I'd believed the succubi killed her.

Marcus put his hand out. "Start a war?" he asked.

"Yeah. Their legends tell them that a tree woman will rise up and battle the Hunters to regain power for all Wilds. It sounds nice and all, at least the end result, but I still don't know how much of that I believe."

His chocolate brown eyes widened and he nodded. "All of it."

I raised one eyebrow. "I should believe *all of it?*"

"Every word. Because the old monks, who went rogue from the church to raise and train the first Hunters, told a similar story. That a Wild Woman would challenge the Hunters. If they were weak and allowed her to win, they'd cause the demise of not only Hunters, but of all civilization. If they gave her a deserved bloody death they'd squelch future uprisings and secure their future as masters over all." A swath of hair stuck out and curled on Marcus's forehead. He swiped it into place, though I thought it looked perfectly fine. "I used to hear that story all the time when I was little."

I set my mother's report on the manila envelope and pushed an empty chair under the table. "So." I let the word draw out as the wheels in my mind turned. Only Hunters knew we weren't human, knew what Shawna had in common with Heather and the harpies' mother, and hated us for it. It was the Hunters who'd called Marcus during our second date and prompted him to leave me alone at the hotel. It was the Hunters who'd stormed the mermaids' island. They were the ones who'd closed the twenty-year-old missing Wilds cases. Every piece of evidence led me to believe that they were behind the Wild abductions. Which meant I'd left Washington in search of my sister who may have been in the next town over from my home. "War or no war, I'm going to get my sister." The fire of purpose raged within me, burning away the bits of sadness still clinging to my mind after seeing my mother's report. "And if she's at the Washington Hunter complex, that's where I'll be going." I raised my eyebrows. "Luckily, I have someone who knows his way around the place."

Marcus stood and made his way to my side. "I'd be happy to service you," he said with a wink.

"Oh, well, there'll be no shortage of that," I said. If I approached this the way I drew a skip out of hiding, the Hunters would never see it coming. "But also, I need your help with Hunter information." I winked back. "Like, show me their hand-to-hand combat training and draw me pictures of their complex and their property and where their security cameras are. If they were to hold a huldra there, where would they keep her?"

"I'll have to see if they've changed anything around. But under the big building where they conduct check-ins is a basement with cells. Unless they've built a new holding area since I left, I assume that's where they'd keep huldra."

"You'll find out for me, get up-to-date layouts of the complex?" I asked, finally feeling more than a spark of hope.

"I will." Marcus caught me off-guard as he swooped his arms behind my back and pulled me to him. "You're so sexy when you're in bounty hunter mode."

The bittersweet scent of excitement mixed with a heavy dose of lust swirled between our embrace. Only moments ago I'd wanted Marcus to fill my mind with information I could use to take down my foes. Now my mind blurred with yearning for him to fill me in another way. I didn't know how much more I could handle without tossing him onto the bed and seeing if sex with a non-human was as mind blowing as I imagined. "Had he been holding back that night we were together because he thought I was human? Is that why he didn't want to have sex?"

I didn't realize I'd voiced my thoughts until he answered, "Yes," in a gravely whisper. His eyes darkened. He licked his lips. "Would you have held back? If we'd had sex. Tried to keep a handle on your physical strength?"

I could only nod. If I opened my mouth it'd be to tangle my tongue with his.

"Yeah, holding back like that isn't something I'm great at." He cupped my face, and for a second something lived and breathed in the lack of space between our bodies, an energy so alive, so fierce, so real. Marcus closed his eyes. The mere suggestion caused me to close my own. He pressed his lips to mine, ran his hands down to my hips and pulled me into him.

I found the curve of his lower back and grabbed at it. I wanted his smooth skin under my touch. I bunched his shirt, fabric in each hand, and pulled. The shirt tore. Marcus chuckled while his tongue connected to mine. I shoved him backwards and slammed him against the wood-paneled wall. He let out a grunt from the force, but quickly went to work unbuttoning my jeans.

"No holding back?" he asked through kisses near my ear and down my neck.

"Not even a little bit." I tilted my head and arched my spine.

"Good." He picked me up like I weighed ten pounds, and tossed me onto the bed. The muscles on his bare chest moved like a perfectly choreographed dance. I hoped he'd perform that dance on top of me.

In an instant he was above me, tearing my cami from my body.

"I can't wait to see your wild side," he said in quick breaths as he kissed my breasts.

"You're not afraid that I'll set off your inner red flags?" I asked, referring to his earlier response to seeing bark crawl across my knuckles. I purposely didn't use the "Hunter" word.

"I hope you do set me off," he said in a deep, throaty voice. "Let's see how well I can channel my adrenaline into pleasure. You game?"

I laughed and jumped out from underneath him—as much as I enjoyed that view—to turn him in place and straddle his waist. With my right hand I held his wrists together. Viny branches extended from my fingertips and wrapped around his wrists like my own organic handcuffs.

He gave a heavy laugh. "That's amazing. I take this is a yes?"

I didn't speak. I only smiled and moved down his body as my branches extended, pinning his wrists to the headboard above his head. I circled my tongue around his nipples and traced his abs, determined to return the favor he'd given me after our first date. A shiver ran through his body and I smiled at the reaction. His back arched for more and I retracted my vines. The moment Marcus was free he rolled me over onto my stomach and ran his fingers down my spine. His gentle lips found the bark patch at the small of my back and I melted inside. Whatever flags my huldra was setting off in his Hunter, they weren't rage-filled.

NINETEEN

I PACED the sidewalk outside my motel room, squinting from the early afternoon sunlight. I exhaled a white puff of breath into the crisp air. Maids wore jackets as they pushed their cleaning carts.

My coterie listened on speakerphone from our common house in Washington as I explained the new developments, pausing each time a human came within earshot.

After I explained Marcus's and my belief that the Hunters were behind the recent abductions as well as those perpetrated twenty years ago, because why else would they try to cover it up, Aunt Renee asked, "Is there a chance Naomi is still alive?" It was odd hearing my aunt refer to my mother by name. I had been four when my mother disappeared. My aunts had gone through all the proper channels—reported her missing with the police, contacted the Hunters—but nothing came of their efforts. And with four little girls to raise, they gave up, believing that the succubi galere had taken territorial revenge on her for sharing affections with a human male they'd already claimed as their own. Nothing could be done short of my aunts getting their own revenge, which would be difficult with the added responsibility of a little orphan huldra to raise.

Knowing Shawna was somewhere at the Hunters' compound killed me inside. I couldn't imagine how much it'd break me to think she was dead...forever gone. I supposed that's why I had wanted to become an investigator so badly—to make sure what had happened to my mother would never happen to another woman. But it had, hadn't it? And to Wilds no less.

A dog barked in the background and Aunt Abigale's promises of a treat if it'd quiet down like a good girl followed the sound.

"Since when did we get a dog?" I asked.

"Oh, your aunt took her in from Shawna's rescue center. Poor thing missed Shawna so badly that she wasn't eating. The people at the rescue center reached out to Abigale and asked if maybe she could take the dog for a while. They thought it'd be worth a try to see if the little thing would eat if it lived in Shawna's surroundings, with her scent," Aunt Patricia responded.

"Is it working?" I asked, eager to see Shawna's face when she found out our coterie had taken in a dog. I wondered if huldra had ever owned pets in the history of Wilds. Dogs and tree-jumping don't mix well. We really were becoming civilized, housing domesticated animals. If anything, I would have thought we'd own cats, seeing as some of the stories surrounding Freyja included a cat-drawn chariot. And cats climb trees.

"She's on her way to being fat and happy," Olivia yelled a little too loudly into their side of the connection.

I laughed and pulled the phone from my face so it wasn't blaring into my ear. "Can you send me a picture?" Knowing there was a little animal out there who loved Shawna so much that it stopped eating when Shawna left made me love the thing. I suspected I wasn't the only one. It also made me deeply sad, and determined.

"But Faline, is there a chance Naomi is alive? That she's at a Hunter's complex, like Shawna?" Aunt Renee asked again. Anxiety laced her words.

"There is," I said. If Marcus was right, if the Hunters had a calculated plan with the disappearances, then my sliver of hope seemed justified. My heart sped and my lips tugged my cheeks into a full-face smile. Just the idea that I'd possibly meet the woman who occupied my dreams, but too few of my memories, made me want to go storm every single Hunter complex this evening with nothing more than what I had on me—a new switchblade and a pair of boots. But I had to be smart about this. No one group of Wilds, not even the mermaids, had the power to take on a whole complex of trained Hunters on their own turf. And my coterie certainly couldn't overtake the Washington complex, which was first on my list. If we wanted this to work, the different groups of Wilds had to come together to study the Washington complex grounds, discuss a plan of action, and train by tapping into their natural abilities. I had witnessed the abilities of the succubi as well as that of the mermaids. Now I needed to figure out what battle tactics the harpies and rusalki had. Olivia and I had a lot of research to do.

"So prepare the common house for guests. I haven't made contact with the rusalki to know if they've lost someone, but if each group, other than the mermaids, has lost a member in the last six months, and twenty years ago they also lost at least one member to the Hunters, I'm crossing my fingers that they'll all be on board to visit the beautiful state of Washington for a meeting like none other."

"When should we expect them?" Aunt Patricia asked. "And what about food? Do they eat different things than we eat?"

The other day Gabrielle had mentioned saving the rusalki for last due to their difficult nature and their lack of residence. I didn't know much about the Wild group outside of human legends that spoke of ghostly pale women who lived underground and in dark lakes, and who could kill with a single snip of their birch scissors.

"If Gabrielle and I can catch a flight to Maine tonight, and the rusalki aren't too hard to find or too hard to convince, I'd say to expect us in four days. Hopefully sooner." As I broke down the logistics to my sisters and aunts, my personal way of thinking took a step back and my bounty hunter-trained mind stepped forward. There was also a possibility that the Hunters hadn't let their captured Wilds live.

But I couldn't think about that right now. "Succubi don't seem to have a certain type of food they eat," I said to get the conversation moving so that I could pay the harpies a visit and head off to meet the rusalki. "Mermaids prefer sea food, and they aren't against eating it raw, so the fresher the better. The fish markets in Seattle or Anacortes would probably be your best bet. I have no idea what harpies eat, but I'll ask today. And seeing as I've never met a rusalka, and I'm not even sure they'll agree to joining us. I'll have to get back to you on that one."

"All right, hun. Well you stay safe and thanks for the update," Aunt Patricia said.

I considered requesting to be taken off of speakerphone so I could ask about Aunt Abigale's emotional state. When I left Washington she'd been inconsolable, as any mother would be if her child were abducted. But I thought better of it. It'd hurt too much either way and right now I needed to harness my hope, not my hurt.

I ended the call and shot Gabrielle a quick text asking if I should meet up with the harpies at their place. She responded with a yes, so I headed into my room to gather my things.

I'd left the curtains pulled to let Marcus sleep. I walked into the dark room and gently shut the door behind me. The sound of his rhythmic breathing filled the small space and I found myself watching him. He had that just-worked-out swollen look. He lay on his stomach, his pillow pressed against the wooden headboard secured to the wall. The flower-covered comforter sat in a heap on the floor near the bottom corner of the bed. Light green sheets wrapped around his body, inches below his tan arms. His Hunter's tattoo struck me as beautiful and grotesque at the same time. Beautiful in that the ink had been artfully done and the canvas was easy on the eyes. Grotesque in what it stood for.

Last night I'd slept with a Hunter. I was pretty sure that made the top five list of ways to utterly betray your coterie, not to mention your foremothers, who'd died at the edge of a Hunter's blade.

I crept closer to inspect the tattoo across his back spanning from one shoulder to the other. Some of the symbols that looked to be an ancient form of writing were foreign to me. Others, the thick two-strand twists and knots, reminded me of tribal tattoos. Night vision was among my huldra abilities, but I'd need a flashlight to clearly see these details.

Marcus rolled over and I moved away. He cracked his eyes open.

His lips lifted in a grin. "Hey beautiful," he said lazily. He reached for me, but I hesitated.

He peered down in recognition and then looked up at me, still holding his lazy grin. "Do you want me to put on a shirt first?" he asked. "I understand if it bothers you."

"Does it bother you? Having Hunter tattoos across your body?" I asked. His ink was remnants of a lineage he'd since turned from, a belief system he no longer accepted.

"On some days, yes, and on others, no." He sat up, resting against the headboard. The yellow blanket and green sheet fell to his lap exposing his pecs and abs. His dark, tousled hair practically begged me to run my fingers through it.

"Have you considered lasering them off?" I asked.

"Not all of the Hunters' ways are awful. Children are highly regarded as the future of the world. Family is important to them. They have a close-knit society where they can depend on each other. Growing up, I never felt alone because I always had cousins to play with. On the holidays we had huge gatherings with food and wine and games, sometimes lasting days. I didn't have my own mother, but the women of the complex were more than happy to mother me and make sure I had meals cooked from scratch and clean clothes."

I bristled at his words. My coterie was closer than most families, but because of the Hunters we were unable to foster relationships with other Wilds, our cousins, and were led to believe that the others wished us nothing but harm.

He brushed my leg with his knuckles. The whole huldras-don't-enter-serious-relationships thing wasn't what held me back anymore. I'd recently seen functioning Wild groups who didn't live by that rule. Plus, Marcus wasn't a human, so it was okay that he knew I wasn't one either. But he wasn't a human because he was born a Hunter. Ironic was an understatement.

"Thank you for coming here and revealing yourself to me," I finally said, after thinking better of a few other statements floating on my tongue.

"I'm the same person I was when we had dinner together, the same person I was all those times we talked about movies and our embarrassing childhood memories over the intake desk. When we realized how much we have in common." Marcus sat up a little taller. His brow furrowed. When he held his hand palm-up on my leg and I failed to entwine my fingers with his, he sighed and pulled it away.

"And that's the problem," I said. "We have too much in common. We're both pawns in a scheme created by a shadow society except you're on the top and I'm at the bottom, preparing to cut the top off and throw it in the trash." The need to control myself warred with my desire to be free, to be a Wild.

"If you're trying to push me away with this enemy stuff, we both know that it's bullshit and it won't work on me." Marcus stood and pulled his jeans on. "I've seen you bring in the most notoriously difficult skips. I know when you want something you eventually get it. And I know you want me like I want you. So one way or another, this is going to work."

I considered his words as I grabbed my jacket where it had been draped over the chair beside the table.

His tone changed from gravelly to irritated. "I hoped when we made love last night that you were okay with my past. That you understood it's not my present and will never be my future. Or were you pumping me for information and getting your rocks off at the same time?"

I stood within inches of Marcus. His eyes bore into mine.

His distrust cut me, probably the way my questioning had cut him. "I'm not playing games," I whispered on a harsh breath.

"Neither am I."

I shook my head. At what, I wasn't sure. Maybe at everything. I was to lead a war against the Hunters, the brotherhood of this man whose touch melted me. But the Wilds trusted and depended on me. To them it wouldn't matter that Marcus wanted to help, that he'd left the brotherhood. Hunter blood ran through his veins, the blood of our enemy, our oppressors. The burden, laced with guilt, bore down on me.

Marcus gripped my shoulders. "Last night, we didn't have to hold back. Have you ever been able to do that with another man? Because I've never been able to do that with another woman. We got a glimpse of freedom. And I want more."

"Right now my priority is my sister," I said. "And frankly, what's about to transpire is bigger than you and me." I sat on the bed and he sat beside me.

Marcus ran his free hand through his hair and nodded. "I get that." He exhaled, as though he too had a weight draped across his back. And he did, didn't he? Of course he didn't agree with the brotherhood, but if he helped me he would be actively hurting them. That couldn't be an easy decision to make.

"I have to go talk to the harpies and then get on a plane to find the rusalki." I didn't know what else to say, so I stated the obvious. Maybe I didn't have his level of hope; with everything that'd happened lately I was running low on the stuff. I couldn't figure out a scenario where a relationship with Marcus was possible. And the harder I tried, the more I wanted it, the more I fell into hopelessness. Even if everything worked out, my coterie would never accept him.

"After this is all done we can unpack the whole you and me thing, okay?" Marcus said.

Who knows, maybe Marcus knew of a way around the Hunters-and-Wilds-are-mortal-enemies thing. "If you help me that means you'll be outnumbered, around groups of Wilds who loathe the fact that your kind exists," I warned. "Your Hunter response will kick in, too. You'll get bigger, stronger." The thought of never hugging him again, never feeling his mouth on mine left me wanting. My racing heart slowed. I took a cleansing breath. "But I'd appreciate the help."

"That's all I'm suggesting." Marcus stood and closed the gap between us. "Well that and a hug goodbye." Smile crinkles formed beside his chocolate eyes. "And the getting stronger thing isn't permanent. It flares up around Wild Women, goes crazy when they change near me. But it dies down when I'm not around them anymore. It's only temporary."

I wondered if he understood the meaning behind his words: our relationship could only be temporary. But I kept my mouth shut in favor of feeling him wrapped around me one more time before I left. "I could take a hug," I said, opening my arms and accepting Marcus into my embrace. "And a crap-ton of good luck." His scent engulfed me. Calming, my mind spun a little slower.

"Good luck." Marcus kissed the top of my head.

I lifted my chin to meet his lips with mine.

An idea blossomed and I pulled away. "How much are you willing to help?" I asked.

"Why does that question scare me?" he joked as he draped his arm over my shoulder.

"What if you were to re-join the brotherhood? It'll be easier to break in and find Shawna if I have help from the inside."

"I was going to bring that up after you confirmed all the Wilds were on board. Because if I do this, most all communication between us will be severed until after you attack," Marcus said. "I won't be able to help you with anything on the police end either."

I considered his words. "I think we're past the point of police reports," I said. "They're a show anyway, at least the ones referring to missing Wilds." A snag occurred to me. "Unless you think they'll notice that you've gotten stronger? They'll know you've been cavorting with the enemy."

"No. I'll tell them I've been hitting the gym in preparation to re-join." Marcus blew out a puff of air. "It shouldn't be too hard to get back in." His chest rose and his smooth skin touched my face.

His heartbeat sped and I knew he was lying to keep me from worrying too much. There had to be some form of atonement he'd have to pay for abandoning the brotherhood. I looked into his eyes. "You're going to step back into the role you were born into so that I and my kind can have the freedom to live in the abilities we were born to have. Thank you for doing this for me."

Marcus's eyes softened. "Don't get me wrong, I do agree that you and your kind deserve the freedom to be who you were born to be. But I'm not only doing this for you."

He didn't need to declare his motivator. I was sure his mother filled his thoughts as much as mine filled my own.

"Well then, I hope that one day you're able to find her so that she can glow with pride for her son." I kissed Marcus on the lips, grabbed the manila envelope of paper and zipped it into my suitcase. I left the tacky hotel room with the gorgeous Hunter inside, hoping beyond hope that I'd see him again.

TWENTY

THE SPRUCE and fir trees of Mt. Mitchell, North Carolina called to me. My body responded with yearning, begging me to sit among the plants and take in their offerings. I jumped from an old evergreen and landed silently on the balls of my feet. Ferns grew from the pine needle-covered dirt, reaching my knees.

I stood with my hands on my hips and took in the deep greens and browns for one last time before retrieving Gabrielle and leaving the state. Hopefully she'd convinced the harpies to join our cause during their time together and we could be off to our next destination. I inhaled the pine scent with a smile. Truth be told, I liked that the mermaids called me a tree woman. If my heart held a connection to anything, it'd be the trees.

When I approached the harpies' home, soft rays of the autumn sun sparkled across Gabrielle's scales as she lounged in the glass-lined pool.

"Your tail," I said, rudely staring at the Wild I'd known for all of three days. I hadn't seen her or any of the mermaids in this form during my visit to their island. Emerald scales sprinkled her body and covered her thick tail. Her fin looked a lot like a folding fan opened so tightly that it may tear at any moment.

Gabrielle slapped her tail into the water and splashed me. I wiped the droplets from my face. Ugh. Saltwater.

"I know what you're wondering. Why do I have my tail on in such a small place where there's nowhere to swim," she said.

Her comment settled it for me: mermaids weren't able to read minds. "No, I wasn't thinking that at all," I said. "I've always known mermaids had tails, but it's different than I imagined. Shorter and more..." I searched for the word. "Buff."

She swam to the edge closest to me. "You can touch it if you want."

"Does it feel like a fish?" I asked. "Or the scales on your arm?"

She nodded. "Like a fish, but not as slimy."

"I'm good, then." I stood with my hands on my hips and stretched to the side. My night with Marcus had pulled a muscle behind my shoulder blade and tree-jumping had brought it to the surface. It was worth it, though, on both accounts.

"Where are our harpy friends?" I asked, looking around.

Gabrielle pointed to the glass bottom of the pool where the harpies' room appeared, blurry through moving liquid. "Sleeping."

"Seriously?" I squinted my eyes, which didn't help with visibility whatsoever. "We need to get moving."

"Harpies hunt at night when they're hidden by darkness," Gabrielle explained as she played with her hair. "Rushing them will only be counterproductive. Trust me; it'll be worth the wait."

I rolled my eyes and rested them back on her shiny tail. Her resemblance to the stereotype of her kind almost made me smile. "Do you know everything about every group?" I asked.

"Uh, no, I most definitely do not. But probably more than most groups know. We don't have to fear the Hunters, so we're able to research, learn more of the truth without being detected. Well, we *didn't* have to fear them." She narrowed her eyes. "What's so funny?"

"You just need a mirror and a rock and you'll belong in a child's coloring book." I shook my head and snickered.

"Oh please," she said. She jutted her fin from the water. "The public's rendition of mermaids is either soft and sweet or murderous. I'm in the middle, but my fin cuts through flesh. So maybe I'm more murderous."

I squatted at the edge of the pool and took the opportunity to stretch as I leaned forward. Gabrielle closed her fin. One line of what looked like green, flesh-covered bone stuck straight out from her tail. She fanned it open again. "I pull this open nice and tight, and the edges slice through the skin and muscle of anything thinking it can attack me. It's like my own personal knife."

Eonza, Salis, and Lapis sauntered up from the stairs with messy hair and sleepy eyes. They each wore loose, flowing silk night shirts and pants that mimicked a lighter shade of their wings. Not that their wings were in view. On first glance they, like the rest of us, looked like human women.

"Your talking woke us up," Eonza complained.

"Good. We have business to discuss," I said as I stood and faced them, only barely wincing in the process. I knew Gabrielle wanted us to wait for the harpies to give some hint that they were ready to talk, but I'd been patient enough.

Lapis groaned and sat on the cement, clearly too tired and pouty to stand.

"No, I'd prefer we not talk out in the open. We never know who's listening," I said.

"No one comes up here. Trust me, we're alone." Eonza crossed her arms.

"That's what we thought, too," Gabrielle said, swimming toward the steps of the pool. Her green scales faded into her skin and each long bone of her fan-like fin retracted to form toes before she pulled herself from the water to join us.

"I suspect the Hunters know where we all live," I said.

Lapis stood. "Where is your proof?"

Gabrielle must have spent more time in the pool than she'd spent recruiting the harpies. The thought ticked me off. A lot. I had trusted her to do her part, to be in as much of a hurry as I was. Yet her entire attitude screamed the opposite. It made me want to yank her from the water.

"They've been coming to the homes of Wilds, to their work," I said, as a painful memory of Shawna speeding away in the backseat of a Hunter's car played through my mind. "They can find us by our last names, based on which goddess we worship, which goddess our priestess foremothers served."

"Then we should continue this in the house," Eonza said, as though it were her idea in the first place. She led us down the cement steps, into the crevice in the mountain that was their home.

When the large wooden door shut behind me, I asked, "What do you three hunt at night?"

"Small woodland animals. It keeps us sharp," Salis answered.

"And you attend the monthly Hunter screenings?" I asked.

"We do, but they don't screen us for eating animal meat. Humans eat meat every day," Eonza added. "They screen us for hunting men. For luring them with our voices."

I couldn't begin to imagine how the Hunters would know if a harpy called to a man in her siren voice.

"We have the siren voice, too," Gabrielle added. "Sometimes we practice using it, because we never know when it'll come in useful. We create a storm first, so nearby boaters won't absently hear us and feel drawn to our island."

"I've never tried to utter a sound of it," Eonza said. "They'll know. Every month, during our screening, they prod us. They don't care that we grow feathers, or if our wings are strong. It's our voices that they deem dangerous. So they jab us with a cattle prod."

I winced, and not because of my right shoulder blade, which now seemed worlds away. I imagined waiting in line with my sisters, not to have my lower back examined, but to be electrocuted. I wondered if the Hunters took pleasure in watching. I bet they did. Then I thought of Marcus. Well, maybe not all of them, but most, surely.

"When the electricity enters us, we open our mouth to cry out," Eonza continued. "They measure the octave with another device. The Hunters wear devices over their ears to protect themselves. If we've been using our siren's song, traces of it will come out in our screams. It's impossible to control it with such pain." Eonza lifted her shirt to show the remnants of a red circular mark on the right lower side of her stomach.

I considered her words. When I was a teenager, our coterie held a sacred ritual for Olivia and Celeste's commitment ceremony—when my two older sisters had become adults and pledged loyalty to our coterie. While walking through the woods to the place of ceremony, I had tripped and landed in a blackberry bush, thorns and all, and yelled a colorful array of curse words. One of my aunts, shocked at my foul mouth, reminded me that the words a person uses in the comfort of daily life tend to sneak from their mouth in their moments of lost control. Eonza and her sisters did not practice their siren's song for fear it'd sneak out under the Hunter's force.

"I'm so sorry you have to go through that. It's awful." Gabrielle shuddered. She turned to me. "Our siren songs are a higher octave than most humans can hear audibly, but their brains hear it, or register it, and are pulled in. The human has no idea why they feel the need to come to us. We speak to their natural instincts. They're unable to interpret which instinct: run for your life or come hither. So they usually come hither."

A memory rose to the surface of my mind, of one of the few times my mother took me tree-jumping without the others. It was summer and we'd traveled east of Granite Falls, toward White Horse Mountain. After hours of tree-jumping we neared a fast-moving river and my mother bounded for the riverbank and plunged her feet into the cool water. She'd urged me to do the same, but I muttered something about mermaids getting me. My aunts had told my sisters horror stories of other Wilds, including mermaids—no doubt taught to them by Hunters. My sisters had in turn told me.

My mother didn't force me to put my feet in the water that day, but she did have me sit beside her while she told me stories of mermaids using their powerful abilities for good. One in particular stuck with me. According to my mother, a group of Vikings had plundered a town where a mermaid had been recently hung for witchcraft. As the Vikings rowed away, their boats heavy with spoils, another ship, whose captain resided in that town, gave chase out to open water after the Vikings. The mermaids wanted the townspeople to pay for hanging their sister, and they figured helping the Vikings was a great start. After the captain's ship began to close the gap on the Vikings, a number of mermaids circled the fleet of Viking ships and created a roaring storm from the outside, but kept it calm on the inside. The other mermaids focused on the British ship. They began singing what sounded like a hymnal at first, but it quickly transformed into what my mother called a "choir of water angels." Within minutes the crew on board were reworking the boat's lines, in an effort to sink the ship and be closer to the angels in the water.

The Vikings were able to see the ship go down, and they say a mermaid told their leader what was happening as it happened. They brought the story home with them, which is how the huldra heard it and passed it down through the generations.

I wondered how hearing both mermaids and harpies sing the siren's song in unison would affect the Hunters. Badly, I hoped.

"We're told our siren song will put us into a killing frenzy and we'll lose control." Lapis leaned against the cement wall beside the life-size impression of her winged goddess, Inanna. "We've never seen or heard it."

Gabrielle answered, "It doesn't work on Wild Women, but we can certainly hear it. It's glorious, like the most beautiful musical instrument played by the most talented of them all. The frenzy part is a lie conjured to make you fear your voice."

We all stared at Gabrielle. She ran her fingers lightly along the shells attached to the roots of her hairline and then smoothed down her hair. "What?" she asked, realizing we'd been watching her.

"Have you hunted men?" Lapis asked.

Every female in the room held her breath. Pin pricks crawled along my skin. The harpies hadn't seen my bark. I wondered if they knew mine wasn't supposed to be as dark and pronounced as it was.

Well, I knew. I knew I was the only Wild in the room that had killed a human man.

"No, of course not," Gabrielle said. "Although, my boyfriend does like me to sing to him. And on those nights when I feel like driving him crazy with want, I sing my siren's song. He has yet to complain." She gave a wink and I smiled. "It's probably one reason he stays with me, though we can't see each other on a regular basis."

If mermaids lived in Nevada they'd make a killing—in profits, not in death. Well, maybe in death too, if they wanted.

"I didn't know you had a boyfriend," I said, wishing hope for Marcus and me wasn't the first place my mind took her comment.

"Yeah, maybe you'll meet him sometime," Gabrielle said. "He's in the Navy."

That made so much sense and included more than a lot of irony, too.

I shook my head and put my hand out in front of me. "We're getting off topic. Sorry, my fault."

The others leaned in, ready to get down to business. Sunlight filtered in through the floor-to-ceiling windows overlooking the forest below and settled on our little group of Wilds. Gabrielle's skin glistened.

I turned to the harpies, reminding myself to ask Gabrielle later if her scales stayed below the surface. "Lapis, Eonza, Salis, I know you said your mother is an only child, but did she ever have sisters?"

"Yes," Lapis answered. "One."

"And she went missing." I said. "About twenty years ago."

The three tall females nodded.

"How'd you know?" Eonza asked in her steady voice, revealing no emotion.

I retrieved the envelope Marcus had brought me from where I'd stuffed it under my shirt before tree-jumping up the mountain. I explained the correlation between their mother's disappearance and disappearances twenty years ago. "These females never made it home, but they could still be alive. We think—" I stopped myself and started again. "I mean, I think, they're being taken for the same reason now as they were twenty years ago."

We needed them to flip the bird to the Hunters and learn how to sing their siren's song. It's one thing to have a mermaid sing the song and lure a Hunter into the water where she's strongest, but a harpy can sing it on land and hold the Hunters like putty in their talons.

"Together, we can save your mother, and possibly her sister," I said. "But it won't be safe or easy."

"Tell us, and we will do it," Eonza spoke for her flock.

"I'm glad to hear that." I stood. "If everything is understood and agreed upon, Gabrielle and I will pay a visit to the rusalki. After we meet with them, we'll fly back to Washington. We'll be ready for you then, in about three days."

The harpies nodded. Salis furrowed her brow and Lapis worried her inner cheek. I watched Eonza, though, who seemed ready for anything, including battle. Something told me I'd be thankful to have the stoic harpy on my side.

"I guess it's time to go then," Gabrielle said, opening her arms for hugs goodbye.

Eonza cut off the hug headed toward her by sticking out her arm. She shook Gabrielle's hand instead.

I stifled a laugh as I compared the Eonza who talked up the bartender last night to the Eonza standing before me. Night and day. The lengths some people will go to procreate.

Lapis held the door open as we left the three harpies who were still in their pajamas and probably planning to return to their beds once we were gone.

Gabrielle and I headed toward the concrete steps when I turned toward the opened door. "Oh, and Eonza?"

"Yes?" she said, poking her head out.

"Do me a favor?"

"It depends on the favor," she said dryly.

"If you're going to continue trying to get pregnant, can you wait until after we've fought the Hunters?" I thought about suggesting the use of condoms until then, but then remembered that she didn't much care for sex.

"Easily done," she said, closing the door behind her.

TWENTY-ONE

DRIVING to the Ashville Regional Airport: easy.

Returning the little red rental car: easy.

Getting two tickets to Maine: easy.

Sitting at the gate, waiting an hour for our flight: not so easy. It made me want to lose my mind in the worst way. The bustling airport terminal had taken way too long to access because a woman in the security line had decided to look her best in heeled boots and jewelry she didn't want to remove.

It was a classic hurry up and wait scenario, and I didn't do well with those. Waiting turned to thinking, which turned to worrying. Gabrielle had left again to call her sisters about thirty minutes ago, so I sat by myself watching humans rush by.

We had one more visit before I could hurry home and make my plan to retrieve Shawna a reality. Every time I thought of how I'd get Shawna back, I was reminded that I'd possibly rescue my mother as well. Once, when I was little, I overheard my aunt scolding Olivia, using my mother's disappearance as a lesson for why good little huldra must never behave rebelliously. Later she denied ever saying such a thing, but looking back I assumed she'd been referring to my mother's affair with the man already claimed by the succubi. I wanted to ask her, why him? Wilds make up such a tiny portion of the country's population. What kind of luck—bad or good—did this human male have that he'd been the object of affection of both a succubus and a huldra? It couldn't have been an accident.

With all my worrying and wondering, I'd practically gnawed off my inner lip by the time the flight attendant announced our flight to Bangor would begin loading soon. Gabrielle rushed toward me from who knows where and grabbed her suitcase, which had been sitting on the seat beside mine.

"Ready?" she asked as though she'd been the one waiting for me the whole time.

I stood and stretched my arms. "Let's go to Maine."

* * *

Other than our two layovers in Philadelphia and Charlotte, the seven-hour flight to Maine proved uneventful. Well, if you didn't include my little run-in with a man who clearly believed he deserved to use half of my seat on the flight from Charlotte to Philadelphia. Marcus, a Hunter complete with wide shoulders and nineteen-inch biceps, would have been able to fit in his own seat better than the man sitting beside me. I treasured my precious smidgen of space. So when he spread his knees as though he'd been carrying a FedEx package between his legs, I spread mine in response.

It only escalated from there. And for the life of me, as I drove the rental car from the airport, I couldn't remember anything about the guy's appearance.

Now that I thought about it, I could have just asked him to scoot over, but in the moment only one alternative presented itself after he scowled at me and refused to budge. I leaned right, toward him, scooched my butt over toward the arm rest between the two of us, and laid my head on his shoulder.

"What's your problem?" he'd asked, jumping out of his seat. A look of revulsion covered his face.

"Oh," I said, peering up at him. "I thought we were sharing. It's your turn to share."

"No, I don't want to share," he said in a thick southern accent.

"Good, because neither do I." I sat upright and eyed him. "So stay on your own damn side."

I'd never much liked the scent of entitlement. It reeks of mold, and not the pretty green fuzzy kind—the black putrid stuff. For the rest of the flight I had wished desperately he could one day be on my bounty list to hunt because cuffing him would be delightful. Not that I wanted him to hurt anyone to get on that list.

So when Gabrielle said, "You don't need to flex your anti-entitlement muscle whenever you're around men, you know," while I drove the little black rental we'd picked up at Bangor International Airport, it pissed me off.

Clearly, days of non-stop travel were wearing me down. But that wasn't really it. Concern ate at me, devouring my patience, my tolerance. I wanted to get this over with and get to the part where I saved my sister, and maybe even my mother.

I stared at the road in silence, thinking better of voicing my response to Gabrielle. The night sky loomed overhead as the car pointed toward Moose Lake and the forest surrounding it.

"I witnessed your exchange with the gentleman on that second to last flight." She pulled a nail file from her purse and went to work on her nails.

"How'd you get that through security?" I asked, still irritated that I had to throw away my switchblade in North Carolina. I hated traveling by plane, having to leave all my helpful weapons behind. Though, I supposed I could grow branches now and stab with those, so...

"I didn't. I bought it at a little kiosk while you were in line for the car. The same kiosk you bought your poor excuse for a weapon after you finalized the rental car." She referred to the only sharp object I could find—a letter opener.

"You already made your opinion on my need for weapons clearly known." I tapped my finger on the wheel, ready to move on.

"I just don't see why you cling to trinkets when you can grow real weapons." She yawned. "Back to what I was saying, though. After your unfortunate behavior on the plane I feel the need to remind you that men aren't the enemy."

"I never said they were the enemy. But when someone thinks they're entitled to half of the seat I paid for, I have a problem with that." I gave her a quick glance before returning my attention to the road. "If we're being completely honest, which it seems we are, you've had the window seats this whole trip, so you have no room to talk. And I highly doubt you've flown or traveled much."

"I need the window seat. Remember, I need movement or I get non-motion sickness," she said.

"*Oh, I remember*," I answered in irritation. "But next time try experiencing the thing you're doling out advice for first, before, you know, *you dole out the advice*. It gives you more credibility."

She turned in her seat to look at me with her whole body.

I sighed and rephrased my last statement before she could respond. "I really do appreciate what you did for me on the island. And you clearly have more knowledge of our old ways than I do. You've been able to hold to the ideals and abilities of our foremothers and that comes with a plethora of wisdom, but you need to realize that the rest of us haven't been so lucky."

"I'm not going to apologize for being enlightened past your understanding or comfort," she said calmly, but with an edge in her voice.

"Fuck you, Gabrielle. While you've been off gaining enlightenment, the rest of us have been treated like cattle and tortured." I gave her a quick look and released the tight muscles along my brow and jaw. "You haven't dealt much with humans, other than those who know of and revere your kind."

Gabrielle turned to face the windshield and stared ahead. "You're right. I haven't."

"Then support those of us who have," I said. "And don't ridicule us when we get angry over things we clearly ought to be upset about."

Among the blue-lit interior of the car and the thick fog of silence hanging in the air, Gabrielle's regret surrounded us with the acidic sweetness of an orange that had been cut open and sat on the counter for too many days.

I moved my hand from the wheel and placed it on her arm. "When all this is done, it may be your shoal teaching the rest what it looks like to stand in our own power on a day-to-day basis. Mermaid therapists to the Wilds, swimming upstream to make house calls."

Gabrielle let out a snort. "I think I speak for all of my shoal when I say we'd be more than happy to make house calls. Except, we don't do stagnant water, so if any of you live near a slow moving river or a lake, you're SOL."

I grinned and returned my hand to the wheel. "No, it's the rusalki who prefer bodies of water filled with algae and fish feces," I said.

Gabrielle nodded. "The hippy recluses in the world of Wilds."

* * *

Our rental cabin near Moose Lake wasn't much—a tiny two-bedroom with a kitchen nook, a loveseat, and a table with two chairs. I didn't want to stay somewhere yet again and waste a precious night in which Shawna was undergoing Freyja only knew what kind of horrors. But we needed the rusalki, and Gabrielle insisted it would take time to find the elusive Wild Women. Especially if they didn't want to be found.

Our surroundings, a patchwork of pine, spruce, maple, and birch trees as far as the eye could see endeared me to the rusalki for their choice in living environment. Gabrielle had insisted on a two bedroom cabin, saying that unlike with the harpies, she needed her own room to stretch out and refused to stay with the rusalki who live in the forest...not in a house, but in a burrowed-out hole in the ground.

The goddess that their high priestess foremothers served was called Mokosh. The word meant moist mother earth. The rusalki took their reverence literally. It helped them to live off the grid. From what I'd gathered, the Hunters couldn't know their address because they had none, only a forest they were known to frequent, which spread out beside a large lake.

And it was no coincidence that their home, if you could call it that, sat near a lake. Rusalki were like the succubi in that their abilities were not as physically obvious as the mermaids, harpies, and huldra. They were like the mermaids in that some spent hours a day in the water, or more. They were like the huldra in that they lived in the forests and connected to the plants. The rusalki were a little of all our groups and nothing like us at the same time.

I remembered my lessons about them well. They'd never used modern conveniences because adapting to the changing times was not in their character. They were the most mystical of Wild groups in that their abilities didn't show on the outside, other than their slightly pointed ears and the way their pale skin glowed in the moonlight. They didn't have scales or bark or feathers. They were not physically strong or quick. But rusalki were the most deadly of us all. After plucking only one strand of their victim's hair, they're able to end the person's life by cutting that strand in half, or decrease their years by cutting snippets from the ends.

According to my mother's stories, my huldra foremothers had once tried to reach out to the foremothers of the rusalki coven, to connect over our common affinity for nature and forests. But like mama bears protecting their cubs, the rusalki stood proud and tall, threatening the huldra that if they didn't leave immediately, they'd cut their lives short or kill them where they stood.

They probably still had bad blood with the huldra, and to be honest, I wasn't sure how I'd react if they threatened me. They needed a strand of my hair to end my life. I only needed to "branch out" to end theirs. I hoped it wouldn't come to that.

"Should we approach their dirt hole together, or should we separate and I find their home away from home in the lake?" Gabrielle asked as we trudged through the woods.

Because my last couple days had been filled with energy-depleting revelations, I wanted to rest up before meeting the rusalki. We'd slept through the afternoon and left our cabin an hour ago, as the sun set in reds and purples along the hilly horizon. I could have been going much faster if I tree-jumped, but I didn't want to leave Gabrielle behind.

"Their 'dirt hole' *is* their house. Why don't you just call it that?" I asked.

"I know," Gabrielle said, pushing a bush branch out of her way. "Normally, I try to be respectful. But it's hard with the rusalki. I mean, we live off the grid too, but at least we know how to be civilized."

"'Civilized' is a matter of perception," I said, eyeing a fern as I carefully stepped over it, making sure not to damage its bright green leaves. "Or have you met them in person?"

"No. I don't think any Wild Woman alive today has met a rusalka, other than a rusalka, of course," Gabrielle said.

With a grimace, I eyed Gabrielle's feet as she tromped on living plants. I reminded myself to offer the same understanding to her that I urged her to offer the rusalki.

"Is it true they practice divination?" I asked. Brown leaves and dead pine needles crunched beneath my boots as I wove around living things. I yearned to feel the soil beneath my bare feet. But if I wasn't tree-jumping or running through the woods, there was no reason to remove my boots. Plus, they hid my newest knife beautifully.

So far, Gabrielle and the other mermaids seemed to have knowledge on every Wild group. But this time her knowledge was sparse. "I've heard they do. I wonder if they use it on the Hunters."

I stopped and gave a questioning look.

Gabrielle shook her head and kept walking, clearly not watching where she stepped. "They're elusive, more so than my own shoal, which is saying a lot, as you know."

I nodded and then jogged to catch up to the mermaid. An owl screeched. She jumped behind me.

"It's only an owl." I laughed.

Gabrielle threw her hands in the air. "I hate the forest. So many animals sneaking around, waiting to eat me."

Thinking of an owl's normal diet of mice, I said with a laugh, "Maybe if you had a tail." Then I remembered she did have a tail sometimes. I laughed harder.

"I'm glad you're enjoying yourself while we're out in strange woods, probably being hunted by wolves and bears and watched by rusalki." Gabrielle turned to walk in a different direction.

"Hey, where are you going?" I ran after her. "I was just joking."

"The lake is this way. I'm going to search it for rusalki, find them before they find us. And if they're not in the water, I'll swim to the far end of the lake. It'll get me to their hole quicker than walking."

"I thought you didn't want to swim in fish poop," I said.

"It's better than waiting to be eaten!" Gabrielle stomped off through a line of bushes as she removed her clothes and wadded them together in a ball. Yeah, she was pissed. I'd never seen her treat her clothes with so little concern.

That's fine. I'd gladly travel alone. I pulled my sharpened letter opener from my boot and stuck it down the back of my jeans, handle side out. I tied my boots together to string around my neck before I took a running leap and landed on the branch of an old fir tree. I grabbed the branch above me and swung my body to the next tree. The fresh smell of pine and crisp night air blanketed me in absolute goodness.

As I tree-jumped through the oldest and tallest evergreens of the forest able to carry my weight, I wondered how Marcus was getting along, what the Hunters were forcing him to do to earn their trust and to pay for his betrayal. For his sake, I hoped it was nothing like what they did to the harpies on a monthly basis. No one deserved that... except maybe the Hunters. Reality smacked me like a thin branch in a wind storm.

Marcus *was* a Hunter. And whether he held allegiance to them or not, he'd always have their blood running through his veins, their tattoos inked along his shoulders, chest, and back. Being around me for any prolonged amount of time would always trigger his muscles, set off red flags in his subconscious.

Obviously, sex with Marcus blew every other sexual experience I'd had out of the water. But in a couple of years it'd be time for my sisters and me to create the next generation of huldra. And I would never damn my daughter to the bloodline of our enemy—present or past.

I noticed an odd lump in the ground and jumped from a fir tree to inspect it. Two evergreens stood on one side of it and a patch of birch trees on the other. Between the trees nestled a flat wall of large stacked stones with a small square wooden door. Above this wall was a type of roof with tall grass growing from wooden boards. Animal bones hung at the left corner of the makeshift roof. Flat stones covered the front opening like a patio. Snake shaped branches propped against the rock wall.

I pulled my boot strings from around my neck and set them down beside the tree I'd jumped from. I grabbed my envelope-opener for protection (because old habits are hard to break) and lifted my nose to breathe in the scents more thoroughly.

A scent that was both natural and otherworldly gently found its way to my nose.

"I can smell both of you," I whispered into the night.

"Then you should also be able to sense your need to leave, huldra." The female's soft voice came from above me, but I didn't look up. I didn't want her to know that I knew where she perched.

"I cannot do that," I said, still staring forward at their earthen house.

"Then we cannot keep from ending your life," the female said.

I had hoped to show my innocent intent in keeping my hair down, that I wasn't there to cause a problem, but clearly they hadn't taken notice. I slowly tucked the tip of my makeshift knife in my pocket. I pulled the elastic hair tie from my wrist and brought my hair up into a ponytail and then a tight bun. If a rusalka stole a strand of my hair it meant game over.

"I'd prefer that you talk to me first—Wild Woman to Wild Woman. But if you insist on trying to kill me, I'm warning you now, I'll stab a branch through your heart quicker than you can run for a pair of birch scissors." I stuck my hands out in front of me and flexed my fingers.

"You bluff. Huldra haven't been able to fully use their abilities for generations." The branch above me cracked as the rusalka moved.

"This one can, sister," a second female said. "Her mind says she speaks the truth." Her voice echoed from the ground, a few trees away, probably hiding behind the thick trunk to my left.

"This huldra," the second, more wispy voice continued, "is the mother of war. Of the dark things, the roots, hidden beneath soil, begging to push through the surface and be greeted by the moon's light."

Chills ran down my spine. In the last week or so I had been attacked by Hunters, had my energy drained by succubi, took part in a kumbaya with the mermaids, and learned Marcus was a Hunter. But nothing compared to the creepy sensation of having my mind read by a rusalka. As though long, glowing fingers ran through my hair, massaged my scalp, and parted my brain to look inside.

"You are right, sister," said the first, soft voice. "I can see that now. Though she cavorts with the enemy."

Shit. They knew about Marcus. I scolded myself for thinking about him while traipsing through rusalki territory.

"But she does not come to harm us," the wispy voice reminded.

"My huldra ancestors hadn't come to harm you either, but your kind didn't seem to care then," I said without thinking. The more I traveled, the shorter my fuse became. Not that I'd had a particularly long fuse to begin with.

"Your ancestors sought to create an alliance, to use our abilities for their own gain," the wispy voice said.

I kept my hands out in front of me and allowed tiny buds of branches to grow from my fingertips. I had to be ready to turn and fight with less than a second's notice. I had been concentrating on their scents, the slightest sound of their movements, so I hadn't noticed two more rusalki, accompanied by a pissed off mermaid, approach from my right side, from the lake.

A short, thin rusalki with milky pale skin and black hair so long that it swished across the backs of her knees peered up at the female in the tree above me. "This mermaid was trespassing," she said before she noticed me and froze.

I looked down. Every exposed piece of my skin was covered in bark, thus her difficulty in seeing me at first.

"It's public land, not yours. I'm not trespassing any more than you are," Gabrielle argued. "Let me go!"

With all eyes on Gabrielle's temper tantrum, I shot out from underneath the fir tree and stopped on the rock patio of their earthen home, turning my body to face everyone.

The soft-voiced rusalka crouched on the branch above where I'd stood earlier. She watched me with ice blue eyes and brown hair about as long as her sister's. The female standing beside the thick trunk narrowed her light green eyes and swept a strand of her long auburn hair from her cheek. The dry rusalki wore short animal-skin skirts and a necklace of long fern branches to cover their chests. On their heads were crowns of woven grass, tiny pine cones, and dried flower petals. The females clasping Gabrielle's hands behind her wore nothing but bone necklaces and seaweed crowns that dripped lake water down their shoulders and chests.

"They cannot let you go," the green-eyed female said, stepping away from the tree. "Your intentions are not admirable. You have not come for the same reason the huldra has come."

TWENTY-TWO

I SNAPPED my head from the green-eyed female to Gabrielle. My eyes widened. I thought Gabrielle and I had been on the same page this whole trip: unite the Wilds and rescue our sisters and mothers from the Hunters.

"Don't believe them, Faline," Gabrielle pleaded. "They live in a hole in the ground. They swim in filthy water. They wear animal skins. You know me. You know my sisters. You know we want nothing more than to see all Wild Women thrive. These rusalki are delusional; they're out of their minds."

"Yeah, but they also *read* minds," I reminded her.

The naked female holding Gabrielle's right arm reached over the mermaid's head in the blink of an eye and within half a second held a long strand of black hair out in front of her face.

"Goddess, no!" Gabrielle yelled. She flung her elbows to push away. The rusalka pinned the mermaid's arms tighter to her back.

"No! She's with me," I said, rushing toward the threesome. Branches shot out from my fingertips. "Don't do it!"

The two rusalki holding Gabrielle didn't flinch. Their arms gripped her tightly. They wore smiles of tranquility despite the angry mermaid. Their skin glowed iridescent, making their white teeth look dark. The other two rusalki joined their sisters, standing on each side, creating a line of four glowing beings with a trapped mermaid in the middle.

"Faline! Stop them!" Gabrielle writhed and screamed. "I can feel them; they're in my head, all of them!"

I didn't know what to do. I couldn't take on four Wild Women at once. But I had to try. I shoved my arms in front of me and willed my branches to grow longer, stronger, from my fingertips. My fingers separated, creating a V on each hand causing the vine-like branches from each finger to join the other and double up in strength. They shot out farther until a woody vine wrapped around each rusalki neck. Still, they smiled and glowed.

I tried to tighten the branches around their necks, but for some reason I couldn't. I didn't want to. I shook my head and my vision blurred. The feeling of long, cold fingers massaging my scalp returned.

"Stop," I pleaded. "I'm not the enemy."

Then don't become one, a female said into my mind. *She has betrayed you. The mermaid has made herself your enemy.*

With blurred vision, I looked toward the iridescent light, bright figures in the surrounding darkness.

"How?" My fuzzy mind failed to grasp a whole sentence.

The female answered, but I couldn't understand as my consciousness floated on what seemed like clouds heading for the stars. My eyes eased shut without my consent and geometric patterns rose and fell behind my lids, starting as pin pricks and growing out. I tried to pull myself away from the mandalas multiplying behind my eyes, but they only doubled in size and brightness. I fought through it, barely. My vision returned slowly.

Gabrielle opened her mouth as only a short squeak left her lips. Her wide eyes and pleading stare lasted less than a second, though the image burned itself into my being, and returned my senses to me and plucked the massaging fingers from my mind. I blinked to see my dark-haired mermaid friend crumbled in a heap on the dirt.

The soft-voiced rusalka held a wooden pair of scissors in one hand and half a strand of Gabrielle's hair in the other.

I wanted to lunge forward and somehow tear the rusalka's head from her body—my own form of killing by hair cut—but something in me, a knowing, told me to be still. My bare feet anchored to the roots of an old oak tree. My feet tingled. I looked down at real vines growing from my toes and rooting into the ground.

"You just killed my friend," I said with a shaky voice. I balled my fists and swallowed down the acid rising in my throat.

Their skin dimmed. Their relaxed facial expressions told me they were unconcerned.

"She was no friend of yours," the soft-voiced female finally said. "Not a friend to Wild Women." I waited for her to explain further, but she only stood there, staring, as though that one piece of reasoning had been enough.

It hadn't. Not for me.

"She was trying to help me save us!" I screeched through a burning throat. Tears filled my eyes.

"Yes," the wispy-voiced female said. "That was half of her intentions. But she also had another half—secretive and vile."

I scratched my scalp to remove the tingles left by whatever they'd used to pry my thoughts from me in what I assumed was an effort to realize my intentions. "This doesn't make any sense."

The wispy-voiced rusalka walked toward their home, and the others followed. "Come," she said to me. "Come inside. Sit, rest, and I will explain."

I shook my head and scoffed. How could they read minds and yet still be so clueless. "I'm not going in there," I said, motioning to the entrance of their home, decorated with sticks and rocks.

"We will not harm you. This is not a trap," another female said without looking my way.

Could what they were saying be true? What could they have possibly read in her mind? I needed to know. I'd come this far, I couldn't walk away without knowing more. "Are you missing members?" I asked, wanting to complete the reason for my visit and put this place behind me. "Were they taken?"

The green-eyed female stood in front of the small square make-shift door and turned on her heel. She cocked her head. "You know the unknown as well?"

"She does not," another female sang. "Or she would have killed the mermaid days ago."

My scalp tingled again and I gave an irritated groan. I should have kept my mouth shut. The mind burglary didn't last long, thankfully.

A female opened the small door and bent low to enter the hole in the front of a mound. The others followed. "Come, huldra," one said from inside.

I gazed at the animal bones beside the door and hoped they symbolized a respect for life rather than sacrifice. The rusalki's abilities would be amazingly helpful in an attack on the Hunters if they agreed to help in the war they said I would be the mother of. I wondered what they would find in Marcus's mind if given the opportunity to explore it, if they were able to explore the mind of a Hunter.

I peered at Gabrielle's body, void of life, crumbled on the ground. Had she really betrayed me? What was her second plan, if not to help the Wilds? Maybe even more important, had she been acting on her own or with her whole shoal's consent?

I turned to the earthen home, what looked like a mound of hollowed out den with a small makeshift wooden door propped open for me. Four females waited inside. If those four females didn't agree to help, this whole mission could implode before it got off the ground. I couldn't settle on an exact plan to attack the Hunters until I saw how each Wild group worked with the others. But we had to do it the day my coterie showed up at the complex for our monthly check-in. If the rusalki was able to sneak up on me and Gabrielle, they could do the same to the Hunters, which would be incredibly helpful to our cause.

Unless, because of the rusalki, this all fell apart. The mermaids would hate the huldra for letting one of their own die. The harpies would hate me, too. Unless, they were also in on it. Gabrielle had spent plenty of alone time with them the night Marcus and I were together. Had she already taught them how to use their siren's song, enabling them to turn on us? No, she'd said it didn't work on Wilds.

In less than a day I'd gone from feeling supported by many to feeling absolutely alone. I caught myself gnawing my inner cheek. There was only one way to find the answers to the questions creating a tornado in my mind.

"I'm sorry," I said under my breath to the fallen mermaid as I passed her empty body.

I bent to crawl into the rusalki's underground den. Once I entered I had to stand with a hunched back to keep my head from hitting the dirt ceiling. Moss carpeted the small, round space. Wood lined the walls and chopped tree trunks made up the table and chairs. Bundled branches hung along the wall creating shelves. Red paintings, like those you'd find in ancient caves, decorated the wooden walls with images of the moon's cycles, and their Russian goddess, Mokosh, growing from a great tree, raising a bowl and a horn above her head with what looked like the full moon behind her.

The four rusalki sat on short tree stumps along the rounded walls in a circle, leaving two open. The green-eyed female motioned for me to sit on the stump beside her. The two previously naked females had since covered themselves, one with a large animal skin wrapped around her shoulders, and the other with a fern skirt and top.

"She thinks us odd," one said to the others.

They stared at me as though I was the odd one for thinking that.

"My name is Faline," I said, eager to begin the discussion.

"We know that," the green-eyed female said with a smile.

Their knowing smiles and eager eyes gave me chills.

"You're scaring the huldra," another said and the green-eyed rusalka's smile dropped.

"She is Drosera." The female with ice blue eyes and black hair pointed to the green-eyed female. "She is Vernonia." She pointed to the female with light hazel eyes and dark brown hair, one of the rusalki who held Gabrielle hostage. "She is Daphne." She pointed to the other female who'd held Gabrielle, the one who wore the bone necklace. "And I am Azalea."

"I'm confused," I admitted, leaving out the other more pissed off emotion I felt in an effort keep the peace long enough to get their help. "You do realize you just made what I'm trying to accomplish even more impossible?" I needed the mermaids' assistance in rescuing my sister and these rusalki just built another major hurdle between Shawna and me.

"Confused is one step better than scared," Daphne said.

I rubbed the palms of my hands on my jeans as a calming technique. "I prefer to be neither."

"She's angry. She wants to know why we killed the mermaid," Vernonia told the others.

I worked harder to smother my growing resentment for the women rummaging through my mind. After Shawna was home and safe I planned to remind her of this exact moment as proof of my selfless love for her.

"We didn't kill her friend, we ended her physical life," Drosera said lightly.

"The huldra doesn't know the difference," Vernonia said.

I was beginning to see why other Wilds avoided the rusalki, aside from their ability to kill with swiftness. They seemed to live outside of reality and be recluses at the same time—suffering a disconnect with the world around them. And their communication skills needed help.

"Faline, all life is continuous, whether it be in the physical form or not. The mermaid still exists, only you cannot see her current form." Azalea stood, though not completely, and walked to a tall stump holding a hollowed-out wooden pitcher beside hollowed-out wooden cups. She poured water and offered to pour me a cup.

For Shawna, I accepted the drink as a peace offering. "Yes, please," I said, realizing I was parched. "Let me be honest. I'm not interested in your coven's beliefs on death and life. What did you see inside of Gabrielle's mind? What was the second plan, her back-up plan you talked about?"

Azalea handed me the cup and sat. "We have lived here, in peace, without outsiders or any trouble, for many years."

I forced myself not to roll my eyes in frustration.

Azalea continued. "We do not possess the same sense of smell you huldra have. And we weren't expecting the men when they came."

"The Hunters?" I asked.

"We too suffer the monthly screenings offered by the Hunters," Azalea said.

I moaned inwardly at getting her off track.

"Oh, we don't suffer much," Vernonia offered.

Azalea spoke to me. "We are able to make them think they've

tested us properly when we visit and that our results prove that we have not been using our abilities. Our great grandmothers taught us from a young age to invade their minds at each screening."

"But we did not see that they planned to take two of our sisters," Azalea said. "They must not have planned it."

"They came whilst we slept," Vernonia said, shaking her head. "Tossed a small metal contraption into our home. It blew a foul-smelling smoke at us."

Azalea nodded. "I was able to reach into the nearest Hunter's mind before the smoke pressed its sleep upon me. A mermaid had given him our location in exchange for her shoal's continued freedom. She'd told him the best way to rend us powerless. I succumbed to their smoke before learning why or where they were taking our sisters." She sighed and put her head down. "We have moved since then."

Daphne rubbed Azalea's back. "You did well," she consoled her sister.

"So you're saying Gabrielle was behind the abductions?" I stood to pace, but hit my head on the dirt ceiling and sat to nurse a budding headache. Bits of dry dirt sprinkled down around me.

"Yes," Azalea said as she raised her head to look at me. "Her and her shoal."

TWENTY-THREE

MY HEART RACED and anxious energy twitched my muscles. "Then why was Gabrielle helping me to gather the Wilds if she was also helping the Hunters?"

"She thought she was being clever, helping the Hunters and the mother of war at the same time. No matter the outcome, she would find her and her shoal on the winning side," Azalea answered. "Never underestimate a mermaid; they are a cunning kind."

"But why tell the Hunters anything to begin with?" I asked. "If she hadn't given them the information, they wouldn't have been able to take our sisters, and there'd be no war." It didn't make sense. Unless. "Their technology is making it harder for us to hide our identities. If we changed our names, there'd be a paper trail leading the Hunters back to us. And staying off the grid is nearly impossible when every electronic transaction, from credit card to internet to cell phone use, is stored and monitored. Even functioning without those things, only using cash and living off the land, won't secure the mermaids' safety for long because of the recent advances in satellites and facial recognition technology."

"She knew it was only a matter of time before the Hunters would no longer need her intelligence. She had to act before it was too late to align with them. While she had something they did not," Daphne said in a quiet voice.

"But they attacked her island anyway," I explained. "While I was there."

"There was nothing in her mind about that occurrence," Azalea said. "So I cannot answer your statement."

"The Hunters attacked. She'd said they must have used drones to find the mermaids. I killed two of them that night." I had to get home. I had to warn the others.

"Yes, we see that in your mind." Azalea took a sip of water.

"Your mother and sister have been taken captive," Daphne said, staring into my eyes.

I nodded. "Yeah, though my mother's disappearance happened twenty years ago, and Shawna was taken last weekend."

Daphne chewed her bottom lip and lowered her chin, still staring at me with blue eyes. "The Hunters had a plan twenty years ago. The mermaids helped them perfect it to try again. It is why they took our sisters. It is why they took yours." Her eyes widened and she inhaled sharply. "It is why they tried to take you, but unleashed your huldra instead. Bloody night that was."

The others nodded and made grunting sounds of agreement.

I paused from biting my lip. "You can see what happened that night? I don't remember. I blacked out."

Daphne nodded. "The outcome is where the importance lies. Not the action."

"What's the Hunters' plan?" I asked. "What do they want from us?"

"The mermaid's mind did not tell us these things. If she would have known, I would have seen it," Azalea said. "And I was not able to extract the answer from the Hunter."

"Do you have any ideas, then, why the Hunters are doing this? What they're trying to accomplish?" I asked.

"Speculation is useless," Azalea answered. "Not worthy of the time spent wondering."

Okay. I tried a different approach. "How could the mermaids help the Hunters perfect their plan if the mermaids didn't know what the plan was?"

"Oh, this I did see from the Hunter's mind," Azalea said with the hint of a smile. "He saw the mermaid as foolish for sharing Wild Women secrets freely in conversation. Though, to me he is foolish for believing mermaids share anything without motive."

"You can see the rough outline I've devised as a plan for attack," I said. "How your abilities could help us succeed."

One rusalka nodded.

"Will you help me, then?" I asked. "Will you come to Washington and join the others in helping us to attack the Hunters and get my sister away from them? Help us to rescue all of our sisters and mothers."

The four rusalki eyed one another, communicating telepathically, I assumed. In one soft, fluid movement they all turned to stare at me and said *Yes* into my mind.

"We will leave in the morning," Azalea said. "And meet you at your coterie's home."

"I can fly back with you," I offered. "I have a ticket to fly home tomorrow morning anyway."

Daphne laughed and shook her head. "Silly huldra, we do not fly. We have no wings."

"I don't either. I use an airplane," I said dryly.

"We do not. We will travel by other means." Daphne smoothed her hair as though the thought of flying messed up her already tangled tresses.

"By train? That may take a while," I said.

The four rusalki shook their heads. "We have our ways," was all Daphne would say.

"Okay, but can you make sure to get there in the next day or two?" I asked.

"Yes, we can promise that." Azalea stood and blew out the many candles along the outer edge of the circular wall. "After we rest, we will be on our way."

I stood to leave, ready to have alone time to process everything, ready to be away from the four mind-benders living in a hole in the ground.

"It is not safe to return to the cabin," Azalea said. "It is your choice. But she had thoughts of the cabin before her physical life ended. The small inadequate one with two rooms, correct?"

I nodded. If Gabrielle had been in contact with the Hunters, she may have told them about the rental. Ugh. Okay, now I wanted to strangle Gabrielle for forcing me to spend a night in a dirt hole with mind-readers who spoke in circles.

"Thank you," I forced my lips to say. "I'll stay." I looked around. "Where is the shower? The toilet?"

The others stretched across the moss-carpeted floor for the night. I breathed in the natural scents of soil and moss with a hint of iron and mold.

"You may relieve yourself to the south of our home, about fifty steps or so. And you may wash yourself in the lake. I'm sure you know where that is," Vernonia said. She closed her eyes and rolled away from me.

I wanted to ask how they lived like this, without modern conveniences like refrigerators and televisions and cell phones. But I wasn't in the mood for a long, patchwork answer, so I kept my question to myself. And then I kicked myself for thinking the question.

Azalea raised her head and motioned to me, patting the soft green moss beside her. I lay next to her and stared up at the dirt ceiling.

"We live like this because it is closest to Mokosh," Azalea whispered under her breath. "We live within the moist mother earth, in her womb. If we are taken from her, we lose our abilities. Our umbilical cord is severed."

"That means your sisters, the ones who were taken, they aren't able to defend themselves by messing with the Hunters' minds," I whispered.

Azalea wiped a tear winding down her temple. "That is precisely what it means."

So her sisters were unable to telepathically communicate over a distance.

"How will you help us fight the Hunters then, if you're away from home?" I asked.

"We will stay on your coterie's property, but not in your home."

Azalea closed her eyes and soon her breath matched the others in the den—the rhythmic breathing of deep sleep.

* * *

When I woke, the four rusalki were already gone. I sat up and wiped my eyes. Everything looked as it had last night, so they hadn't taken much with them. If they were walking they wouldn't arrive in Washington for weeks. I hoped they held to their word of helping us in the next day or two.

I crawled from the hole in the ground and stood up tall to stretch my muscles. My spine popped and I sighed with relief. I didn't consider washing off in the poopy lake. I'd take my chances with the cabin and risk a Hunter attack.

I looked right and then left, but I couldn't find Gabrielle's body. Sniffing the air didn't help. I hadn't thought to ask the rusalki what they planned to do with the mermaid last night. The lake's scent wafted to me as I sniffed the air and it occurred to me that they'd probably placed her in the lake, in the water where she belonged.

My throat tightened and it hurt to swallow. I believed the rusalki, but I also didn't blame Gabrielle. Helping the Hunters was awful, but I understood the desire to do anything to protect my sisters and aunts. I walked past the trees and bushes to the side of the lake and looked out over the dark water. Reeds swayed at the edges and strips of seaweed poked from the glassy top.

"I really wish you hadn't betrayed us," I whispered out to Gabrielle —to the water. "I was starting to trust you."

A pain stabbed at my heart and I fell to my knees. Tears wound down my cheeks. Exhaustion clawed at me, compelled me to quit, to give up. It was like the olden days all over again, when Wilds turned against Wilds. Shawna was missing. My mother might be alive, but I hadn't a clue as to where she was. Wild groups were falling apart, disintegrating in what little power, strength, and numbers they held. And while I'd gotten them all to agree to meet together and devise a plan to get our loved ones, some were double agents. I'd taken two steps forward and three steps back.

And the mermaid I called my friend lay dead somewhere, probably at the bottom of the lake. Yes, she betrayed me, but she wasn't the only one secretly speaking with a Hunter.

Nothing made sense anymore. The more I dug, the more I realized there was no such thing as deep enough. I wiped my face and stood. I brushed my jeans off and walked to the fir tree where I'd left my boots and socks.

I had to keep going. I had to get home to warn my coterie and plan a battle. But first, I needed a hot shower to wash the tears from my face and a serious breakfast to fill me with enough strength to attempt the impossible.

* * *

I sat at a Denny's about a block away from the Bangor International Airport and cut into my rare steak. Blood oozed from the meat, covering the plate and seeping into runny yolk.

I fingered through the stack of old missing persons reports Marcus had left with me. No one had been in my cabin while Gabrielle and I were gone. I'd sniffed around to make sure. Once I'd gotten in, I'd taken a shower, brushed out my tangled hair, put on a new change of jeans and a V-neck t-shirt, and then headed out. I'd grabbed Gabrielle's suitcase along with mine, because I don't know why. I'd also checked my phone and found no new texts or messages.

Marcus had warned me that he'd have to cut contact if he rejoined the Hunters, but I'd hoped to hear from him by now. Maybe just a quick text that everything was on track. It'd help to know what I was flying home to. It would have also let me know he was okay. After Gabrielle, I was desperate to know.

I had called home during my drive to Denny's. They had nothing to report, other than their new dog's ability to now sit and lay on command. I reminded Aunt Abigale that Shawna would be thrilled when she arrived home to her favorite rescue dog performing tricks in her own living room. That seemed to brighten my aunt's mood.

I swallowed a bite of egg when my cell phone rang. I peered down at the screen. Marcus.

"You don't know how happy I am to see your name on my phone," I said instead of answering the traditional way.

Marcus chuckled under his breath. "They watch me constantly," he said. "I'm in the bathroom now, the one place they don't want to watch me."

"That explains the echo. So what have you found?" I asked.

"Not much," he said. "They don't trust me. When I walk into a room they stop talking. I have to wear a vest over my black shirt with a huge red circle on the front and the back, as a warning that I can't be trusted."

"You mean like a target? You're joking, right?" I said through a mouth of perfectly cooked hash browns.

"No, a ruby. As in the ruby on their dagger hilts that symbolize the fiery pits of hell as the resting place of all evil." Marcus turned the faucet on.

"Fire doesn't sound restful," I joked.

"There's a woman here you'll want to know about." Ah, the reason for the added faucet water to cover his words.

I sat up straighter in my chair and set my fork on the plate. "And?" I asked. I rustled through my purse for a pen to jot down any notes he had to share.

"That woman who skipped bail, the one taking the rap for the human trafficking ring that was in the news, she's here."

"Clarisse? What's she doing hiding out there? Have you made contact with her?"

"She's a Hunter. I mean the daughter of one. And no, I can't get near her. She's betrothed," he answered as though I should have known one equaled the other.

"What's that got to do with anything?" I asked.

"It's inappropriate for a woman who's promised to a Hunter to be alone with another single Hunter." Marcus answered my next question before I had the chance to ask it. "She could cause the single man to stumble and make advances on her and then she'd be used and unwanted by any of them. Not to mention the fight it'd cause between the brothers."

I groaned and rolled my eyes. "Please tell me you don't believe any of that bullshit."

"I wouldn't be on the phone with you if I did. But if I'm going to work my way back into the fold I need to act like I believe it wholeheartedly." Marcus sighed. "I think they'll let me in tonight. There's a big meeting. Some higher ups from other complexes are coming in for it and I'm sure our complex leaders will want as many strapping young Hunters on display as possible, to show off our force. Sans the vest," he added.

The waitress walked toward me with the coffee carafe, but I covered my cup and shook my head so she kept walking.

"Hey, I missed talking to you," Marcus whispered.

My heart fluttered for a quick second before I put a stop to that nonsense. Huldra do not do heart flutters.

"Me too," I said and then quickly shifted the topic so the heart flutters would stop. "How was the hazing?"

"Not as bad as I thought. They need all men on deck. A violent hazing would keep me down for a while." Marcus turned off the sink faucet. "I'll call you when I can."

"I look forward to it," I heard myself say. And then I had to backtrack and re-mold the meaning of my statement. "I mean, I look forward to hearing more so I can better devise a plan."

Marcus's quiet chuckle sounded like soft base. "All right, Faline," he whispered and then ended the call.

I shoveled the rest of my steak, eggs, and hash browns into my mouth and chugged down my coffee and orange juice. I had a flight to catch, a bunch of upset Wilds to gather and compose, and Hunters to take down.

TWENTY-FOUR

I FLEW into SeaTac International Airport—located between Tacoma and Seattle—right on schedule. As I heaved Gabrielle's and my suitcases from the conveyer belt at baggage claim I wondered if leaving my car in California was such a great idea. Asking the mermaids to pick it up from the airport was no longer an option. I could always ask before they arrived and before I delivered the bad news, but that felt dishonest. I'd get it myself when this was over, hopefully with Shawna. A road trip with her sounded like the perfect way to move forward.

I didn't have to wait outside on the arrivals curb for long before Olivia's Jeep fought through the traffic. I landed a kiss on her cheek the moment I was close enough. I'd missed my sisters and aunts terribly. The grey skies were an added welcome-home gift from nature. I fought the urge to clap when rain splashed onto the windshield as we made our way northbound on interstate five.

I filled Olivia in on everything, but she was most interested in how the different groups lived, especially the mermaids.

"So, they don't drop men once they've mated?" she asked, astonished. "What happens when they get pregnant and it's time for the male to go? He can't return to the human world with what he knows, right?"

"They don't see it that way," I said, still unsure how the mermaids dealt with breakups. "They don't have a limit on how many offspring they create or what years they're brought into the world."

"So there's all different ages of mermaids running around?"

"And men." I laughed, glad to be with my sister, with someone who grew up with the same values and rituals as I did. "The lead succubus had a man lying on a couch, mostly naked, while we discussed business. She asked him if he wanted a threesome with the both of us."

Olivia took her eyes off the road and stared at me with her mouth agape.

"No, I didn't do it," I said, laughing and shaking my head.

"Why not? That sounds like a pleasure-filled night to me," she said.

"Because I had other things on my mind."

Olivia's smile dropped and she exhaled. "Right."

I wanted to cheer her up. I figured the mood around our home had been somber at best this last week. "Plus, the leader, Marie, is batshit crazy. You'll see."

It worked. Her mood lightened. "How?" she asked.

I told Olivia crazy Wild stories, which had her rolling, until she parked in front of our common house.

I nearly kissed the ground the moment I swung open the car door. I missed home: the scents, the trees, the familiarity. I yearned to scale up my tree and sprawl out on my bed. To eat in my own kitchen and read a book on my porch.

But the joyful familiarity was cut short. I lifted my nose. "Do you smell that, Olivia?"

"Thank you," she said as though I'd confirmed her suspicion. "It started this morning, but none of us can find where it's coming from. Somewhere on our property for sure, though." She took the two suitcases I'd grabbed from the trunk.

I unlaced my boots and pulled them and my socks from my feet. The scent reminded me of lake and fir trees and tangled hair. I dropped my boots and socks and jetted for the woods. Low hanging, light green moss grazed the top of my head as I ran under tree branches. Ferns smacked at my legs. I catapulted myself into an evergreen and jumped from its branch to the branch of the next tree.

I neared the edge of our one hundred and sixty-two acres of forest and spotted the hole dug into a mound of dirt. I dropped from the tree with a light thump. "I can smell you. We all can. Why are you hiding?"

Four rusalki walked out from behind tree trunks.

"We are not hiding," Drosera answered in her wispy voice. "Do the fish hide?"

I shook my head. "I have no clue what that's supposed to mean, but I'm glad to see you." I motioned to their makeshift home in the ground. "How'd you get here and make this so quickly?"

Azalea patted her messy black hair. Pieces of plants poked out from the knots. "Time and space are only configurations of the mind, easily transcended."

"Okay..." I said, putting my hands on my hips and scanning the area they'd made comfortable for themselves. "We don't have a lake. I hope that's fine."

"Oh no, you do not, but your creek will do nicely." Daphne pointed to a small stream brought on by weeks of rain. Her movement caused the bone charms hanging from her neck to jingle.

"Well, are you ready to meet my coterie?" I asked, eager to see my aunts and Celeste, and to meet Shawna's favorite rescue dog.

"I think it's customary for you to lead the way," Azalea reminded, waiting.

Well, there goes my break from crazy-confusing. I hoped they couldn't read my mind in a way that they'd see what I'd told Olivia about them on the drive home. I quickly scolded myself for thinking about it in front of them, and leapt into a tree. "Follow me," I said, and jumped to the next tree, heading home.

I wasn't sure how they followed me because I hadn't seen them do it, but when I arrived outside my common house, they did too. They all dressed alike now, with animal skin shawls draped over their shoulders. Fern leaves connected to what looked like a string wrapped around their chest and back, under their armpits, and draped down to cover their breasts...mostly. Brown-furred animal skins hung around their waists to their mid-thighs. And yes, they smelled. Not putrid... natural. Earthy, wet-dog, and moss kind of natural.

I was going to ask them if they were ready, but I couldn't be sure what type of answer I'd get, so I escorted them into our common house. A small statue of Freyja stood on a ledge beside the front door and I touched it gently before crossing the threshold. Oh, how good it was to be home.

A little barking dog greeted us, sniffing excitedly at my feet. I bent down to pet it until the rusalki entered behind me. The dog ignored my presence and ran to them, though its barking quieted. Azalea reached down to pick up the white fluff ball and cradled it in her arms.

"Faline!" Aunt Patricia ran to me and wrapped her arms around my neck, holding me in a tight embrace. "You don't know how good it is to see you." She sniffed me and then lifted her head. "What is that smell?"

"Allow me to introduce what's left of the rusalki coven. Azalea, Vernonia, Daphne, and Drosera Moks," I said, stepping aside to make the introductions.

The three Wilds behind me nodded. The rest of my coterie joined us in the tiled entry. I interrupted the early stages of a staring battle. "Let's go to the living room. It's getting tight in here."

"Is it?" Daphne asked. "It feels quite spacious to me."

"It would, compared to your home," I said, leading the group toward the white couches, and realizing I probably didn't want them to sit on the cushions and ruin the fabric.

"We are happy to sit on the floor," Azalea told me, clearly having read my mind. She and her sisters sat where they stood, on the dark wooden floor opposite the couch. Shawna's dog sat in Azalea's lap, a content look on its face.

"The rusalki read minds," I warned my sisters and aunts. "They've also created a little living area on the outskirts of our property so they won't need a room here."

"Well, you are more than welcome to stay wherever you like," Olivia said. She sat on the couch. "But this arrangement works best. The mermaids are on their way, and they weren't specific as to how many were coming."

"Ending the mermaid's life was necessary," Vernonia said.

Awkward silence filled the room.

"I didn't say it wasn't," Olivia muttered.

"No, but you thought it." Azalea seemed completely composed sitting on the floor with her legs folded, petting Shawna's dog.

"Well, yeah, I did. The Wild Women groups haven't come together in over a couple hundred years. Faline makes that happen, gives us hope to not only get our sister, but get our lives back too, and you guys go and kill a key player who's a member of the largest and richest group of Wilds." Olivia scrunched her eyebrows as she spoke, clearly irritated.

"I'm concerned as well," Aunt Patricia added. "Our goal is to fight the Hunters, not one another. I'm not sure how we should approach this topic when they arrive."

"She betrayed her kind," Azalea said.

"Okay," Olivia said. "But did she betray the mermaids and the other Wilds or just the other Wilds? Are the mermaids on board with her? These are things we should know."

Azalea looked up from the white dog and peered at Olivia. "You are not the sister in your family who's plagued with anxiety, yet you exhibit such behavior."

Olivia looked at me and raised her eyebrows with an *are you serious* expression. Azalea did have a point. Normally it was Celeste who fretted over everything, but Celeste sat on a white chair, listening. "Um, no. Not unnecessary anxiety. I'm trying to plan how this is all going to go down. Are we about to fight the mermaids? Because yeah, that possible scenario makes me a little anxious."

"I will explain everything to the mermaids," Azalea said.

"No, that's not the best idea," I chimed in. A plan popped into my head and I ran with it. I motioned toward my coterie. "When they first get here, we will behave normally. The rusalki can read their minds and see if the other mermaids are working with the Hunters, too. If the rusalki don't interrupt us with news that the mermaids are traitors, we'll tell them what happened. I've brought her things to give to them along with our condolences."

"And what if they're *all* working with the Hunters?" Olivia asked me.

"Then we'll tell them something else happened to her and try to get Hunter information from them. It'd help to know how much and what they've shared with the enemy." I spoke while wondering what my sister would say if she knew that I too was sharing information with the enemy.

Azalea's head turned sharply toward me and tilted to the side.

Shit.

I kept talking, hoping Azalea hadn't just read my mind about Marcus. "I don't like being dishonest, but we can't afford the time and casualties in a fight with them when we need to be focusing on saving our sisters and mothers."

Olivia nodded. "Desperate times..."

I waited for Azalea to expose my secret about Marcus. She only raised one corner of her lips. I hoped that meant she agreed with the plan.

Either way, I had to change the subject before she exposed me—a metaphor about a bird leaving its nest or something. "You said the mermaids were on their way?" I asked my Aunt Patricia.

"Yes."

"Are they flying or swimming?" I asked.

"Swimming," Aunt Patricia answered. "At least ten of them, from what I gathered. But like Olivia said, we don't have an exact count."

Azalea stood and the other rusalki followed her lead. She softly placed the dog onto the floor. "We have made one another's acquaintance, and we will now take our leave," she said. "Please summon us the moment the mermaids arrive." The rusalki showed themselves out.

Olivia opened her mouth to speak, but I put a finger over my lips and waited until I could no longer hear their steps outside along the gravel. The moment I lowered my finger, she started in.

"What the hell was that?" Olivia said. "Weirdos."

"Powerful weirdos," I corrected. "They were being nice today, probably respecting our home and territory. But when I showed up at their home they got into my head. The way they keep the Hunters at bay, they check in for their monthly screenings and then get into their minds, make the Hunters think they'd already tested them and that all the rusalki passed the test."

Shawna's white fluff ball of a dog pranced toward me and sat at my

feet, eyeing me with the look of "you know you want to let me up."
And I did want to let it up. I scooped the animal from the floor and
placed it into my lap. "The mermaids are cunning, but they're also into
peace and having an elevated consciousness, so I don't think they'll
come at us with violence once I break the news, if it gets that far,
which it probably will. I don't think the rusalki will find them to be
traitors." But then again, I didn't think Gabrielle was a traitor either.
"And just to be sure, while I explain exactly what happened to
Gabrielle in Maine, the rusalki can read their minds then too."

"So, you're saying the mermaids will be the most civilized group?"
Olivia asked.

"They would have been if a rusalka hadn't killed their sister. Now
I'm just hoping they practice what they preached to me on their island,
about Wild solidarity. The harpies are also civilized, in their own way.
They're emotionless and pretty stuck up. Private. Think of tall, thin,
human-looking owls that stare at you. Oh, and they want to share a
room." I sat the dog on the cushion beside me and padded into the
kitchen to grab a bottle of water from the fridge as I spoke. "The
succubi will be the most difficult to control. They absorb energy and
can manipulate it. They had me on the ground, unable to move at one
point, and then offered a threesome a few minutes later. They're all
over the place."

Celeste's eyes widened at the threesome comment and I shook my
head. I couldn't help but laugh a little. Yes, it was good to be home.
But more importantly, it was good to finally be close to saving Shawna.

I chugged my water and checked my phone. I yearned for a shower
and clean clothes.

I had to take the stairs to my house with Gabrielle's and my
suitcases in tow. I flung my bag on my bed and took a moment to
breathe in the scents of home.

If my mother was still alive and I rescued her, we'd share this tree
home. Would we get along? Would our personalities mesh? I'd always
been resigned to watch mother-daughter relationships from the
outside. Would it ever feel normal to experience from the inside?

TWENTY-FIVE

I STIRRED the chopsticks in circles, entwining the few noodles left in the bowl. Any other night my sunken-in couch would wrap me in comfort almost as much as the terrycloth robe I wore. I'd delight in the sounds of nature echoing through the woods. But this night I sat rigidly on my couch, itching to get out of my robe and into boots and a holster. I dropped the chopsticks and sat my bowl away from me. I hated this. Hated the waiting while Shawna suffered goddess knew what.

"So weird, how it's all spread out like this," a female said from below my tree. Gravel shifted under her feet.

I jumped from the couch and perched on my porch. Finally. Twelve mermaids walked barefoot, wearing thin flowing dresses of different colors, headed for the common house.

"Do they dislike being together?" another said.

"You've met one. Would you like being around her all the time?"

I rolled my eyes. Mermaids.

"They have impeccable hearing," an older mermaid reminded her sisters. Azul.

I took a deep, cleansing breath, and then scaled down my tree trunk to meet the mermaids in front of our common house. "We certainly do have impeccable hearing, Azul," I said. "Welcome. I'm so glad you could come."

Azul offered me a hug and I returned the gesture. "Where will we be staying?" she asked when we parted.

I pointed to the large building. "There are rooms ready for you," I said.

I had them follow me to the common house—twelve mermaids with barely any clothes on, shells woven into their hair in various places and pendants of their finned goddess hanging from their necks. Among the Pacific Northwest's rainy, wet, wintery woods, they stood out like a flock of scarlet tanagers perched on an empty branch in the fall... Or like fish on dry land.

I opened the door to our common house and invited them in with a sweep of my arm. Several of them eyed the ferns that stood in most corners and lush vines that wound from one shelf to the next, filling our walls with greenery. The lack of water had to bother them, but no one said anything.

I made the introductions between the mermaids and my coterie, in which many stiff handshakes were shared. I had a hard time differentiating the mermaids' scents to identify their emotions with all the saltwater seeping from their pores and hair. I waited anxiously for the rusalki to sense the new arrivals and come walking through the front door. They'd told me to summon them, but didn't say how.

"I don't understand," a black-haired, tall mermaid said. She peered around the large living room area. "Where's Gabrielle? Why isn't she greeting us instead?"

I kicked myself for forgetting Gabrielle's bag in my tree home, but then decided maybe it wouldn't have been appropriate to greet them with their passed sister's suitcase in tow.

"Let's go into the kitchen," I said, walking toward the room lined with stainless steel appliances and dark wooden cabinets. "We can sit at the table and discuss the newest turn of events." If you could call it that.

Our common house's kitchen was large and fit a narrow, long, dining table made from an old cedar tree that had fallen in a storm one winter many years ago. Bark still clung to the slightly rounded bottom side of the table, though the top had been sanded flat and lacquered. We'd lacquered the bottom too, but it didn't shine because of the bark. I really hoped a fight didn't break out that would destroy that table. Shawna loved that table.

We rarely had visitors enough to fill the table, but dissecting the great tree seemed sacrilegious. Today our decision proved worthwhile. Only a few younger mermaids had to stand for lack of chairs and table space. It was obvious that they'd left their youngest members at home, and a few of their strongest for protection.

I understood. I appreciated all the help we could get. Though, I couldn't be sure that they'd help us once they found out about Gabrielle.

"Why are we sitting here instead of kissing our sister?" one mermaid asked another. She'd allowed a sprinkling of light orange scales to creep across her forehead from one temple to the other above her eyebrows like a crown.

I peered around for the rusalki. Where were they? They were supposed to be here, reading minds. The mermaids stared at me. One stood from her chair to tower above the sitting huldra, I assumed. Damn it, I had to tell them.

You may, someone spoke into my mind. I looked around the room, but spotted no ruaslki.

Can we trust Azul? I wondered.

They will move forward with you as promised, the voice answered.

Again, she hadn't answered the question I'd asked, but with the mermaids staring at me and tension threating to brew over, I trusted the rusalka.

"Because Gabrielle didn't make it out of Maine," I said.

Azul shot me a hard look. "What does that mean?"

The members of my coterie tensed. The air in the kitchen thickened.

"We tried to visit the rusalki, to enlist their help, but they found Gabrielle unworthy." Bark tingled as it crept up my wrists. I pulled my hands from the tabletop to hide on my lap.

"You're not being clear." The mermaid I'd met in the bathroom, Elaine, hit the table as she spoke with a raised voice. "We're all tired from our travels," she said to her shoal. "Too tired to be jerked around and forced into playing huldra games." Her gaze settled back on me. "It's beyond me why we thought we could trust you with our sister's safety. You couldn't even keep your own sister safe."

I stood in a flash and dug my nails into the wooden table top.

Another mermaid with green scales along the tops of her shoulders pushed her chair out from under her and loomed over the table.

"You want it straight?" I said as I worked to restrain myself. They had every right to be upset, but bringing Shawna into this crossed a line. "Because I wasn't playing games. I was trying to be respectful of the loss of someone I came to call my friend. But if you could give two shits about how the message is given—"

"Loss?" Elaine asked through clenched teeth. A monstrous look flashed through her eyes.

Another mermaid tapped the table and shook her head. "No, no, no," she muttered.

"She was killed," was all I could push through my burning throat before I had to pause and swallow. A chaos of yells and questions filled the room, but I continued. "She was my friend. I tried to protect her, to stop it from happening."

"How dare you wait to tell us now," Elaine seethed.

"I thought you should be told in person," I countered.

Elaine threw her hands up. "I'm done here. I want no part in helping this huldra or her sister."

Azul closed her eyes, inhaled through her nose, opened her eyes, and exhaled through her mouth before she spoke. "As awful as we all feel, I am sure Faline speaks the truth. There is no reason to be cross with her or her coterie." Azul leveled a gaze at Elaine. "And our shoal knows that this is not simply about a missing huldra. We are here for a reason much bigger than one Wild."

"I don't want to stay in this home any longer." Elaine backed away from the table as if she were preparing to leave.

Aunt Patricia placed her hands on the table and spread them out, one in my direction and one in Elaine's. "Death is never an easy thing to discuss. Let's bring this down a notch or two before your coming here defeats the purpose."

Azul chimed in, "I agree."

Elaine and I held an intense stare from across the table. Neither of us sat. Her eyes shifted to my hands and I hid them behind me.

Azul patted Elaine's backside and Elaine sat. A few of the other standing mermaids fell to their chairs as though the lack of a fight left them to collapse in their pain.

I sat, careful to hide my hands beneath the table. I didn't need my bark triggering an already on-edge mermaid. I knew, too well, how quickly travel exhaustion can escalate to defensiveness.

"Please, Faline," Elaine said through tight lips. "Continue in telling us about our fallen sister." Tears slid down her sisters' faces as she spoke. Her own eyes glistened.

"The rusalki read minds," I said. "It's one of their abilities. They caught us on their land, or what they deemed as their territory, and reached into our minds. They said she had been working with the Hunters, and they ended her life for it."

A few soft sobs broke the short stint of shocked silence. Elaine shook her head. Azul folded her hands together and closed her eyes. The mermaid with the scales across her shoulders jumped up and ran from the room, sobbing uncontrollably.

"So the rusalki think they're judge, jury, and executioners of all Wild Women now?" Elaine asked, clearly pissed.

"We think of ourselves as no such thing." Azalea spoke from the kitchen entrance with the living room at her back. Her rusalki sisters stood on each side of her.

I hadn't heard the door open, but maybe they hadn't needed the door.

Daphne explained, "While one's thoughts can be deceiving to themselves, their intentions are powerful and clear, like raindrops, magnifying all."

"Please." Olivia stood and invited the rusalki to the table. "Join us."

The four females with tangled hair, dressed in animal skins and leaves, glided into the kitchen and stood together at an empty end of the table.

"We should have never tried to help." Elaine wiped an angry tear from her eye. "Gabrielle agreed to go with you, to walk beside you, and now you sit here and she doesn't. We should let the Hunters do whatever they will with your sister." Elaine stood and pushed the empty chair toward the table. "I will take no part of this."

Olivia pounded her fist on the table. "Your sister being a traitor does not mean mine deserves to be left for dead." She ground her teeth and her cheeks reddened.

Aunt Abigale buried her face in Shawna's dog who sat on her lap.

"Watch your words, weak huldra. I could slaughter you in my sleep." Elaine seethed.

Olivia stood and swiped her fist above the table, barely missing Elaine. Elaine bared her teeth and hissed. Gold and sapphire scales popped up along her shoulders and down her arms. She reached for Olivia and caught a fistful of hair. Olivia grabbed Elaine's head and wrestled to slam it onto the table.

Two mermaids flanked their sister and reached toward Olivia from across the table, tangling their arms with hers. Celeste growled and jumped onto the table, shoving the mermaids into the wall behind them.

"Stop!" I spread my arms toward the fighting Wild Women. "The Hunters have done this to us. They've turned us against one another. Gabrielle *did* give them our secrets. Maybe it's her fault they were able to successfully take Shawna, and the sisters and mothers of other groups. But she did it for her shoal. What she did was wrong, but we can all understand why she did it."

Olivia scoffed. Aunt Abigale cried softly. A few mermaids muttered complaints to one another.

"The Hunters oppress us," I continued. "They threaten us—cause us to live in fear of thriving, because they live in fear that their control will be stolen. They believe that if we thrive, we'll snuff them out. They want to control our abilities, use what is ours for their own gain."

And that's when a new level of understanding hit me. My rant took an abrupt pause as I stared into nothingness.

"She believes she knows why the Hunters have taken the Wild Women, why they've tried to take them in the past," Daphne explained.

I couldn't find my lips to speak. Anxiety tightened every muscle in my body and bark covered my skin, though I didn't move to hide it. The long ghostly fingers rummaging through my mind bothered me, but not so much that I lost focus. Why? Why would the Hunters want our abilities?

Azalea spoke, "Faline believes the Hunters have taken our sisters and mothers in an effort to claim our abilities as their own. To become what they deem as better versions of us, in male form," Azalea said.

Branches grew from my fingers and I didn't try to stop them.

Olivia gasped. Sounds of shock from Celeste and my aunts quickly followed.

I snapped out of my thoughts and looked down at my hands and feet. Vines wrapped up my calves and branches wound around my fingers like intricate wooden rings.

"You can do this, too," I told my sisters and aunts. "Huldra never ate men. The myths were all stories to make us look like animals set on mayhem, unable to think and out for blood. They were stories propagated by the Hunters so that villagers would be repulsed by us and think we were out to get them. Somehow, my mother knew this. The Hunters wanted us to believe the stories, to be ashamed of our foremothers and fear our abilities, to suppress our strength. And now they want that power for themselves." My mother must have tapped into that strength and been taken for her effort.

Azul's quiet contemplation ended when she raised her voice to address the group. "We are all descendants of high priestesses who were forever changed when their goddesses breathed her life force into them. We should rise as one and crush the Hunters for what they've done to us."

Mermaids gave shouts of agreement. Huldra nodded.

The rusalki stood at the end of the table, staring. Reading minds, no doubt.

"The harpies have landed on your patio," Drosera told me quietly. "And the succubi are driving up your driveway."

The others around us cheered and patted shoulders, as though the fight moments ago had never happened. I figured the rusalki mind tricks had a little something to do with it.

Our patio led into the living room through a large set of doors.

Three tall, lean harpies stood outside the glass doors. Feathers along their bodies ruffled in the wind and talons clicked along the stone tiles. A set of powerful wings protruded from each of their backs.

Olivia ran to open the patio doors, having to tilt her head up to invite the feathered females in. The harpies gave tight smiles, but refused the invitation, unwilling to retract their talons and wings. They peered around the living room with short, controlled head movements.

In my mind, I asked the rusalki if any other mermaids were working with the Hunters.

Yes, one responded. I couldn't tell who answered because the words were without voice, but more like my own musings that I hadn't thought up. *The grey-haired female with the scales of midnight. She will adhere to her promise to you, in her own way.*

I shot a glance to Azul. What a shame, with all of her talk of sisterhood. The mermaids looked up to her. They followed her wisdom and support. I couldn't let the rusalki end her life too. Not yet. Not if she'd lead the other mermaids in helping me to get Shawna. Her punishment must come later.

We will wait for the attack, one of the rusalki said into my mind. *We will force a Hunter to end her life, a most ignoble death compared to the cut of a rusalki, but if you wish.*

I nodded. Either way, Azul would suffer the consequences. The rusalki would make sure of it.

The doorbell rang and Aunt Patricia opened the front door. Marie let herself in without a verbal invitation from my aunt. Five succubi followed their leader into our common house. Marie wore a short, tight black and red striped skirt. Tattoos stretched down her thighs. Her high heels clicked on our hardwood floor. A low-cut, black, tight V-neck top revealed cleavage and nipples pushed through the thin fabric.

I half expected her to bring a male for downtime pleasure, but only succubi flanked her. She looked right and caught Elaine's gaze. Her smile widened. She peered left at the harpies refusing to come in.

"Ugh." Marie groaned. "Your anxiety is leaking into the room. It makes me want to vomit."

Immediately the harpies' talons and wings retracted, no doubt due to the relaxing energy Marie shot their way. Their shoulders eased down as skin replaced feathers and they crossed the threshold into our common house.

"That's better," Marie said, running her fingers through her hair and shooting Elaine a lusty smile.

Elaine twirled a strand of her hair and licked her lips. I quickly made my way to Marie and put my arm around her shoulder, turning her away from Elaine and toward the kitchen.

"Stop making her want you," I whispered under my breath, though I knew most of the females in the room heard me.

"Do you blame me?" she asked with a snicker. She turned and gazed at Elaine. "She's gorgeous, and attracted to me. I'm doing her a service, helping her to let go. The fun we could have..."

"She's taken, in a committed relationship with another mermaid who has stayed in California to care for their daughter...that they share...together," I said.

Marie laughed and patted my arm before she pulled away. "That's cute, but succubi don't believe in committed relationships. We believe in pure, raw energy." She left my side and made her way into the kitchen. So far, no one else had died. I had to count that as a success.

TWENTY-SIX

THE KITCHEN TABLE proved too small for all thirty-one Wilds, as did the living room and patio. After a quick round of introductions my aunts showed our guests to their rooms and invited them to unpack and get some rest. On the way to my personal tree home, in the dark early morning hours, my phone buzzed. A message from Marcus. Once inside the privacy of my home, I opened up my messages.

In two words he confirmed my belief that the Washington Hunters held my sister captive. "She's here," he'd typed. I scoured those words for additional meaning, wishing he'd included which building I'd find her in, or if she was hurt. The day I'd asked for help in finding my sister, John had told me each complex is highly trained in dealing with the Wild Women they're supposed to handle, so I was certain the "she" Marcus referred to was Shawna.

He also included a rough drawing of the complex. I downloaded the drawing to my phone and pulled up the coordinates on a Google Earth app to compare the two. I'd been there plenty of times, but only to the main building and only from the front gate. Never had I seen it from an aerial view. The tops of evergreens blanketed my screen in a deep emerald green, but lines of brown walking paths and rooftops peeked through. My kind could use those trees to our advantage. A river ran alongside the complex, but farther than I would have liked. Still, other Wilds could make use of it. I took a screenshot and sent it along with the drawing to every Wild on my property whose contact information I had saved in my phone.

I ached with need to call my coterie members, wake them up, and tell them Shawna is alive, and so very close to us. I didn't, though, because I couldn't for the life of me think of an excuse as to how I came by that information—one that didn't involve an alignment with a Hunter. It wouldn't be a tidbit I could attribute to my bounty hunter connections like I planned to use for an explanation as to how I got the hand-drawn map of the complex.

We'd decided to reconvene in the woods behind our tree homes an hour after sunrise, to give everyone a chance to catch some shut-eye. I figured each group would use a bit of that time to privately go over the maps before meeting up. I neither slept nor discussed the map with my coterie. Knowing Shawna was so close and alive kept me on edge; picturing her in a cell underneath the main complex building didn't help.

After the kitchen incident, though, I'd mentally prepared for the regathering to result in more arguments. But as the sun barely hung in the sky, everyone seemed to have calmed down enough to listen intently as I announced we'd attack the local Hunter complex the day of the huldra check-in—a week and a half away. It tortured me to wait that long. While the Hunters might not be killing our kind, they weren't exactly having them over for tea either. But we had no choice. We couldn't get in until then, and if we couldn't get in, we couldn't rescue anyone. An all-out siege on the complex would only end in more of us dead.

I assured the Wilds that as the date approached we'd create a more solid and detailed plan, but first we should train and assess each group's strengths and weaknesses. What I left out was the tidbit about collecting intel from Marcus that'd help me to strategize better. Not that the Wilds noticed much; they seemed more eager to flex their abilities than to plot tactics, though a few did thank me for sending the map screenshots. Other than the mermaids, they each had a loved one depending on them for rescue—learning to use their Wild abilities was their only hope of overpowering the Hunters, who'd had years of training and experience.

As the day wore on, my heart-broken Aunt Abigail stood back and watched the other Wilds practice hard, take direction, and try again… except for the rusalki, who kept away from the group, watching, listening, and probably reading minds. They garnered a few puzzled stares from the mermaids and succubi, though the harpies seemed unfazed by the rusalki's oddness.

"Like this?" Olivia stood with legs parted and bare feet crunching the dead leaves. She separated her fingers and light patches of bark grew up her arm. "Why can't I grow branches?" she asked, shaking her hands.

"I wasn't able to until I had my first kill," I said. "But according to Gabrielle, that's not what caused my body to remember the dormant ability." I'd thought of taking my group on a bounty hunter outing to access their abilities about three times since we'd started training. Each time I'd decided against it. We had too many witnesses on our property at the moment. Plus, it was illegal.

"Then what's. It. Caused by?" Olivia asked between ragged gasps. She'd been practicing hand-to-hand combat with a mermaid who'd clearly gone against a few sharks and won.

"She said it's because I had stood in my strength, fought back," I explained.

Olivia groaned. She stopped training and put her hands on her hips, using the opportunity to catch her breath. "So, what, I'm not going to get lifesaving abilities until after I go up against a bunch of people who want to kill me? Yeah, I can see that going real well in my favor." She adjusted her dark blue yoga pants and loose cotton top. "Sounds counterproductive, if you ask me."

I could ask Marcus out to the property to train my coterie and help them access their powers, but bringing him to my home, with thirty other Wilds… No, it wouldn't go over well. And anyway, other than the map email, I hadn't spoken to him since he'd called the night before to tell me that he'd returned to the fold. And that he'd seen Clarisse at the complex, but she was a problem for another day.

"I'm no huldra," Azul said as she walked away from the others to join Olivia and me. "But if you go into the complex full of confidence and a couple moves at the ready, you'll light that spark inside of you."

"Just drug me and I'll wake up when it's over with a few Hunter's bodies at my feet like Faline." Olivia pulled her hair into a ponytail. Sweat glistened from her temples.

Azul's eyes widened and she shot me a glance while my sister wasn't looking. I only stared—didn't confirm or deny. I hadn't mentioned my abilities' origins to any of the groups and I had no intention to share the story now.

"Gabrielle is...was," Azul corrected herself with a slight shake of her head, "a better teacher than me at these sorts of things. But I'll give it a go."

I wondered how long the two of them, Gabrielle and Azul, had been working with the Hunters. And what had started the unnatural relationship. I also wondered if any mermaids left on the island knew their secret and had joined them in their risky dealings. Thankfully, the rusalki were keeping a mental eye on the mermaids we currently dealt with.

"Your greatest strength is in the legs," Azul explained to Olivia. "Use it. Crouch down and kick me with everything you have. Swipe my legs out from under me. Try to land a foot in my gut to knock me down. Once you have the Hunter on the ground, you've got more options at your disposal."

Azul evened her footing for balance. Olivia crouched before jumping up and using the momentum to jab a foot into Azul's stomach, though it didn't make contact. Azul quickly bounced out of the way, allowing Olivia to lose balance and fall forward into the dirt and leaves. Olivia huffed as she stood and brushed the dirt from her jeans.

"You didn't tell me I'd have to catch a moving target," she complained.

"Hunters are not stupid. They won't stand around, waiting for you to knock bruises into them." Azul got into position.

Olivia thrust her foot out again toward Azul's stomach, but again, Azul jumped to the side causing Olivia's foot to only swipe at air. This time, though, Olivia didn't lose her balance. She swung around, crouched, extended her leg lower, toward the ground, and knocked Azul's feet from under her.

"Perfect!" I yelled before leaving the two to visit with Celeste, who leaned on a nearby tree. A large fern glistened with rain drops beside her legs. I bent down to touch the wet leaves.

"I can't do this," Celeste said before I opened my mouth. "There's so many variables, most all of them with outcomes that are not in our favor. Statistically, we'll lose."

"Is that your logical mind talking or is it your fearful mind?" I asked. "Because sometimes they sound the same in our heads."

"Aunt Abigale isn't training. She knows there's no hope." Celeste watched our other coterie members practice. She wrapped her beige sweater shawl around herself.

"She doesn't *know*. She's scared shitless. And who can blame her? She's not scared of how well she'll be able to protect herself. Her daughter was taken by the same organization who taught us to not only fear them but to fear ourselves and what we were created to do." I put my arm around my sister's shoulder. "Fight your fears. Combat those who put that fear in you. I promise, once you overcome those who want to dominate you, you'll overcome your fear of them."

I peered up at the great evergreens towering high above us. A harpy swooped down from the branches and knocked a mermaid on her ass before flying away just as quickly as she came. "That was great!" the mermaid yelled as she grabbed a handful of dried pine needles and threw them in the harpy's direction. "I didn't see you coming!"

I never imagined such a scene would ever play out in my lifetime. A rusalka and a succubus stood ten feet from one another, staring, probably trying to out-maneuver each other—the rusalka getting into the mind of her opponent and the succubus shifting the energy around hers. Harpies pretended surprise attacks on mermaids. A grin pulled at my lips until my face hurt. If Shawna could see us now. She would, very soon.

As the day wore on, though, excitement wore off and irritation took its place. Dark clouds loomed in the evening sky. Rain drenched our hair and dribbled down our faces. The mermaids' skin drank in each drop of water, so while we wiped our eyes and wrung our clothing, the mermaids practiced undisturbed.

"I'm only saying there's a river near the complex, it'd be best for us to attack from that direction, swim up the river and surprise them," a mermaid said as she absently pinned a harpy to a tree. "I don't know why that's so hard for you to grasp."

"Oh, I can grasp it all right, but that doesn't give the idea any credence," Aunt Patricia responded sharply. "The river is nowhere near the complex. That leaves us down twelve females who could be fighting alongside us from the moment we enter."

"How about we call it a night?" I announced, interrupting the disagreement between the huldra and the mermaid. "Maybe over dinner we can discuss the strengths and weaknesses we discovered during training and come up with possible plans of attack." I'd never organized gatherings like this. That was Shawna's forte. So it only just occurred to me that the huldra shouldn't have to do the all cooking and cleaning up. "Since we'll be doing this for a week and a half, we should also come up with a schedule for cooking meals and training."

Wilds nodded, glad to be done for the day. They brushed dirt, leaves, and other debris from their clothing as they came closer. Harpies perched on evergreen branches. Rusalki sat on the soft moss growing along a fallen log, out away from the group. Some succubi stood in the center of the group while others sat. The more vocal mermaids sat in the center while the stoic ones paced the outlying area. Aunt Abigale leaned against a tree and petted Shawna's dog, while the rest of my coterie took part in the discussion. Celeste stood quietly beside me.

But before I could think of a suggested schedule, another mermaid joined the river argument. "The harpies probably won't be walking into the complex with you," she pointed out.

Aunt Patricia furrowed her brows and spoke slowly. "They can fly directly to the Hunters. You can't swim right up to the Hunters. The distance between the main complex and the river shows that your idea isn't feasible."

A few Wilds pulled their smart phones from their back pockets to examine the maps, as did I. The Hunters' main training building also housed our "classroom" and monthly check-in area. I'd never been given the opportunity to walk the grounds, but according to the map, smaller structures scattered the property connected by pathways extending out from the main building. What looked like a large home with a porch stood off to the side of the property, away from the circle of buildings. None of them, however, were remotely near the river.

"Do you mind?" the mermaid asked, holding her hand out for the nearest phone, which happened to be mine. "I left mine in the house."

"Sure, here," I said.

"See." The mermaid tilted the screen toward my aunt and pressed her fingers to zoom in on the map to show the distance between the river and the main training building.

For a short second no one spoke as a few Wilds, including my aunt, gazed at what the mermaid wanted them to see. And in that short second, my phone let out a screech. A certain type of sound that I'd programmed to alert me of bad news. The members of my coterie all jerked their heads to me. I stared at my phone.

"Um, it says you got an email," the mermaid said, handing the phone to me.

I absently accepted the device, but didn't look at the screen. I knew who it was from. The warning sound from the desktop computer in the common house sounded, and those of us with heightened hearing abilities turned toward the house despite our inability to see through the trees.

I addressed the crowd of Wild Women. "It's an email...from the Hunters."

I looked down and swiped at my phone's screen. We had a special email account only for their correspondence. It didn't used to be this way. Before the internet, because they weren't allowed to know our names or where we lived, we had no communication with them other than our monthly screenings. But now we were at their beck and call through the advances of technology. I hoped to soon use technology to our advantage, starting with the map of their complex on our smart phones.

I opened the email and sighed. The note shouldn't have shocked me, though it did. They knew about me. They knew what I'd done the night I'd blacked out. They may have even known what I'd done on the mermaids' island.

"It's a summons," I announced.

Wilds gasped, but I couldn't pull my eyes from the screen to see which Wilds.

"I am to report to the complex tomorrow morning, by myself, for a *random* screening." Random, my ass. "I'll fail and they know it." They had me where they wanted me.

"But we still have another week of training and planning before we're ready," Azul said.

"They want to dispose of her before we're able to dispose of them," Aunt Patricia said.

She was right. The punishment for killing a human or a Hunter was death. And from the dark bark patch on my back, it was obvious I'd killed since my last check-in. While I'd been able to take down two Hunters on the mermaid's island, there was no possible way I could fight off a whole complex of them by myself.

I peered past the Wilds to the evergreens behind them. How could I be sure there weren't Hunters right now, on our property, watching us? Azalea caught my eye with a shake of her head as she stared straight at me. I'd forgotten about the powerful Wilds from Maine. Who knew a rusalka's presence could bring me such comfort? There was a first for everything, I supposed.

You all are, she spoke into my mind.

She had a point. We each were powerful in our own right, however deep those powers were currently buried.

I'd gone through so much to bring these females together, to align them. They'd traveled so far. We were supposed to organize a proper attack, and those take time and a lot of strategy, not one night of training and a couple of crap ideas thrown out there. If they followed me to the complex in the morning, they'd be annihilated. I'd brought all the American Wild Women together to be slaughtered in one fell swoop. I might as well have handed our kind to the Hunters on a silver platter and said bon appetite.

These women came to help with hopes that rescuing Shawna would lead to the rescue of their own loved ones. And now, without the proper training and planning, all they could do for me was die. I refused to ask that of them. Dying wouldn't return Shawna to my life. It wouldn't help my mother or the others, and if any survived, they'd hate the huldra with everything in them. If I survived and this went badly, I was damning my daughter and my nieces. Shit, maybe I was placing a big red target on all huldra throughout the world.

I wasn't sure if I'd regret it later, but I shot Marcus a quick, nondescript text asking if he'd heard anything new, if I should be on the lookout for anything. I waited a few seconds, still racking my brain for my next step as though it would magically appear to me moments after plowing into a roadblock.

I looked up from the cell phone and addressed my guests. "You should all stay and train, and continue on as planned, attack the complex during the regularly scheduled huldra check-in. I'll enter their complex tomorrow morning and if they choose to hold me, for whatever reason they're abducting Wilds, then I'll hopefully be reunited with Shawna and be waiting to help from within when you attack. If they try to kill me for failing my check-in I won't go down without a fight. I'll try to thin their ranks as best as I can."

"No," Olivia exclaimed. She walked to the other members of my coterie and stood beside them. "We're not going to let the Hunters take another member of our coterie. We walk into the complex together, or we don't walk in at all."

I forced myself to smile. Out of every Wild Woman in these woods tonight, my sisters and aunts were probably the least prepared to go up against the Hunters. We hadn't had a cattle prod pressed against us or mastered the art of controlling the energy of another. We hadn't lived a life of freedom on an island or learned how to control minds. My sisters and aunts still had an inner huldra waiting to come out. And if their experience would be anything like mine had been, their transition and learning to work with their huldra would take time, guidance, and practice. Three luxuries they no longer had at their disposal.

"They are huldra, Faline. You are huldra." Vernonia of the rusalki stepped forward to join the group. Her coven had been hovering at the group's edges, watching. Her brown hair fluttered gently in the breeze. "Huldra were the Wild Women's first protectors." She addressed the crowd of females. "They have a mind for strategy, for survival, for engaging and subduing the enemy."

The sensation of ghostly fingers massaging my scalp came on strong and I wanted to sit to enjoy the pleasure more fully. I caught Vernonia's eyes. She gave a slight grin and continued working her magic. My brow unfurrowed and my forehead relaxed.

I knew the rusalka was placing these thoughts of confidence in my coterie's and my minds, but the belief grew in my heart where the rusalka could not penetrate.

"What time did the email say you're to report to their complex?" Aunt Patricia asked, unknowingly pulling those ghostly fingers from my mind and snapping me into the stark reality of the moment.

I blinked a few times before answering. "Seven in the morning."

"Is she not the Mother of War?" Vernonia asked, changing her focus to a cluster of mermaids. "Should we not follow her into battle?"

"No, you shouldn't," I said.

Aunt Patricia wrapped her arm around my shoulder and leaned in until our temples touched. "This coterie has always made decisions based on what's best for the group, not the individual. Losing your mother felt as though someone hacked off an arm from the body of our group. Losing you and Shawna would kill us. Not to mention it was you who brought all these Wilds together, and without you I suspect this will all fall apart."

My aunt pulled away and addressed our guests. "If Faline is to lead us in recovering our abducted Wild Women and overthrowing the Hunters, her death will only stop the revolution before it's begun. The mermaid's wise woman spoke of Faline for a reason. We can't just hand her over to the enemy." When a few Wilds nodded their heads, my aunt continued, "The Hunter's complex is about a thirty-minute drive from here. Those who decide they want to join us, we'll be leaving at six-fifteen."

"I fully trust the premonitions of our late wise woman. We will join you," Azul said. She flashed deep blue scales across her chest and allowed them to fade into her tan skin. "But we will enter the property by way of the river."

We didn't have time to argue anymore. Aunt Patricia nodded. "As long as you're able to get to the complex in time to help us overtake the Hunters."

"We will fly in," Eonza of the harpy flock called out. "We have not yet learned our siren's call, as Gabrielle had promised to teach us, but we are still strong and our talons can do much damage."

The rusalki coven and the succubi galere said nothing.

"Thank you," I said to Azul and Eonza once I relocated my voice. "We appreciate your bravery."

Aunt Patricia closed her eyes and rubbed her temples. When she opened them again she wove her arm through mine. "We must go petition to Freyja for wisdom and strength in battle, and for victory. I suggest you all pray to your goddesses as well."

* * *

The members of my coterie stood around a fire pit lined with river stones behind our common house. Aunt Patricia opened an old splintered box and removed Norse bracelets, one for each of us with one remaining in the box. Each silver bracelet twisted in on itself with braids and a growling wolf's head at the two ends.

The glow from the fire danced along my sisters' and aunts' faces in the night. We wore only the bracelets.

We rarely petitioned Freyja in such a manner. And we'd never come to her as warrior daughters. Yet, it felt natural, as though my soul had memories of similar rituals, hidden deep within my cells.

Power filled the space as we passed a dagger around the circle. Aunt Patricia made a small cut in the palm of her left hand and squeezed to drip a few drops of blood into a copper basin. Each of us followed her lead until Aunt Abigale joined her blood with ours. She then swirled the basin and passed it back around the circle. I held the copper basin with my left hand and dipped my right finger into the blood mixture of my coterie. In this way, we were connected, that we may live by blood or die by blood, Freyja's choice.

The ritual called for complete focus on our intentions. No one spoke. Not until we called to Freyja.

With my pointer finger, I smeared blood onto the wolf-head bracelet and whispered a prayer, verbalizing my intentions. "Goddess of life and death, of war and peace, please be with me as I fight for your honor."

I passed the basin to my right and heard the intentions of my sisters and aunts spoken into the night, to our goddess.

Pride in my species filled me. We were each a link in our circular chain, praying to the goddess who created the huldra, who made us who we are.

Once the basin made its way around the circle, silence filled the area again and we gazed into the dancing flames. My heart moved me to speak. "We pray to Freyja, who gifted us her abilities to root ourselves into the ground, forces to be reckoned with, unable to be pushed over, like the great and mighty evergreen. She gave us their strengths as assets in battle. The trees have always protected the living as we are meant to protect our Wild sisters." I paused and watched wisps of fire like orange silk dance in the wind. "Embrace who she created you to be. Your natural self, your wild self. Release the lies we've been told. We are not weak. We are not evil. We are not monsters. We protect the innocent and the defenseless." I raised my chin and my sisters and aunts met my gaze. "For this we were created and in this will we thrive."

The power in the clearing where we stood vibrated like a tuning fork. I felt something in my coterie members relax, unleash. Smiles beamed from my fellow huldra. Bark grew across their naked skin, originating at their lower backs and embracing their stomachs, stretching north and south.

"Goddess, it's almost as good as an orgasm," Olivia gasped.

I let out a light laugh and watched the others experience what I'd only recently learned about myself. Aunt Patricia reached her arm out in front of her and turned it from side to side. "It looks so thick, so impenetrable," she said. "I'd heard stories as a little girl, but seeing and feeling is certainly believing."

I peered down at myself. I'd never tire of seeing nature's decorations along my skin. "There's strength and power in standing in who you were created to be."

"Hunters have been trying to push us over for years," Olivia stated with awe.

I smiled. "Tomorrow, we push back."

TWENTY-SEVEN

ONLY THE SUCCUBI galere drove to our meeting point near the Hunter's compound. The other Wilds traveled by their own unique form of transportation. The harpies flew. The mermaids swam via the river that led to and through the complex grounds. The rusalki did... whatever they did to get from one place to another in an instant. My huldra coterie tree-jumped through our woods, and then ran and tree-jumped the rest of the way to the Hunter's property.

We met up at 6:45 in the morning behind a gas station a quarter of a mile from the Hunter's compound. There were no homes or businesses between the gas station and the complex; if someone did see us they'd likely be connected to the Hunters. We lacked the time to plan or train, so surprise was our biggest weapon.

The gas station held very few items inside, scattered along broken shelves. Cobwebs covered each window corner. Moss grew across the porous red bricks in shaded areas behind the building. Flattened boxes littered the ground, the cardboard soaked through and mushy from the constant drizzle of rain.

The sun crested the landscape and barely lit the sky behind thick grey clouds. An old streetlight hummed at the front of the building, leaving the back area covered in darkness.

Olivia held her nose from the stench of the rotting building and nearby dumpster as we stood under the overhang and waited for the other groups to arrive. The other huldras enjoyed the light rain on their heads and face, but I had to appear as though I'd just walked out of the house to my car and from my car to the complex. I didn't want to raise suspicion among the Hunters too early—as in, the moment I walked in for the "random" screening.

The rusalki exited the nearby treeline where the parking lot met the forest. They wore their regular animal skins and fern leaf attire, with the added decoration of mud smeared on every inch of exposed skin.

"It is a tribute to our goddess," Azalea said, reading my mind and answering my unspoken question.

"And a tactic to insight fear," her sister Drosera said in a wispy voice. Her auburn hair looked as though she'd brushed it with a handful of twigs. In fact, maybe she had because a small twig stuck out from the top of her head.

It occurred to me that the majority of the Hunters in my region had probably only seen huldra in real life and had never experienced other Wilds aside from pictures. In this, we had one up on them.

Eonza and the other harpies landed on the pavement, their talons gripping the crumbling surface. Eonza's golden wings flapped silently as she made contact with the earth. The harpies wore their specially made shirts with open backs. Eonza's was white. I wanted to crack a joke about leaving the Hunters' complex today with a red shirt instead of a white one, but nothing about her led me to believe she's the joking type. Neither she nor her sisters pulled their wings or talons in. They waited in a huddle, peeking from their circle with jerky movements to eye each noise.

One by one the succubi filed out of my aunt's crossover until only Marie was left in the driver's seat. I'd insisted they drive our car, not theirs, because their Oregon plates could raise suspicion. Especially because the crossover was the vehicle I'd use to drive onto the complex.

"I take it back," Marie said as she jumped from the car and closed the door behind her. "It handles better than I thought." She joined me below the rotting awning and dropped the keys into my hand.

The succubi all wore their own variation of ripped jeans, fitted tattoo-exposing tops, and interesting hair styles.

"You sure you don't need a ride there?" Marie joked.

"I'm sure." I eyed her. "You'll be able to restrain them the way you did me, right? Make them crumpled, powerless heaps on the floor?"

Marie's smile widened, but she didn't break eye contact. Olivia yelped from the parking lot before hitting the pavement as though her spine melted within her.

"Knock it off, Marie," I said, shoving the succubus. "I didn't ask for a demonstration."

Marie's smile didn't waver. She turned slightly to see what I'd been watching. Olivia caught her breath and stood, wiping the dirt from her jeans. She smoothed her hair and pretended to reach out and strangle Marie. Marie didn't seem to take offense.

"You'd better be careful," I said to the succubi leader, who still beamed with accomplishment. "When she learns to bring out her vines and branches, she *will* be able to strangle you from five feet away."

"When do we leave?" Eonza asked, peeking her head from the harpy circle. They reminded me of three birds, huddled together for warmth, with only one poking their head out from time to time to verify the safety of their surroundings.

I checked the clock on my phone and hoped to see a text response from Marcus. Nothing.

"I'm leaving in a couple minutes," I announced. I knew harpies had hearing similar to mine, but I wasn't sure about the succubi or the rusalki. Though, the rusalki knew my words before I spoke them, so hearing wasn't much of an issue.

"Remember the map of the compound," I said, raising my voice a little louder for the succubi. "The river is to the right of the cluster of buildings as you look at it from the front gate, to the west on the map. When my coterie hears scuffling from inside the building they'll know I've begun and will alert the succubi and harpies nearby. They'll then howl to signal to the mermaids to come out of the river and join us at the building. They'll come out from the woods to the left of the complex, or east on the map. You'll all need to come in hard and fast, because I'll already be in the main building, and if you're seen, they may lock me in and lock you out. Going up against ten Hunters at the same time on my own does not sound like a picnic."

Olivia joined me under the awning and wrapped her arm around my shoulder. Celeste followed and stood on the opposite side of me. I missed the old Celeste, the bossy sister who seemed to know everything. She'd become a quiet, anxious person since Shawna's abduction. Clearly, it had rocked her foundation.

I had to leave in a minute and all I could think to do was look around the parking lot at the females preparing to go to battle. While I knew how many Wild Women were entering the compound behind me, I wondered how many of us would survive to exit the compound when this was all over.

A speech bubbled up inside of me. "We deserve freedom. Freedom to use our goddess-given abilities for good. Freedom from painful and invasive tests or scans. The freedom to raise our daughters in peace without fear of angering the Hunters by their mere existence." I paused and swallowed down the fears pulsing through me. What if I was about to enter an ambush? What if they somehow coerced Marcus to reveal that I was likely bringing backup? What if this was the last time I'd see my sisters and aunts? What if we weren't able to get Shawna out of there?

I kissed my sisters and made my way to Aunt Patricia's car. My three aunts showered me with hugs and kisses before I got into the driver's seat.

"We're so proud of you," Aunt Patricia whispered.

"Your mother will be proud, too, when she hears of what her daughter achieved this day and all the days leading up to this one." Aunt Renee placed a warm kiss on my forehead.

"Please," Aunt Abigale said with a hoarse whisper. "Be safe."

Aunt Patricia shut the door and I turned the engine on.

* * *

When I pulled onto the property, everything seemed normal. Except me; I was different. The rows of large evergreens lining the long driveway seemed angry, more glowering than before. The set of wrought iron gates seemed smaller. The compound didn't seem so hidden. It felt within reach—vulnerable even.

I pressed the call button on the key pad at the gate. A camera focused on me and adjusted to look inside the car. I wouldn't say that I was alone, but there was certainly nobody in my car. That night on the mermaid's island flashed into my mind and I wondered if the camera being used also sensed body temperature. Obviously, our little trick of lowering our temperature to remain unseen by their thermal imaging cameras was something Gabrielle and Azul failed to mention to the Hunters when they were acting as double agents. Probably because it concerned them and their ability to protect themselves. I made a mental note to ask the rusalki if the Hunter attack on the mermaids had been staged for my benefit.

The iron gates, with their ornate tops that bent and curved to form dagger shapes as though the blade tip would pierce the sky, swung open. I took the car out of park, rolling forward. I parked in the "Reserved" spot closest to the training building's doors.

The main building looked a lot like the churches that meet in a big square warehouse. I only know this because once I chased a skip into his church and arrested him in the middle of the service. It had been a glorious day, indeed. The congregants weren't singing my praises, but Marcus certainly did when I dropped the slippery skip off at the jail.

Marcus.

I peered around the grounds for any sight of him. Nothing. In fact, barely anyone lingered about on the cement walking paths or in the grassy areas. Only one woman in a long skirt quickly skittered from the side of the main building and out to a cabin. Her hair swung as she turned mid-run to look at me. Clarisse.

Maybe I'd get lucky and take her with me. Dale would probably give me a bonus for catching the infamous human trafficker. I double-checked that the daggers were safely in my boots. My heart pounded as I exited my aunt's car. Yes, I was afraid. I was preparing to stand up and challenge the biggest, baddest bully my kind had ever experienced, on his turf, with an army backing him. Which "him" didn't matter.

They were all "him," all trained to hate my kind. And in my mind, they all held my sister hostage. Every. Last. One. Of. Them.

The fear pulsing through me melted away, replaced by anger. I wanted to don my bark and go all huldra on their asses.

Cameras at the corners of the square building and right above the door repositioned on me. One of the double doors swung open to reveal a Hunter with broad shoulders and biceps so meaty the sleeves on his black shirt protested with each stretch. His facial expression barely registered that he'd seen me.

Normally I would have made a joke about the horrible service, but I wasn't there to defuse tensions. I was there to escalate tensions. And I was pissed. A few more steps into the space narrowed by fencing and the metal detector screamed. I raised my arms and stood perfectly still as four Hunters knocked me to the ground.

TWENTY-EIGHT

IT WASN'T time to put up a fight. The Hunters needed to see that I had no desire to cause any more difficulties for myself. That I had no idea my closest friend and sister was somewhere on this property.

No. I pretended to be the oblivious huldra they thought I was—the nearest human-like species to an animal, only evil.

One Hunter straddled me as the others gave me the pat-down. I inhaled deeply, set on memorizing their scents and giving them my own brand of pat-down later. It would include vines and branches and maybe a puncture wound or four. Especially the one who sat on top of me, using his weight to push my hips into the cement.

Intense, pungent fear wafted around the youngest Hunter with blond, patchy facial hair. My skin vibrated with eagerness. I'd never given much credence to breathing techniques, but now I counted my breaths, my lungs filling and emptying in a decidedly slow rhythm. My racing heart slowed enough to keep my bark under wraps. I had to bide my time. Two Hunters hurried to pull my boots off, remembering the reason behind the metal detector going off during my last visit. A group of men dressed in black formed a circle around us.

My right boot came off first and my dagger fell out, hitting the grey, painted cement floor with a clang. Within seconds my left boot gave the same reward to the struggling Hunter who'd assigned himself to its removal. A few older Hunters in the crowd chuckled at my stupidity in trying to bring daggers into their complex twice in one month.

One made a snide remark to the man beside him about loaning me his dagger and he'd still smoke me. I couldn't help but smile. I'd get my daggers back, both of them, and then use those and my more natural weapons to in turn smoke *his* ass. The enthusiastic boot-tuggers would also get some of my attention when the time came.

"Get her up!" John shouted from behind the circle of males. The greying Hunter stepped forward.

I made it to my feet, glad to be rid of my boots. The branches and vines from my fingers were a given, but now I could also grow them from my sockless toes.

"Wipe that smile off your face," John commanded with a tone of disgust. So this was the real male hidden behind the veneer of kindness he'd previously displayed. "Where's the..." He snapped his fingers. He didn't have to finish before a younger Hunter handed him an electronic tablet. "I need the letters bigger."

The younger man did as he was told.

"ID number?" John barked as he stared at the screen. He led me into the classroom as he spoke. I assumed my summons had to do with my recent "disobedient" activities, that somehow John had been tipped off. His icy behavior and disregard for following the usual check-in procedures worked as confirmations.

I unbuttoned my jeans and immediately the bearded Hunter holding me yanked the side of my pants down. "Damn it," he mumbled. "Why the hell would you decorate your abomination number?" He squatted to get a closer look. "I see an eight and some zeros, maybe a two. With all the vines, it's hard to tell."

I listened to the noises around me, took in the scents and found one scent I knew very well.

In the crowd of men watching from outside the open classroom door stood Marcus. I caught his eye, but he gave me no smile, no wink, no affirmation that he was still on my side. The man who had previously made my heart thrum stood rigidly in the same black

Hunter regalia as the others, who were seconds away from seeing the death warrant of dark bark on the small of my back. A knot rolled in my stomach and I bent forward to vomit from disgust at the sight of that uniform.

Through my dry-heaving, I looked up for a brief moment and noticed Marcus slinking to the outskirts of the crowd.

John snapped his fingers again. "Inspect its back."

I sprang into action and shoved the bearded male. He landed on his butt and I quickly buttoned my jeans. He scrambled to get away from me, crab walking in the process.

John dropped the tablet and lunged for me. I grabbed my daggers from a plastic bin beside the metal detector and raced for the doors to signal my sisters.

Marcus called out my name. I swung to find him in the crowd as he ran to a screen on the wall nearest to him and pressed a few buttons. Darkness cloaked the room. It was something he and I had discussed during our night in the motel room, the fact that every known Wild Woman had night vision to one degree or another, a handy ability the Hunters wished they could possess. Marcus had suggested "misplacing" the infrared goggles kept in the main building as part of his plan.

"Get the power on! Where are the damn night goggles!" John barked orders. He grabbed the tablet from the floor and shoved the device out in front of him, using the shattered backlit screen as a flashlight.

I used it as a beacon like a ship drawn to a lighthouse. I brought my hands out in front of me and willed vines to sprout from my fingertips. I flicked my left hand and the vines whipped the device from his fingers, leaving him in darkness. Fitting. I turned my right wrist and willed the vines to wrap themselves around his neck. His artery pulsed under my thick, brownish-green vines.

Power surged through me as his barking orders turned to choking gasps. I pulled him to me and whispered into his ear. "Where's my sister? Where is Shawna?"

The other Hunters were shouting commands to one another, hurrying about to get the lights back on and secure the proper night vision and defense tools.

"You finally show your true colors," John wheezed.

"As have you."

"Evil. You're all evil," he coughed out.

"See now, your brain must be on the fritz. Losing oxygen will do that to you. Because that's not what I asked," I said.

"Die, demon bitch," he wheezed.

"Oh, don't worry. The demon bitches will be here soon enough." I had been hoping for answers, but his comment assured me he wouldn't be supplying any. I flexed my hand. My vines tightened and doubled around his neck. He patted his pants for his dagger and found it. His trachea crushed beneath my vines. The dagger he held clanged to the floor right before his heart stopped beating and he fell in a rumpled heap.

Olivia burst through the doors first and ran into a crowd of Hunters focused on pulling goggles from a recently opened container on the ground. Light streamed through the open doors behind her as they slowly eased shut. She was met with male screams as she tore through the group.

I stood in awe of my sister's viciousness.

"Where. Is. My. Sister?" she screamed as she used her huldra strength and speed to shove the preoccupied Hunters and throw them to the cement.

The rest of my coterie followed her, allowing light into the room and giving the Hunters an upper hand, seeing as they hadn't yet procured their infrareds. I rushed toward the doors to shut them quickly, but before I could, the harpies landed on the cement slab outside, calmly walked in, and shut the doors behind them.

Their strong wings flapped, shifting the air in the room. A young Hunter yelled out, "What was that?" as talons dragged across the floor. Another commanded the men to fall into formation and ready their daggers.

One male kept his dagger at the ready, but without goggles he had no way to see her coming until he felt her presence too late to protect himself. Eonza kicked him in the stomach. Her talons bore deep into his midsection. When she pulled away, blood covered her foot and she lost her balance, sliding across the smooth cement. The Hunter she'd kicked was dead, but another in formation swung his dagger through the air and made purchase into her arm.

Eonza cried out and within seconds her two sisters were by her side, tearing her attacker to shreds.

A Hunter caught my right arm and jerked me backwards. I spun on my heel and raised my dagger into the air, set on plummeting it into his skull.

"Faline, stop! It's me."

I blinked. Marcus, night vision goggles covering his eyes, held my arm.

"Come on," he said. "I disabled the power and jammed their closed network. They had us put our phones in a lock box before coming in here, so now no one can take video or call for help. I've disabled the security cameras and most of the automatic locks by adjusting their timers. But I'm not the only techy on the grounds, so everything I've done can be reversed in a matter of minutes. Let's go find your sister while we still can."

"The others haven't arrived. I won't leave them to fight my battle," I said.

"I can't control myself much longer," he groaned. "The Wild Women in their Wild form. You know it triggers the Hunter in us." Hunters grew swollen before my eyes, their muscles thickened and pulled tighter. It was so slight, though, that I hadn't noticed until Marcus mentioned it.

Marcus let go of my arm and swung around me, putting me at his back. I quickly righted my stance and stood at his side. He unsheathed his Hunter's dagger and shoved it into a fellow hunter before the other Hunter's blade could stab me. Blood hit my face and arms.

Power surged through me. My heartbeat vibrated.

Marcus peered in my direction as the male fell to the floor. "You okay?" he asked softly.

I gave one short nod. Bark covered my skin, surfacing like a submarine exploding from the water. Green leafy vines crawled up and wound around my calves, making my tight jeans feel tighter.

Marie led her group of succubi as they burst into the room, yet again allowing the Hunters to see. Olivia's focus flickered onto the new arrivals long enough for a Hunter to slice his blade into her arm. She screamed and held her wound for only a quick second as her attacker smiled and raised his dagger to land a killing blow.

I moved to help her, but before I took two steps Olivia let out a growl, the sound of great trees bending in the wind and righting themselves again. Bark the color of alder wood sprang from her skin and covered her wound. Like touching watercolor onto porous paper, the bark spread.

Olivia gave a giggle, which clearly caught the Hunter off guard, and in his millisecond of timidity, she reached forward and placed the tips of her fingers on his chest, right over his heart. With a grin the branches from her fingers pierced his skin and dug into his chest. When she retracted the branches, he fell to the floor and didn't move. Olivia turned to me with questioning eyes, as if to ask if it was supposed to feel that good. I didn't have an answer. I wasn't sure what it was supposed to feel like. Where did we draw the line from protector to monster? In that moment, it didn't really matter.

At least not while Shawna was still locked up in a Hunter building. And possibly my mother.

Hunters dropped like fall leaves as the succubi used their energy manipulation like a strong gust of winter wind. Each succubus seemed to concentrate on one area of the room. Marie walked to the center with not one Hunter's blade pointed at her.

"Demon!" yelled out a brown-haired Hunter as he tried with no success to push himself up from the painted cement.

Marie *tsked* and glared at him. His mouth no longer worked to create words, only grunting sounds behind his tightly shut lips.

I canvased the scene. Of the twenty or so Hunters in the building, seven lay hurt, four were dead, and the rest writhed along the cement under succubi control. The other Wilds regrouped with their sisters and assessed their damage. Blood colored Eonza's right golden wing a deep purple tone. My aunts and sisters flanked me. Celeste's arms held traces of bark, but nothing as rich and thick as Olivia's.

"Were the mermaids behind you?" I yelled to Marie from across the room.

"Faline, I can't...wait anymore." Marcus shook his head. His teeth ground and he clenched his fists.

"I haven't seen them or felt them," Marie answered quickly. Though she ignored Marcus's comment, I could tell by her expression that she was interested by the fact that a Hunter stood protectively beside me.

"Traitors," I murmured, deciding on a plan B. "The communication systems have been deactivated for now, but we need to retrieve my sister before they get it running." And Marcus needed to leave the room full of Wild Women before he went from my ally to my enemy through no will of his own.

"Go then. We'll finish up here," Marie said as Marcus dropped to the floor.

Marie watched me with more interest than I would have liked as I cradled his head in my arms. She smiled and waltzed over to Marcus and me.

"Release him," I asked.

"As enticing as this one is, Hunters do not make good love slaves. They lack the ability to let go and live in the moment of pleasure. A skewed moral compass will do that to you." Marie reached down to remove Marcus' goggles and run her fingers through his dark hair. He twisted his torso to free from her touch. Her energy held him in place.

I wanted to smack her fingers from his face, but I controlled myself. "That's not what I need him for. He's promised to help me retrieve Shawna."

Marie's knuckles brushed along Marcus's cheek and squared jaw line. His brown eyes focused on me.

"How do you know you can trust him?" she asked, toying with me. She could feel his intent. But she could probably also feel those Hunter flags going off in him, telling him to kill Wilds.

"He's already helped me this far," I said.

A light gasp escaped more than a few sets of lips behind me, including Aunt Abigale, who no doubt found my getting help from a Hunter appalling. My whole coterie probably agreed. I dreaded looking around the room to see the disgust in the eyes of the other

Wilds. So I didn't. I kept my focus on Marie and Marcus, like watching a cat and mouse tensely size one another up.

"You've had sex with him," Marie said. She bit her lower lip as though she wanted a turn. "Sex with a Hunter. And...it was wonderful. Shocking. Shocking. The energy coming from this male is filled with the intensity of a great lover. What must it feel like to let your complete wild side out with a male lover?"

"I didn't know his lineage when I dated him," I contended. "And he left the brotherhood years ago. He's only re-joined to help me." I eyed the side door. We needed to leave, to get Shawna. We didn't have time for this argument. But I couldn't find my sister without Marcus's help, and the only way to get Marie to release her hold on him was to convince her of it.

"And yet he yearns to kill your Wild sisters." Marie's lids lowered until she peered through slits at Marcus, who still writhed on the floor.

"We don't have time for this, Marie. I need to go and he needs to come with me," I said.

Wilds shook their heads in disgust.

The auburn-haired rusalka, Drosera, placed a hand on my shoulder and spoke. It was as if she came out of nowhere. "We have seen her interaction with this male from the moment we met her. And it is noble. We see into his mind as well, and he too is of noble intentions. He has good reason to fight the Hunters, equal to the reasons we all hold for our own uprising. Release him succubus, so that we may finish our task and return home to celebrate."

"What if I don't trust you, rusalka?" Marie said with a sneer.

"But you do trust me. You also fear me, that I will expose the secret you've kept shrouded from all but yourself. No, you are unable to keep it all from yourself," Drosera announced, as though she were merely talking about the lunar cycles of the moon.

If Marie was scared—and I believed Drosera—then she was a master at disguising it.

Marie eyed Drosera, probably trying to decide if she could take on the odd rusalka or not. The answer was no. Two more rusalki circled our little huddle around Marcus. It would only take a quick grab of a strand of Marie's hair for her life to be over. And she knew it.

Marie rolled her eyes and let out a groan. "Fine," she said. She turned on her heel to join her sisters, who'd been watching the interaction, preparing to pounce on the rusalki if needed.

Marcus gasped for air and shot up to stand beside me. In a winded voice, he proclaimed the one thing I'd been longing to hear. "Let's get Shawna."

TWENTY-NINE

MARCUS GRABBED my arm and I led us to the side door, past the Hunters who'd either been knocked unconscious, lay dead, or had been forced to their knees with hands above their heads. Only two lay bleeding out across the floor. Five were unconscious. They were probably the lucky ones in the bunch. Thirteen Hunters were herded into a line, forced to move while still on their knees with elbows out and hands on their heads toward the classroom to be locked up. The succubi could have willed the males to move, but forcing them to shuffle on their knees was more demeaning.

Marcus's maneuver to cut the power had worked; the Hunters weren't able to call for reinforcements in time. That didn't mean there weren't Hunters outside of the main building, somewhere else on the property. Once the Wilds were done here, they would scour the rest of the complex and take it down, one building at a time.

"Abigale should go," Aunt Renee said with a low and serious voice right before I pushed the door open and left.

I made the mistake of looking over at Renee. Fire blazed in her eyes. She gave a short head shake, as though she were daring me to speak to her.

"No," Drosera said, though she didn't turn away from the males to speak to my aunt.

The other Wilds stood in a line in front of the stoic Hunters shuffling toward the classroom, but my coterie kept to the side of the room in their own cluster, anxious to be rejoined with their missing member.

"She's her mother!" Aunt Renee reminded.

Drosera turned toward my aunt. "And she is also a liability, emotionally frail at this current time. But I do agree that they will need another, one who is not emotionally involved. Any more than that would be too much. My sister volunteers."

Aunt Renee took one step forward and then paused. "To do what? Watch?"

Azalea joined Marcus and me. Her ice blue eyes stared ahead as though she were talking with someone else telepathically, probably Drosera. She gave a tiny nod and as she walked past Drosera, she pulled birch wood scissors from her long black hair and placed them in her sister's hand.

Drosera stood before a Hunter who hadn't yet been forced into the makeshift jail of the classroom, stared into his eyes, cocked her head for only a moment, and with a blurring swiftness, she plucked a strand of blond hair from his head and snipped it in half. His body slumped to the side and hit the cement before his hair finished floating to the ground.

A young Hunter, two males down, gasped and grit his teeth. The others stared ahead with blank expressions.

Marcus rushed to leave. "I can't watch this."

As we left the building, I heard the muffled thump of another male falling to the floor.

"What did you expect?" I asked, catching up to him as he hurried to a footpath.

"That you'd have to do what was necessary to get your sister, but lining them up and killing them like that? Who knows. Maybe in a month they'll decide, like I did, that this life isn't for them. Your woman in there is taking that opportunity away." He headed deeper into the property.

"My sister knows their thoughts and intentions," Azalea reminded. "She will only end those who wish to end us."

It didn't help that Azalea, like her sisters, showed absolutely no emotion—not a hint as to her motives. Being privy to the rusalki ways gave me the strangest mixed feelings of love and an eerie unknowing. Like I don't know as much as I think I do. This only added to the anxiety swirling like a tornado in my gut.

Marcus stormed ahead. "Years ago, that could have been me in there! Where do you draw the line?"

"I don't know, Marcus. I'm not the one who made the rules; I'm only playing by them." I huffed and peered at the spattering of cabins around us. "Where is she?"

"The big house is straight through these trees. They like to keep it hidden," Marcus said, pointing toward a clump of evergreens that Azalea walked toward. The top of a roof barely peeked out above the trees from my vantage point.

I quickened my pace to catch up to Azalea.

"She is in the building," the blonde rusalka said with a glassy gaze. "Top floor...attic?" She cocked her head as she walked quickly. "Yes. Attic. She does not know how to think."

"What's that supposed to mean?" I asked.

We zigzagged through tree trunks. The grounds had been kept pretty clear for foot traffic, free of bushes or ferns. There wasn't a constructed foot path to the house, but it was easy to see the worn patch of dirt stretching from the main building to the home.

"Who lives in there?" I asked Marcus.

He walked beside me, opposite Azalea, taking one stride for every two of mine. His warm breath created a tiny cloud when his words hit the frigid air. Except, Marcus didn't seem chilly in his black long sleeve shirt and cargo pants.

"The second in command," he said, not looking at me. He trudged forward. "John."

"John's not the leader?" I asked.

"Their leader lives in a secret location," Azalea offered, though no one had asked. "It is not secret to me."

"The second in command carries out the wishes of the leader." I noticed Marcus had said "the" rather than "our" when referring to Hunter hierarchy.

As the house came into view more clearly, I realized I didn't know as much about the Hunters as I should. Once today was over, I'd pick Marcus's brain about everything Hunter. I had to be more prepared next time.

If the Wilds didn't try to kill Marcus first.

Or punish me for aligning with a Hunter.

We reached the front porch steps of the two-story home's wraparound deck. Long, narrow windows framed the carved wooden door. A huge etched cross made of bones sat front and center, separating the four sections of the door.

Symbols carved into the wood made up each section. One portion had what looked like an intricate vine woven around waves and trees and clouds. Growing from the vine was fins, wings, demon-like horns, scissors, teeth, and other symbols I didn't recognize.

I tugged on Marcus's sleeve. He turned with raised eyebrows as if to say "What now?"

I pointed to the carving on the lower left portion of the door. "Werewolves?" I barely whispered and mostly mouthed.

He nodded.

Holy shit. I'd never met a werewolf, figured they were the stuff of fairy tales. But then again, so were mermaids and huldra. Though, huldra were less fairy tale and more horror story.

Marcus peeked through the narrow window on the right side of the door.

"She is in the attic," Azalea whispered.

"I'll burst through first," Marcus instructed. "You two run up the stairs, they're a straight shot when you open the door. When you get to the second floor—"

"I know, Hunter. No need to explain." Azalea looked past Marcus, through the window, though I doubted she needed to. "They are aware of what just occurred. A Hunter escaped to warn them, but they did not have the numbers to engage such a group of Wilds in warfare, so they wait for you here, where they feel they have more of an advantage. The female is inside, pretending to read in the front room.

She is protected by males," she said dryly. "They stand on each side of the door, out of view, and upstairs. She is bait."

Okay, now I was confused. I turned to eye her. "Shawna is bait?"

Azalea shook her head again and I thought I caught her roll her eyes. "The Hunter's female. They do not believe we will make it to your sister."

"Enough talking," Marcus said as he pressed down the bronzed iron latch on the front door and pushed it open. A gush of testosterone flooded through his body and the alluring scent of it caught my senses off guard.

I quickly shoved his tempting scent away from my mind and darted into the large cabin-style home, straight up the green-carpeted stairs. With each foot fall moving me up toward my sister, voices raised from down on the first level: males threatened to kill Marcus for betraying the brotherhood, Marcus agreed to their challenges.

At least until the talking stopped and the punching started. The scent of blood filled the air as I landed on the second floor and caught the attention of two Hunters guarding the door at the end of the hallway. I hoped it wasn't Marcus's blood.

Faint traces of Shawna's scent lingered in the space. Rage filled me and a growl ripped through my lips. These Hunters were blocking me from my sister.

Like a bull teased one too many times, I broke into a run, seeing only red

My one-woman stampede ended in a crash into the narrow door with outstretched arms grabbing both Hunters in a choking embrace. The blond male twisted out of my grasp, but the other wasn't so lucky. I wrapped my fingers around his neck and pushed him up the wall until his feet dangled above the ground. Terror filled his wide eyes as one of his hands struggled to push me away and the other patted at his many pockets, probably searching for a weapon, seeing as he dropped the one he'd been holding. With my free hand I punched his right thigh. It made a cracking sound. He let out a muffled, closed-mouth scream.

Something hard slammed into my back and I dropped the brunette. He fell in a crumpled mess, but quickly dragged himself away from the wall and toward his dagger lying on the floor about ten feet away.

I turned on my heel to see the blond Hunter swinging an iron staff in my direction. I jumped out of the way and the force of his missed strike knocked him off balance.

He reached his arms to catch his fall, leaving his iron staff ripe for the taking. Before the thing hit the floor, it was in my tight grip. The blond pulled a dagger from his belt and smiled at me with perfectly straight teeth.

He must have been a lefty because his left hand wrapped around the hilt of the dagger. It held no wedding band.

"Single, good. I won't be widowing your lawfully wedded slave," I taunted, hoping for a reaction of anger rather than of calculated control. "On second thought, it would be a mercy to any woman."

He sneered, not taking the bait. "Like you could. And I'm engaged, so, soon." He gave a quick glance to my abdomen. "You're not pregnant with demon spawn, and your stomach filled with the remains of its poor idiot father. Shame, I could have got a twofer."

I laughed. I couldn't help it.

"Well, I'm secretly fucking someone in your brotherhood, so... soon." I didn't have the time or the will to stand around and play with my prey. I wanted to see my sister.

Before the blond Hunter's smile could drop, I lunged forward and sunk the iron staff into the center of his chest. His thin lips moved, but only gurgling sounds escaped his mouth. I released my hold of the staff and backed up. His fingers wrapped around the iron as he tried desperately to pull it from his body. It moved maybe an inch as he worked with every last bit of strength he had in that muscular Hunter body of his.

I reached my hand toward the staff, but didn't touch it. Vines grew from my fingertips and wrapped around the iron, encasing it in green. The blond Hunter's eyes widened, but the scent of fear didn't emanate from his skin, only disgust. The vines grew up his chest and over his shoulders, gripping him to hold the staff tightly in place. Panic set in and he dropped the staff to tear my vines from his body.

Each tear stung.

"Ah!" A burning pain pulsated up through my legs. My body faced the blond, but I turned my head to see the brunette Hunter swinging his dagger to hack off another thick woody vine growing from my heel.

Pain blazed up my body again, but this time I didn't scream out. I lashed out.

I pulled my vines from the bleeding out Hunter and focused on the soon-to-be-dead Hunter.

He swung the blade at the vines growing from my heels. The vines growing from my fingers danced around his hand in a flurry of confusing commotion and he swat at them like they were flies. One vine wrapped around the hilt of his dagger. Within seconds the metal burned through my vine and left the vibrant green a black crisp. The dagger dropped to the floor with a thud.

The brunette laughed. "You can't touch righteousness, it burns you with the fiery pits of hell—where you belong."

That's when I laughed. Maybe my vines couldn't touch it—which was news to me—but my fingers did quite fine against the metal. I reached down and gripped the dagger tightly in my right hand. As shock painted the young Hunter's expression a smile grew on my face.

"Let's see what it does to you," I said. I plummeted the blade into his left thigh.

His scream resembled a howl.

It excited the huldra in me and without thinking I allowed my vines to braid together into a thick rope and squeeze his neck, crushing his windpipe and cracking his spine. He went limp and fell to the floor.

I reached for the door. Locked. That's okay. I turned it a little harder until the knob snapped and the door swung open. A narrow staircase loomed before me, boxed in by walls decorated with red stones hanging from hooks. I pivoted on my heel to invite Azalea to follow me, but she was nowhere to be seen.

I rushed forward, unfazed, taking the steps up to the attic two at a time. "Shawna?" I whispered in case she wasn't alone upstairs. "You're here, right? I can barely smell you."

She is, Azalea's voice spoke into my mind. Weird, I couldn't smell Azalea's scent. *But so is he.*

Red rubies hung on both sides of the stairwell walls like framed photos. I didn't smell a Hunter, only traces of my sister. "Who's he?" I asked as the stairwell walls ended and my right foot hit the attic floor.

"Shit," I said as I stared at the biggest damn Hunter I'd ever had the displeasure of laying eyes on. He was close to seven feet tall. Not even his white lab jacket could hide his bulging muscles. He stood beside a queen-sized bed where my sister lay in a daze amidst rumpled sheets. An IV pole held a bag of green liquid that dripped into my sister's arm.

How did I not smell this?

Azalea answered, from who knows where. *The Hunter used rubies to block your abilities in the stairwell. They've have had a spell placed on them by their secret sect of monks, not known by others of the cloth.*

My eyes bounced from my sister to the Hunter, to my sister. Bruises littered parts of her skin that weren't covered by a black t-shirt. We heal fairly quickly, so whatever was in the IV bag must have kept her mind from focusing and her body from repairing itself. *Can she walk on her own?*

No. She is not well. Your male cannot outfight this Hunter. He has been trained to fight, more so than the others, but not more than this one. You must fight. Your male can carry your sister to safety.

I didn't like that idea. I wanted to carry Shawna. She didn't know Marcus from another Hunter. I didn't want to cause my sister more fear, more trauma.

I cannot carry her. I must remain hidden, Azalea answered my thoughts telepathically.

I heard Marcus racing up the stairs from his fight on the first floor.

"Fine," I said out loud and sized up my smiling opponent. I took a wary step toward him and lifted my nose into the air to get a whiff of his emotions.

I coughed on the stench.

"Hand delivered," the huge Hunter said with a deep and hungry voice.

"She's not for you," Marcus growled as he stepped from the attic stairwell.

"For him?" I asked without turning from my newest foe.

"Yeah," Marcus said, walking to the other side of the bed to check on Shawna "You were their original target."

Marcus gently leaned a knee onto the bed to get a closer look at Shawna. She blinked her eyes sluggishly and unsuccessfully tried to roll away from him. I kept my gaze on the big Hunter, but watched my sister in my peripheral vision.

"The hotel," I said.

"We would have made powerful hybrids together," the large Hunter said with a smile. "And unlike this one," he motioned to Shawna, "I wouldn't have used artificial insemination with you."

My breath hitched and I bit my lip to keep from showing anything but anger and assertiveness. But inside, my heart crumbled. My sister. My Shawna. They were trying to... Using her body as though she were nothing more than her womb.

I morphed from seeing red, to seeing nothing.

The last thing I remembered, I was shoving my hands out in front of me as vines grew from every spot possible, charging the huge Hunter with tears of anger rolling from my eyes. And then everything went black.

THIRTY

"FALINE! FALINE!" Marcus's distant shouts neared.

The room's spinning slowed. I blinked with effort. Light careened into my eyes and my temples pulsed. I reached up to hold my aching head, but realized I was smearing blood in my hair and jerked my hand away. The huge Hunter lay sprawled in front of me, his clothes slashed. Blood pooled at his groin. His throat had been slit open. Chunks of flesh were missing from his pecs, shoulders, and biceps.

I opened my mouth to speak and tasted blood on my teeth. I licked my lips and tasted more. Lethargy draped over me as though I'd woken from a restful nap after indulging in a decadent meal. I blinked again and swallowed before turning to Marcus.

"Yes?" I asked calmly, but already knew the answer to his insistent calls.

The wanted woman, Clarisse, straddled Azalea on the bed with a dagger to her throat. "You'll stay," she said through gritted teeth. "I know what your kind can do. You'll prove a handy pet to have around."

"What is Azalea doing here?" I asked to no one. She'd told me earlier that she had to stay hidden. And now here she was for everyone to see.

"I couldn't leave you here for them," Marcus explained. "But I can't carry both you and your sister out. I'll need a free hand for fighting."

You would have killed Marcus if I had not pulled you from your huldra abyss—if he would have tried to awaken you to leave. Azalea's words filled my mind. *I had to step in. It is not his time to go.*

"Enough!" the human woman yelled. Like an animal frightened to the brink of insanity, Clarisse's chest lifted and fell rapidly. She shot glances all around the room. Her wide eyes settled back on the rusalka. "Promise me. I know you have to keep your promises. Promise me you'll stay once they've left." She pushed the blade deeper into Azalea's throat.

She was reading the wrong folklore—I knew nothing about rusalki having to keep their promises, or huldra for that matter. And obviously mermaids were immune to such a supernatural law. She also didn't know the rusalki's beliefs about physical death.

Azalea spoke audibly to Clarisse. "Your intentions are devious. You belong here with your lords. I do not."

The human woman's head jerked to me. "They are not my lords," she whispered. "They didn't tell me to take the fall...for the trafficking. I did it of my own accord."

"Put the knife down," I instructed as calmly as possible considering a disturbed, wanted woman had a sharp object against my friend's skin. I froze in place so as not to spook her into action.

"Not my lords!" Clarisse yelled as she pulled the dagger from Azalea's neck and plunged it into the rusalka's chest. From the sickening cracking sound, I knew the power of the Hunter's blade enabled her to break the breast bone and stab Azalea's heart. "They are not my lords!"

"No!" I yelled, rushing toward the bed to knock Clarisse off of Azalea and onto the floor.

The black-haired rusalka did not cry out from the burning pain of the blade. She did not move. She only closed her ice-blue eyes as I tackled her attacker.

Marcus shifted a squirming Shawna to his right shoulder and leaned over the bed to pull the dagger from the rusalka's chest. He flung it across the room, far away from both Shawna and Azalea.

I pinned Clarisse to the floor and shook her shoulders with each word I spoke. "She wasn't going to hurt you! You didn't have to kill her!"

"They are not my lords!" she repeated.

I shook my head, set on a separate approach. Thoughts of other victims, not just Azalea filled my mind. "You took the fall for the human trafficking ring and now they're hiding you? Why? What are they planning?"

"Their plan has already been set into motion. Samuel Woodry, the man you took to jail, saw to that," she said with a sneer. "I am insurance."

"Samuel was working for you? What's that supposed to mean?" I seethed.

She refused to answer. She only stared defiantly into my eyes.

"If you don't open that mouth of yours I'll have Arlington PD covering this complex like ants on candy," I said, wishing for my cuffs. Oh well, my vines were so much more huldra-like.

"Someone from this compound has probably already called for backup. We needed to leave ten minutes ago," Marcus said.

Marcus was right. I nodded and allowed vines to grow from my fingers.

"Stop, don't," he said.

"You want to leave her? She skipped bail. She's wanted. All those innocent people whose lives she ruined. She killed Azalea, for goddess sake!"

"No," he said, shaking his head and letting out a long exhale. Either Shawna was heavy or I was irritating him. Probably the latter. "There's only two of us, and we have two Wild Women down. I don't know if the reinforcements have shown up, so we may need to fight our way out of the compound. Leave her. Alive."

"Why the hell would I do that?" I asked, reminding Marcus that I do not take orders from him.

Marcus sighed. "Because she's only doing what she's been told to do. She doesn't have a choice. She must submit to her father and fiancé. She's a victim too."

"They're not my lords!" Clarisse screamed.

I wrapped my fingers around her neck and started counting. But I didn't finish, didn't cause the woman to pass out.

"Fine," I said, raising my body off of hers. "Give me Shawna and you can carry Azalea." I wanted my sister. I neared Marcus and Shawna, and gently stroked her right arm.

But Shawna didn't lean into my touch, she pulled away from it and hitched her breath as though I'd hurt her.

"Shawna?" I asked, fighting the tears in my voice.

Her glazed brown eyes lingered on me for only a second before her lids closed and her head rolled onto Marcus's shoulder.

"Fine," I said, reaching to grab Azalea.

"She needs her own kind," Drosera said, stepping from the empty corner of the room as though she'd been standing there moments earlier...which she hadn't.

I glanced at Marcus. Maybe Drosera had been there and I hadn't noticed. But Marcus returned my gaze with raised eyebrows.

Drosera floated to her sister. Her feet hovered above the floor. Without a word she turned and crouched behind Clarisse. Clarisse shot up to sit and peered around the room, wide eyed. Drosera plucked a hair from the human woman's head and tied the strand around her wrist before walking to her sister. She gracefully laid a hand on her sister's wound and in that instant the two rusalki disappeared.

"What just..." Clarisse stuttered, peering up from the floor. She crawled the two feet to my legs and rested her head on the tops of my bare feet in submission. "Please, I'm begging you. Bite me. Make me one of you."

Marcus shook his head with pity. I shook with anger. I pulled my feet from under her as though her touch disgusted me, which it did. I left the room and started down the stairs. I refused to dignify her idiocy with a response.

The narrow steps creaked beneath my feet. I hadn't noticed the affect my weight had had on the wooden slats before. But then I'd had a one-track mind: find Shawna. Now my mind whirled with possibilities of what's to come. And seethed with retaliation ideas. Today was Shawna, next we'd begin the search for my mother.

I fought the urge to hold Shawna's hand or stroke her arm as she cuddled into Marcus's arms as though he were her sibling and not me. He walked in front of me, forcing me to watch the top of my sister's head nuzzle into that spot between his shoulder and his chest. I didn't blame her. And I didn't blame him. I blamed the Hunters. I blamed Clarisse.

"If you take one step out of line you're dead." I threw my voice to the female human at the top of the stairs without turning around.

I decided not to give the human any more details of how the rusalki killed, or that they read minds, or shed light on any of their other abilities. But if I couldn't end Clarisse for what she'd done, or return her to jail, causing her to live every second in fear would be at least a consultation prize. So I added a threat before leaving the attic stairwell and entering the second floor through the broken door.

"That was her sister you murdered. She's going to kill you. Probably when you least expect it."

* * *

In the rearview mirror, I watched the compound grounds burn.

Thankfully, if there'd been reinforcement Hunters called, they hadn't arrived by the time we'd left. And when they did arrive, they wouldn't find much more than the burnt rubble of what once was a Hunters' compound, and what once were Hunters. The moment Marcus and I had left the ruby-lined attic stairwell, the scent of burning wood and flesh had assaulted my senses.

Apparently, the mermaids had shown up. Honestly, I hadn't expected them to. But from what I'd gathered, they'd torched every last building on the compound. Records of local huldra, and maybe records of other Wilds, were gone—burnt. Hopefully there were digital records stored off site, but that search would be for another day. I'd have to ask Marcus, seeing as that's what they'd assigned him to do when he was a young bright-eyed Hunter—scan paper records into the computer.

Shawna sat sideways, molding her right side to the car's leather seat. She moaned and cried the entire drive home. The tension in the confined area doubled each time the car hit a pothole and she cried out. Her mother, Aunt Abigale, sat to Shawna's right in the crossover and I sat to her left. I tried rubbing her back, to comfort her, but she screeched like a frightened owl. Yet each time Shawna's eyes fluttered open, she watched Marcus, who sat behind us on the third row, as though she were checking to make sure he wasn't leaving her. He'd had to carry her all the way out to the vehicle because she wouldn't allow anyone else near her. It made no sense, but now wasn't the time to pressure her.

Aunt Abigale stared at her daughter, unable to touch her. My sisters and aunts looked ahead at the road. There was an elephant in the room...or car...and his name was Marcus. None of them liked the idea of inviting a Hunter into the vehicle, let alone a male. But Shawna would have it no other way. Her words only slurred when she talked, but her screeches, splaying arms, and kicking legs got the point across. Aunt Renee had agreed to bring him along. Begrudgingly would be an understatement.

We rode in silence. No one wanted to upset Shawna any more than she already was.

Some time later we pulled into our forest-lined driveway. I exhaled deeply for the first time since I'd left that morning. Deep down, I hadn't expected to see my home again. Without Marcus's help I would have walked into an ambush, despite the Wilds at my back. I doubted my coterie agreed.

Aunt Renee parked her crossover right up next to Aunt Abigale's and Shawna's tree home. The harpies, mermaids, and succubi stood solemnly around the great evergreen.

"Where are the rusalki?" Olivia asked.

"I'm not sure if we'll ever see them again," I said. "Azalea didn't make it."

Olivia bowed her head and shook it. "That leaves only three of them."

Aunt Renee opened her door first and Eonza approached her as the rest of us emptied from the car. Familiar soil beneath my feet sent comfort through my shaky body. I'd forgotten my boots at the complex, though they were probably burnt to a crisp by now.

"My wing is hurt," Eonza pointed out, slightly pulsing her golden wing as drops of crimson blood dripped from its feathers. A black patch of soot smeared across her right arm. "But I am strong enough to fly your wounded to her home."

Shawna cried out from inside the car, and I popped my head into the vehicle to see why. She reached for Marcus, who sat in the back row, waiting for the second row to be emptied so he could push the seat forward and exit. But Shawna refused to leave without him.

Eonza's gaze darted to the commotion in the car and she leaped away from Aunt Renee. "You brought a Hunter here? To your home? Where my flock is staying?"

"Just..." I raised my hand in the air. "Can you let us deal with one crisis at a time? Once we get her settled, I promise, I'll explain everything. But for now, just know that he's not a Hunter. He's safe, and Shawna won't go anywhere without him."

Eonza gave a sharp nod, though her eyes tightened. I lowered my hand.

Marcus crawled over the back seat to sit beside my fragile sister. Once she calmed, he cradled her in his arms and scooted along the seat, out of the car. Low growls reverberated from the Wilds positioned around the evergreen the moment Marcus's boots hit the gravel.

"You're not welcome here," a voice spit out from the group.

"She clings to her captor," another yelled.

"He's the one who locked her up and she's fixated on him," yet another stated.

"Ignore them," I whispered to him, though I knew they could all hear. "Follow me."

Aunt Abigale walked beside Marcus while I led them toward her home. The other members of my coterie followed behind. As we neared the old tree most of the Wilds backed up to leave a wide girth between them and the Hunter. Blood smeared their arms. Their torn clothing hung from their shoulders and hips. Exhaustion shadowed their eyes. Purple fist prints sprinkled across their skin. Knotted hair poked from ponytails and down backs. I counted three arm slings and multiple legs wrapped with gauze. And though the plan was to repeat the today's battle as many times as needed, at other Hunter complexes to rescue their sisters and mothers, today they fought for us, for Shawna. And their appearance showed just how hard they'd fought.

Still, wings flapped as Marcus passed the women. I noticed Marcus limping on his right leg as he carried Shawna up the first few steps, and I shot a harsh glance to Marie. She quickly looked away and Marcus's leg seemed fine again. She huffed off toward the common house and her succubi sisters followed. The harpies stood their ground with wings out to appear larger. The mermaids only watched; they didn't seem to be bothered.

Aunt Abigale stopped in the middle of the staircase leading to her tree home and placed her hand on Marcus's bicep for all to see. She spoke loudly, a hidden warning for those who'd stop him from comforting her daughter in her tone. "Thank you for helping my daughter. You can use my bed tonight, young man."

I respected that my aunt knew her daughter wouldn't let Marcus out of her sight for the time being, and all she wanted was what her daughter wanted. Whatever helped ease her daughter's pain. I couldn't guarantee that the others would respect it, though.

Shawna lifted her head. She opened her eyes and smiled at her mother, and then leaned her matted dreads onto Marcus's shoulder.

I ached to know what ran through his mind, what the policeman in him was thinking. I'd gone through similar training as him, but he'd had more experience in these types of cases. Was Shawna experiencing post-traumatic stress? Was this Stockholm's syndrome? Or was this behavior a side effect of the drugs, and would it vanish when the drugs cleared her system? Desperately, I hoped for the latter.

THIRTY-ONE

I CREPT from Shawna's home and silently shut her door behind me. She'd fallen asleep with Marcus resting on the floor beside her bed. He refused to accept Aunt Abigale's offer. So she'd gathered blankets and a pillow and made him a makeshift bed on the floor. He'd stayed awake long enough to give me a few details of his time at the complex, but when exhaustion slurred his words, I stopped asking questions. He now snored lightly as Shawna whimpered in her sleep and Aunt Abigale watched her daughter from under her comforter, silently crying.

I had been summoned to the common house. I couldn't put off the other Wild Women any longer. They wanted to know our next move.

The afternoon sun hid behind thick layers of grey clouds as my bare feet crunched along the gravel and padded up the stone walkway. A light mist danced across the air. I paused to breathe it all in: the crisp air, the pine-scented trees, the moist earth. I missed the days when all I had on my mind was the next skip I'd set my sights on. I'd been thrust into the leadership role of an uprising that I knew little about.

But someone had to lead it, or it'd never happen. And it needed to happen.

I pushed through the front door to the common house. The energy in the room stilled with all eyes on me. I was the Hunter-lover. Not to be trusted. Yet I was the leader of this whole thing. I was the one who'd traveled and visited with all the Wild groups. I had the connections and all the details.

I took a deep breath and shut the door behind me.

And then I realized what truly plagued their thoughts, deeper than their dissatisfaction with my choice of male helper. Shawna. She'd been taken after their sisters and mothers were taken, and she'd been in bad shape. They probably wondered how much worse their loved ones were, and if we'd get to them in time. Their anger toward Marcus was only an afterthought.

They needed me. And deep inside, I needed to help them. I couldn't live with myself if I didn't help them, if I didn't uphold my promises.

I made my way to the front of the living room and waited for the talking to quiet. "My coterie extends their immense gratitude for your help in rescuing my sister and destroying the local Hunter compound," I said. "We are ready and willing to return the favor."

Eonza stood behind the couch and nodded. Marie sat on the couch. Her red lips turned upward into a smile.

"We will visit each group's home, stake out their local Hunter's complex, and create a plan to infiltrate and destroy the compound and the Hunters in it," I announced. "We cannot do it the same way twice. We need to assume that someone got away tonight and is spreading the word through the Hunter community of what we did today. The other compounds will know we're coming. We must assume they'll be prepared." Then there was the matter of Clarisse being spared. If she escaped the fire, her people would surely question her.

"It'll be easier for us to access compounds closer to larger bodies of water," Azul said from where she sat on the floor, surrounded in a cluster by the other mermaids. "The river today was not deep enough. We had many problems."

"And that was why you were late?" Aunt Renee asked with a clipped voice. "Not because you're traitors?"

I eyed my aunt and shook my head. We needed to band together, not fight one another. Yes, there was something fishy about the mermaids, but the rusalki only pointed to Azul as the mermaid working with the Hunters alongside Gabrielle. I wanted to get my facts straight before approaching the shoal with what I knew. Since Azul wasn't killed during the attack as Azalea and I had planned, I had to let the mermaids dole out their own brand of justice. And I needed concrete evidence to show the shoal or else their whole group would turn against me. I wished the rusalki were here, but I understood why they weren't.

"Excuse me? Traitor?" Azul said. "I'm not the one whose coterie member is in bed with a Hunter!"

"Are you talking about Shawna?" Olivia shot up to confront the mermaid.

Azul stood. "Absolutely not. I'm talking about Faline, screwing around with a Hunter. What self-respecting Wild Woman doesn't sense that a man's her enemy?"

"This Wild Woman," I said sternly. "The one who's going to lead a revolt against the Hunters and help every single one of you reclaim your right to freedom. Do you have a problem with that?"

Azul sat. Olivia gave a nod of satisfaction and found her chair.

"I'd screw him," Marie added. She licked her lips. "If you're down to share, so am I."

I laughed a short laugh. Ugh, Marie. "Marie, that's not helpful," I said, knowing she'd only made the comment to diffuse the situation without using energy.

"Oh? Because you didn't mention you needed my help." Marie closed her eyes, inhaled, exhaled, and then opened her eyes. A calm, uniting energy filled the room. Tense shoulders relaxed. Clenched hands opened. Gritting teeth separated for a smile.

"Thank you," I offered. "That's better."

"Imagine what else I can do," she quipped.

"Duly noted," I said. I addressed the rest of the room. "I think we should hit an east coast complex, they're less likely to have heard about what we did here in Washington. I'm sure they'll hear bits and pieces, but according to Marcus there's a disconnect between the west coast and east coast. The east coast Hunters are more old school, if you can imagine that, and they've been there longer, so they behave like they're the "big brothers" to the west coast Hunters. Which, if you know Hunters, they don't like to be dominated; they like to dominate." I paced in front of the big flat screen TV. "They probably assume we'll hit the Oregon complex next. So let's throw them off."

My words were met with head nods and agreement.

"What happened to Shawna?" Salis, one of the harpies, asked. No doubt she was worried for her mother.

This was the part I didn't want to share, though I knew they deserved to hear it.

"The Hunters have sunk lower than we thought possible." I considered my words and then continued. "Twenty years ago, a number of Wilds went missing. My mother was among them. At the time, we didn't know that the Hunters were behind the abductions. We trusted that they'd been honest in their promises to protect us." I took a breath to steady myself. "They've started abducting Wilds again, but this time in full force. From what I've gathered, the Hunters are trying to impregnate Wilds, hoping to create hybrid Hunters. Boys with their strength and our abilities," I said. Since Marcus and my whispered conversation over my sleeping sister, the wheels in my mind had been turning. "The more I think about it, the more it makes sense that they'd raise these boys to exterminate our kind."

"But we can't have boys," Azul said.

"I think that's the problem they ran into twenty years ago. But Marcus believes they've found a way around that. Over the last few days he's heard things," I said.

His name caused a few females to bristle, so I counted on Marie to continue to regulate the calm energy in the room as I set the record straight. "Okay, so I'm going to say this one more time and then never again. Because honestly, after what he sacrificed for us, I shouldn't have to repeatedly defend this male." I let that settle into their minds and continued. "He renounced the Hunters years ago. He does not agree with their way, mindset, beliefs—none of it. He is a police officer with a heart to help. And helping is what he's been doing. Through all of this. He flew out to the east coast to bring me intel. She clings to her rescuer, not her captor."

As I spoke my heart melted a little more for Marcus. Marie cocked her head. Yeah, she could feel my energy shift. Damn obvious energy.

"I asked him to re-join the Hunters. He didn't want to, but he did it to help us rescue Shawna. He's not sure if he has a job to go back to, depending on who knows about his actions. You're sitting here cursing him, and me for trusting him, while he's sleeping on the floor beside a Wild Woman's bed because she's so scared from the trauma she suffered that she's clinging to the person who picked her up from that awful makeshift lab bed and removed her from the situation." I thought of how Shawna flinched when I'd tried to grab her from Marcus in the Hunter's house, and hoped her reaction had more to do with the drugs they'd given her than from seeing my wild huldra in action and fearing me.

"Please tell me you killed the Hunter hurting her," Marie said with anger in her eyes.

"I did," I said, and wondered when Marcus and I would talk about what he saw. I had a lot to sort out when this was all over.

"Good." Marie addressed the group. "I trust the male." I appreciated that she didn't call him a Hunter.

The others nodded in agreement.

"But we must bind together if we are going to be successful," I said. "Yes, we are huldra and mermaids and harpies and succubi, but above all of that, we are Wilds. We may not be sisters, but we are certainly cousins, and we should behave as such."

Eonza stepped forward. "We should bind this decision with a traditional Wild Women treaty," she suggested, looking around the room for support.

I wanted to kiss her for suggesting that. The treaty was sacred. No one would doubt it's binding. "I agree," I said.

Others followed in agreement.

Aunt Patricia popped up from the couch. "I'll gather the basin and tools." She hurried out of the room and down the hall.

I eyed the silver braided wolf bracelet on my wrist and reached for the Freyja charm on my necklace, thankful to my goddess for enabling us to rescue Shawna.

"We need water," Azul spoke up. "To participate in a ritual."

"We'll conduct it where the rusalki were staying," I said. "Near the only creek on our property. It's no ocean or roaring river, but it'll have to do."

* * *

Heavy clouds slowed their pace as large rain drops fell on our heads. A piece of me hoped the rusalki would appear during the ritual. Yes, they'd been strange and distant, but they were also comforting. And after all, it was my fault they'd lost a sister tonight. For that, I would always owe them.

But they'd fought beside us, in their own ways, and they deserved to be among us as we joined hands and promised a united front. I'd grown to like the rusalki. In fact, I'd grown to like all of the Wild Women I now celebrated alongside.

We formed a circle in the woods near the rusalki's hole, holding hands and swaying, naked as the day we were born. My sisters and aunts had fought long and hard and viciously. Their earned bark darkened and covered their skin in more than splotches.

The twelve mermaids, six succubi, three harpies, and five huldra sang the songs of our foremothers under our breaths. Pride filled me and tears streamed from my eyes.

We had been taught to compete with one another. Taught to hate our differences, to distrust and conspire against each other. We'd been forced apart, picked off in our weakness. But in this moment we stood together, embracing our differences, trusting, and conspiring to take down the very establishment that tore us apart. If my mother could see us now.

My mother.

If she'd been at the Washington complex, a rusalka would have known. No matter how many complexes I had to burn to the ground, we'd find her and get her back.

A bronze basin stood in the center of our circle, held up off the ground by an iron stand with three winding legs, twisted to look like vines. When the *quberacho* stick was passed to me, I accepted the piece of wood with a sharpened tip on one end and the image of Freyja etched into the other. Blood already soaked the sharpened point, but I added my own by dragging it across my right palm until liquid crimson dripped from my skin. I passed it to the female on my left and exited the circle to squeeze my blood into the basin. As I walked toward my place in the circle, another Wild made her way to the basin.

When the *quebracho* stick had been passed completely around the circle, the humming stopped and so did the swaying. Shawna's absence weighed heavy on my heart. She deserved to be here more than any of us. She'd suffered the most at the Hunter's hands. I promised myself that one day, when Shawna was healed and everything returned to normal, I'd tell her all about this moment. Maybe we'd have a bigger circle, a victory ceremony. And every missing Wild would be rescued and able to join in the ritual.

Aunt Patricia stood in the center of the circle and stirred the blood in the basin with her pointer finger. She pressed her finger along her forehead and then across her chest. We took turns around the basin, placed our combined blood on our heads to symbolize our joined thoughts, and over our hearts to symbolize our love for one another—the love of family tied together by both bonds and blood.

The last Wild completed the ritual. Aunt Renee sang out a prayer of thanks and the rest of us followed. Normally, we'd run through the woods, tree-jump all the way home, to end the night, but out of respect for the mermaids' ways, we ran towards the creek. We yipped and laughed and tossed water on one another in utter freedom and hope for our future as a species. For the future of our ways.

As the ritual wound down, the mermaids ran to the common house by way of the creek, splashing all the way home. The harpies flew through the evergreens. The succubi ran along the dirt, touching the trees and ferns, harnessing their energy as they moved.

The others made their way to the common house, but I was exhausted and wanted nothing more than a shower and a bowl of steaming hot noodles. I jumped from the tree onto the moist dirt. I figured the group would understand. I hit my stairs at a run, too tired to climb the trunk.

I pulled the noodle packet from the fridge and placed it on the counter. No, shower first and then food, on the couch, in comfort. I didn't have to shed any clothes, seeing as I was already naked. I only willed my bark to melt into my skin and climbed into the shower.

In the middle of sudsing up my hair, the front door creaked open. I tilted my head under the water to rinse my hair and not be caught off guard. Marcus stood in front of the glass shower door as bubbles streamed from my temples.

"I woke up and your sister and aunt were sleeping, so I thought I'd visit you," he said. "Have anything to eat here?"

His dark hair was disheveled and he still wore the black Hunter outfit from earlier.

"I want to burn that uniform," I said as I finished rinsing the suds from my long hair.

"I'd have to take it off first," he responded.

I didn't want to think anymore. I only wanted to feel. And I only wanted to feel good. I'd had enough of feeling shitty to last me a lifetime.

"What's stopping you?" I asked.

He pulled his shirt over his wide shoulders and pushed his pants and boxers down past his ankles. Cuts, scrapes, and bruises covered his body. I'd forgotten. Before I was in the attic losing my mind, Marcus was downstairs fighting a room of Hunters, singlehandedly.

He ran a hand through his hair and looked at his palm. "I've got blood in my hair," he said with remorse.

"Me too." I sighed. "Come in and wash it out." I opened the shower door and he stepped under the water with me.

"Brrr, it's cold." He jumped from the stream of water.

"Oh, sorry. I don't feel temperature so well." I turned the knob toward "Hot" for him.

He stepped into the water and relaxed his shoulders. I wrapped my arms around his waist and leaned my head against his chest. This. I wanted to feel this. Comfort, security, hope, pleasure.

I don't know how long we stood in the shower holding one another. But I broke the silence. "Do you think she'll be all right?"

"Tomorrow morning, or maybe the afternoon, after she's slept off the drugs, she'll realize where she is and who you all are. She'll be much better." He kissed my forehead.

"But her mind...the trauma. I've see what it can do to people."

"If she's patient with herself, and maybe gets therapy, that'll heal in time too." He ran a hand from the crown of my head and down my hair. "The worst is over for her. She's safe at home surrounded by nothing but support and love."

I gazed up at Marcus. His defined jaw. His soft lips. His soulful eyes. "Thank you. For everything. I mean it. Thank you."

When I first went out with Marcus, I'd only intended to have a little fun with him, break my dry spell. But now, two weeks later, he had done more than break my dry spell. He'd stood beside me as I broke my old ways, as I threw a rock into the Hunters' expectations and cracked their establishment. One day, hopefully soon, we'd shatter it to the ground.

THE END

Thank you for reading!

Please consider leaving a review.

Thank you for reading! For more from Rachel Pudelek, check out her website and find her across social media.

Twitter: www.twitter.com/rachelpud

Website: www.rachelpudelek.com

* * *

Please sign up for the City Owl Press newsletter for chances to win special subscriber-only contests and giveaways as well as receiving information on upcoming releases and special excerpts.

All reviews are **welcome** and **appreciated**. Please consider leaving one on your favorite social media and book buying sites.

For books in the world of romance and speculative fiction that embody Innovation, Creativity, and Affordability, check out City Owl Press at www.cityowlpress.com.

ACKNOWLEDGMENTS

This book would not have happened if it weren't for its champion, my agent, Jacquie Flynn, who is nothing short of a magical book doula. Thank you, Jacquie, for seeing the importance of this empowering story. And if Jacquie's my book doula, my editor, Heather McCorkle, is this book's midwife. Thank you, Heather, for helping to bring Freyja's Daughter into the world.

To my coterie who's never stopped believing in me, Geno, Christany, and Isabel: if it weren't for your loving support, I'd still be penning story ideas and first chapters, but never actually writing the books. Geno, thank you for anchoring me in every storm that comes my way. Christany, thank you for reading my many first drafts and encouraging me to keep going. Isabel, thank you for being genuinely proud of each little accomplishment I achieve in this process.

Years ago, among the trees of a Washington forest, I made a promise to Rayna Stiner and myself that I'd one day become a published author. It only makes sense that my debut novel is about a huldra with the bark of an evergreen. Thank you, Rayna, for years of encouragement and your willingness to meet me in the woods for all-day hikes that consist mostly of book talk.

To my mom, Cathy, and my sisters, Wendy, Michaele, and Dani, thank you for the kind of never-ending friendship stories are made of. To my dad, Gary, who gave me a love of learning and the stubbornness to achieve my dreams, I miss your hugs the most.

Thank you to my family, either by marriage or by blood, whose acknowledgment of my dream has encouraged me far more than you'll ever know.

Lots of hugs to my critique partners and beta-readers, Amanda Benally, Maria Medina, and Jessi Gage. And to my writerly friends who've been there since the beginning and beyond, your friendship means the world to me...Wendy Higgins, Hilary Harwell, Sarah Glenn Marsh, Stacey Lee, Kendare Blake, Tara Sheets, Jennifer Alvarez, Megan Paasch, Amy Patrick, Amber Bardan, Anne Greenwood Brown, Jody Holford, Annie Sullivan, and everyone in the Authors '18 debut group. Also, many thanks to the supportive team at Sno-Isle Libraries.

ABOUT THE AUTHOR

RACHEL PUDELEK is a dog-hugger and tree-lover. Growing up with three sisters sparked her passion for both women's history and women's advocacy, which led to her career as a birth doula and childbirth educator. These days she channels those passions into writing fiction. When she's not writing, Rachel enjoys hiking, attempting to grow her own food, or reading.

Rachel lives in Seattle, Washington with her husband, two daughters, two dogs, a cat named Lucifer, and two well-fed guinea pigs. Freyja's Daughter is her debut novel.

www.rachelpudelek.com

ABOUT THE PUBLISHER

City Owl Press is a cutting edge indie publishing company, bringing the world of romance and speculative fiction to discerning readers.

www.cityowlpress.com

Made in the USA
San Bernardino, CA
22 May 2018